I0835078

EDGE OF ESCAPE

EDGE OF ESCAPE

LINDA J. PARISI

CITY OWL PRESS

EDGE OF ESCAPE

CITY OWL PRESS
www.cityowlpress.com

Cover Design by MiblArt. All stock photos licensed appropriately.

Edited by Tina Moss.

For information on subsidiary rights, please contact the publisher at info@cityowlpress.com.

Print Edition ISBN: 978-1-64898-327-6

Digital Edition ISBN: 978-1-64898-326-9

PRAISE FOR LINDA J. PARISI

"Parisi makes this beach town in *Reunion with the Single Mom* feel so real. this is a place I want to visit. The family dynamic, the food, and the warmth of the people, all make for a fantastic read! The visceral imagery made me feel like I could almost smell the salt air and feel the ocean breeze on my skin. I truly loved this book and was seriously bummed when I got to 'The End'." – *Shari Nichols, author of Midnight Desire*

"This book hit the mark, amazing characters, suspense, and the mystery behind the rogues. I loved every second of the book and read it in one sitting, now all I have to do is wait for the next book in the series which hopefully won't be too long." – *Paranormal Romance Guild*

"Stacy and Chaz light up the page together and are downright unforgettable. Plenty of steam and just enough danger to keep the plot zipping along at a fast, thrilling clip combine to make this a phenomenal read in the vein of JR Ward that fans of paranormal romance will adore as much as I did." – *April the Book Dragon*

"A charming story that was a nice derivative of a standard vampire story…I loved the drama and danger throughout the book. The insights into vampire politics were fascinating. Well written and very easy to read and understand, it was a great start to the series, and I'm looking forward to what happens next." – *MP Book Reviews*

"The story was well written in a way that the reader could stop after this book and not be disappointed. A great read for a cold weekend." – *Readers Favorite*

"*Blood Rogue* took me on a journey filled with suspense, danger, humor, and romance." – *Totally Addicted to Reading*

"The debut novel to a new paranormal series, *Blood Rogue*, is a fast-paced, action-packed fantasy from page one...It is an entertaining story readers can devour in no time." – *InD'tale Magazine*

"With a gritty urban backdrop and plenty of intriguing clan dynamics, *Blood Rogue* is a perfect vampire romance. Plenty of steam and just enough danger to keep the plot zipping along at a fast, thrilling clip combine to make this a phenomenal read." – *Kat Turner, Author of Hex, Love, and Rock and Roll*

"*Blood Rogue* is a well-crafted, smart adventure of the unlikeliest of lovers...reminiscent of lore's age-old heartbreak, how can two beings that belong in separate worlds ever be together? A great read!" – *M. Kate Quinn, author of Endangered Diamond*

ALSO BY LINDA J. PARISI

Reunion with the Single Mom

Blood Rogue

Honorable Rogue

Destiny's Rogue

This book is dedicated to each and every one of you out in the world who have a book in your heart, and no choice but to write it.

CHAPTER ONE

THE DELICATE NOTES OF THE PIANO IN THE BAR CLASHED with the hustle and bustle of the hotel lobby. Crystal chandeliers and gilt crown moldings quarreled with the picture windows filled with sun, sand, and the ocean not more than a hundred yards away. The building was just as much juxtaposition as she, for if there was ever a place Dr. Morgan Mackenzie didn't want to be, this was it, right down to her last dime and her final hope.

"Friend of the bride, or friend of the groom?"

Morgan froze. She placed a hand on the check-in desk counter of the hotel to steady herself, turned her head, and inhaled the scent of an intriguing, spicy cologne. She released that breath, hearing nothing now but the roar of her heart inside her chest.

"I beg your pardon?"

He leaned toward her as if this were an everyday occurrence. He was so tall she had to tilt her head to look up at him. His midnight black hair gleamed in the artificial light as he raked over her from head to toe with his killer blue eyes. "No need to beg. I'm yours for the asking," he answered, a slow smile growing on his face.

Her gaze swept over him, then the receptionist interrupted, "Excuse me. Will you be using a credit card today?"

Morgan pulled out three one-hundred-dollar bills, trying not to wince. He stayed her hand and pushed past her. "Put the lady's room on my card." The man pulled out a black piece of plastic.

"Wait a minute, umm, excuse me, but that's quite all right. Very kind of you, but not necessary. I mean, I don't want to...oh hell, I don't even know you."

"Ahhh." He smiled, handing over the card, which the receptionist was too eager to take. "But I know *you*."

Morgan's knees liquefied. Her stomach sank. She gripped the edge of the counter to keep from falling but had just enough sense of self-preservation to paste a smile on her face. "Look, I'm not quite sure what kind of game this is, but you need to stop right now." She turned to the receptionist. "I can't allow him to do this. You need to give him his credit card back, please."

The receptionist smiled, and Morgan found no hint of remorse. "Sorry, I already put the charge through." She lifted her gaze to the man's and added, "And your room, sir?"

With the aplomb of centuries of male ego, he said, "Don't have one." Then he stared directly into Morgan's eyes. "Do I need one?"

She opened her mouth. She shut her mouth. Her fingers trembled. She couldn't get a wisp of air through the lump inside her throat. "Guess I do," he grinned. "Any openings?"

"Just the Hamilton Suite, sir."

"Sounds fine."

"The suite comes with a complimentary bottle of champagne. Shall I have it sent up?"

He arched his brow, and she fell right into the heat of his gaze. If only dreams did come true. She shook her head, and he turned to the receptionist, his shoulders lifting and falling. "Guess not."

For whatever reason, the receptionist handed him both keys. Maybe because he paid for both of them? Morgan would never know. "Later perhaps," he added.

The roar of her heart could've drowned out the ocean at that moment, so much so that she missed his question. "Sorry?"

"Guess I'll have to repeat myself. Are you a friend of the bride or a friend of the groom?"

"Neither. I'm not here for the wedding."

He pulled his thick dark brows together as he frowned. "You're not?"

His gaze scorched her from head to toe. She shivered and wondered to herself if the new Morgan made that much of an impression? Gone was the tight chignon. Her newly colored, newly styled hair now brushed the tops of her shoulders. Say sayonara to the khakis, the sweaters, the comfortable Dexters. Instead, she wore shiny new Ferragamos, a tailored pantsuit, and a turtleneck to hide a throat already full of rope burns.

"Listen," she replied, feeling the noose tighten once again. "You've been very kind and I'm flattered as hell, but I need to go. I'm already late."

He wrapped his fingers around her arm lightly, and suddenly, they were walking out of the lobby. "For what?"

"I don't think that's any of your business," she snapped, trying to shrug out of his grasp. "I don't know you. I didn't ask you to pay for my room. And I'm under no obligation to stay with you."

"I know. But I promise, if you do, you won't be sorry."

What? He reached around and looped his arm through hers, not letting her pull away. He guided her down a hallway toward a raucous ballroom, but she hesitated before they drew near. She had no business being anywhere near this wedding or this man, yet she didn't stop him as he turned and led her through a set of doors and out onto a balcony.

Cool ocean air rippled across her skin. He noticed and drew her into his arms. "I'll warm you up."

Confidence or arrogance? After a moment, she stopped trying to decide. They began to dance, and Morgan stiffened, lying to herself that he'd caught her by surprise. The sad fact was she couldn't afford the luxury of dancing in a man's arms. Not when she was on the run. She looked up to see him smiling down at her.

Ah, hell. Dimples. For a moment, they almost made her forget who she was.

As "Unforgettable" floated through the air, she realized she was smiling with him. Against her will, against all sane thought, Morgan relaxed into him and the space between them vanished. His heat enveloped her, as did his arms, one hand cupping hers tightly to his chest. Rough calluses along his fingers spoke of hard physical labor, not surprising considering the rock-hard muscles beneath her fingertips, fingertips that longed to explore. Morgan admonished them to behave.

His other arm curled around her waist, pulling her closer. Caught, she wanted nothing more than to give in. Hell, she was *this* close. Then, the picture of a computer screen filled her mind.

The moment died a slow, relentless death. And if she didn't get her act together, she would die too.

Morgan tried to bolt, and he tightened his arm around her waist. "Easy, kitten. There's no need to run."

There's every need. "Look, I know you were just being kind. Or maybe you thought…"

He looked down, his brows nearly touching. "Thought what?"

"That I was an easy mark for your bed." There. She said it and now it couldn't be taken back.

His face fell. "You're not married, are you?"

"Why in the ever-loving hell does my marital status matter? I'm not going to sleep with you. Do you understand?" She blew out a frustrated breath. "End of discussion."

He laughed. "Fine by me. Besides, I wasn't in the mood for talking, anyway." He cocked his head. "And?" he asked, completely ignoring her statement.

"You're incorrigible. No, I'm not married," she cried out, wanting to gnash her teeth together. God, he was impervious and brazen, completely pig-headed and freaking egotistical. Yet, as his hips continued to mesh with hers, her core opened, and a flood of desire filled her belly. Sweet, sweet temptation despite the price. And if her life was the only one involved, Morgan would never have hesitated. "I don't even know your name."

"Jack."

"Mr. Jack? Jack in the beanstalk? Jack-in-the-box? What?"

He leaned back and smiled. *What could be more deadly than that smile*? "No. Just Jack."

"Oh, okay. I get it. Jack as in Ripper."

His nose scrunched up as he winced, yet laughter rumbled through his chest. "As in Jackson. Jackson Kent. Thanking my lucky stars my mother drew the line there and didn't name me Clark."

Morgan couldn't help herself. Her lips twitched.

Jack bent down to bring his eyes level with hers. "Come on. I saw that. Go ahead. You won't die. Smile."

Yes, she would, especially if she didn't get her head screwed back on. The people coming after her would be professionals. They wouldn't be inclined to hear her side of the story. Still, she had to try to extricate herself. "Look, I need to leave now."

"So you keep saying." He drew in a deep breath and let the air out in a whoosh. "I'll let you in on a little secret." She didn't ask. She didn't dare. "I'm not here for the wedding either."

Said with the most innocent of faces. And the dimples no less. He had to be kidding. "Seriously?"

"Scout's honor." He even let go of one hand and held it up, curling his thumb over his bent pinkie to leave his middle fingers pointing at the sky with not an ounce of remorse in his expression.

"Wedding crasher?" she asked.

"Nah. You wouldn't believe the real reason."

"Try me."

He stilled. His grin faded. His gaze turned serious the way gazes do when they are ready to impart earth shattering news. "I fell in love with you the moment you turned the corner."

Morgan laughed, unable to hold back the heat filling her cheeks. But inside her stomach was doing an act for *Cirque de Soleil*. "I'm sorry. That wasn't very nice of me. But you don't expect me to believe you, do you?"

"Told myself you wouldn't. But how can you fault a man for trying?" he asked, barely above a whisper.

"I can't."

His head tilted toward the buffet that lined the hallway down from the patio. "Sorry enough to let me buy you dinner?"

This time she laughed and didn't feel guilty. He was too outrageous. "Buy?"

He shrugged. "A matter of semantics."

Spoken with a grin that could melt a woman's bones. She started to decline when her stomach growled loud enough for both of them to hear.

"Sounds like you've had your mind made up for you."

Morgan could feel herself blushing. She could also feel the sharpened steel of an axe coming down on her head. "Guess so."

"Hey, don't look so upset," he said, his face as innocent as it was beautiful. "You'll kill my ego."

"I highly doubt that's possible," she retorted with a roll of her eyes.

He arched a single brow. "You'd be surprised."

The song, long over with, stuck in her mind as he let go. He trailed his hand possessively down her back, and for a moment, she wondered what it would be like to have a man who cared.

"Glass of wine?" He quirked his mouth. "Or would you prefer something harder?"

"Don't you ever give up?"

He shook his head, his gaze promising things Morgan knew she had no right acknowledging, let alone dreaming about.

Not trusting herself to answer, Morgan let him lead her to the bar, knowing she shouldn't indulge. "A glass of white. Pino," she said.

"Red for me. Cabernet?" he asked the bartender.

They touched glasses once they were poured. His eye filled with devilish delight. "What should we toast to? A chance meeting? An enchanted evening?"

Either would have made her day, even her week, a couple of weeks ago. Now they felt like sheer impossibilities. "How about... to life?"

He tilted his head in question. "No," he said in a warm tone, "to love."

Damn. He really needed to stop making her insides flip. "Do you tell that to every woman the first time you meet her?"

"No."

She watched his lips curve over the edge of the wine glass wondering how they would feel on her skin. "Oh, come now. You tried to buy 'us' a room. It's a great line, you know. Must get you laid quite a bit."

At first, just his hand stopped, right before he was about to take another sip. His gaze shuttered, but not before she saw the hurt. Genuine hurt. Still, his tone enveloped her as he answered, "Just women in pinstriped pants suits wearing outrageous high-heeled shoes and carrying handbags with a very expensive name written on them."

Wow. He pursed his lips and drew his brows together. She watched his fingers tighten around his wineglass. She'd angered him. "I wasn't playing with you. I swear."

Impossible. No one but a good actor could have said so much with such a straight face. "Look, I don't know what your game is or why you decided to pick me up, or what I'm even doing here. Most men wouldn't have the smarts or the gall."

His gaze traveled her length yet again. She shivered, not quite sure if her reaction was from excitement or fear. "I'm not most men," he said, his voice wrapping her in silk even as he stepped back away from her.

That was for sure.

"But don't expect me to believe out-and-out bullshit, all right? It's demeaning to both of us." Morgan felt like one of those cartoon characters with the angel and the devil sitting on her shoulders. One part of her desperately wanted to stay and the other part of her wanted to run and keep on running.

She should never have threatened BioClin.

But she had threatened BioClin and now she had to pay the price. The problem was, the price was growing exponentially. *Would it ever stop?*

"I apologize. I see now how my desperation must look." He paused, shaking his head as if to clear it. "I know you think I picked you up to get you into bed. But all I wanted was to meet you. And just so you know, I'm going to have a devil of a time trying to explain to my boss how that room charge got on my expense account."

"A BLACK EXPENSE ACCOUNT?"

He lifted his forehead and then rolled his shoulders. "I travel all the time."

Her stomach growled again, and he grinned. "Sounds like someone is hungry. At least have a bite with me. Please."

She let him lead her back inside. They trolled the hors d'oeuvres, piling two plates high with everything from crab puffs and scallops wrapped in bacon, to thin slices of rare fillet.

"I know it's a bit chilly, but would you like to eat outside?" he asked.

"Less chance of getting caught?" she asked with a wink.

"Wouldn't want to end up in jail over a crab puff," he replied, popping one into his mouth.

Morgan couldn't help but laugh. "Caviar, at the very least." She inclined her head, allowing him to escort her back outside. "I'd prefer the noise reduction," she answered. In truth, she wanted to be alone with him, even though she didn't deserve the gift he presented. What she'd done was wrong. What she was doing now, well...that was worse.

Several tables and chairs were empty, probably because of the temperature. She shivered, and as soon as she put her plate and glass down, he whipped off his jacket and covered her shoulders. Then, he pulled out her chair as she sat.

"Anyone ever tell you how gallant you are?" Morgan asked, wondering how chivalry remained alive in today's techno-solitary world.

He palmed his chest. "Me?"

She nodded, savoring a bite of tomato and mozzarella. So much better than the fast food she'd been surviving on. "This is heavenly. You really need to try some of this."

She held out a forkful, but he shook his head. "I'm a meat and potatoes man. This is all a façade," he replied, sipping his wine. "Trust me."

She couldn't, and that was a shame. She would have liked to. "What façade?"

"I'm all about beer and football." He waggled the wineglass at her. "Not my norm."

He was lying. He was obviously used to better. Both the wine and the company. He'd swirled his glass and sniffed before wrinkling his nose at the taste of his first sip. The funny part was he seemed sincere. She wrenched her gaze away from him and looked around. Despite the din of the wedding, she could hear waves crashing against the shore. The day, so warm from the sun, now cooled with the ocean breeze. She looked up to see a seagull fly overhead through the pink swirls lingering in the sky. She wished she could be so free.

He sat back, his sapphire gaze swirling with banked desire. "Come upstairs with me."

CHAPTER TWO

GAUNTLET THROWN. MORGAN FROZE, FORK IN MID-AIR, shocked he'd crossed the line even though their whole meeting flirted with the possibility. She said she wouldn't sleep with him. "You can't be serious."

"I'm not?" He cocked his head as if trying to read her most secret place. The tension in his shoulders eased. "You're right. I just wanted to see your reaction."

She watched his Oxford shirt stretch beneath his broad shoulders and knew that a week ago, the possibility of jumping his bones would never have entered her mind. A man like this was simply out of her league. Once a geek, always a geek. Now, he was hers for the taking. Damn.

"Really? Exactly what was my reaction?" Anger bubbled inside, at fate, and the realization that he was probably playing with her. "Are you reading my mind?"

"How could I be?" He leaned back over the table and dug into his food with gusto. "I'm having dinner with a woman who hasn't even told me her name yet."

"I haven't?"

His long, slow, knowing, smile scared her more than anything else did. Then, she realized his gaze hadn't softened. "No, but it's kind of neat, though. Like one of those romantic mysteries."

Morgan stared at him. *Who are you, Jackson Kent?* "Strictly an oversight, I assure you. My name is Mariah."

"Not Carey," he said, taken aback.

"No. Like you, my parents stopped just shy of that."

Funny how lying came so naturally to her.

"At last. Something in common. Mariah—?"

Did lying come to him naturally also? Morgan inclined her head. "I didn't realize. Didn't the receptionist say it?" He shook his head. "Mariah Darmachzen," she lied, using one of her tech's last names, one she figured no one would know.

"That's a mouthful."

"Yes. My friends call me Mac."

"Am I your friend, Mariah Darmachzen?"

Amazingly enough, he'd pronounced the name correctly. It'd taken her a week. "Jury's still out on that one."

His smile belied the temperature. "I'd like to be, if you'll let me."

"Liar," she whispered.

"Yes." He stood and tossed back the last of his wine. "Come on. Let me walk you to your room. Nothing more, I swear."

Morgan rose, still befuddled. Desire twisted and crawled in the pit of her belly only to become frozen as the idea reached her mind. "You really are brazen, aren't you?"

God help her, there was that grin again. "That and a whole lot more."

"And if I do come with you?"

With an exaggerated sigh of disappointment, he replied, "Look, why don't you grab a sweater or something and we'll have coffee and desert on the deck? My treat. We'll watch the waves. And if you're adventurous, maybe even have a nightcap."

She knew she shouldn't. She should get in the car and run. Indecision slammed through her. "No pressure?"

He laughed. Morgan liked the sound. "No pressure. Just coffee."

Did she dare?

A fight ensued between logic and desire. *No one's going to know who you are.*

His gaze softened, coaxed.

You're stuck here until morning.

He licked lips that screamed for attention.

Until the next ferry.

Desire argued: It's Cape May, New Jersey, for crying out loud. Off-season. It doesn't get much quieter than this.

It's too dangerous, reason answered.

I need to rest.

Her psyche won. "Just coffee."

He moved closer. "Coffee... and..."

She took a step back. "No bargains."

He gave her his best request face. "None at all?"

She shook her head, unable to hide a grin. "No."

"Very...well."

"Then you can call me Mac."

And with that, she started walking away.

They sauntered along the deck to two sun chairs. Fresh paint and the huge hanging pots of purple, pink, and white impatiens sold her. They shouted *home*, exactly what her soul craved. And the waves? They calmed her soul the way only the ocean could.

Morgan had to believe no one would recognize her. She'd hit every ATM in Boston, cleaning out every one of her bank accounts. Not a lot, although enough for her to get lost for a while so she could do what needed to be done.

Changing her appearance was easy. Hair color and colored contact lenses. *Too many television shows*, she thought with a sad smile, never imagining in her wildest dreams, she'd be living one. Just as she reached the first chair, a light touch at her elbow reminded her of where she was and with whom.

"I think I lost you there for a sec," Jack said.

She winced. "Sorry. Baggage handling."

His gaze turned serious. "You want to talk about it?"

How she longed to tell him. Even though she felt she knew him, he was a stranger. He wouldn't judge. He'd simply listen. Then, Morgan realized, one word and he'd share her fate. They'd stop at nothing to keep their secret.

As a scientist, she imagined something new around every corner, something wonderful, something that would save the world. To discover those possibilities, Morgan had pushed the edge of the envelope. She dared to go where no one had gone before and look where that had gotten her.

They weren't going to let her get away. They were going to try to stop her. She had to believe that meant dead or alive. *Damn them all to hell and back again.*

Jack nudged her. "Hey, I lost you again."

She smiled, steel reinforcing her spine. Because they'd all forgotten about right and wrong and one little word. *Justice.*

"Hope that smile's not for me, 'cause if it is, I don't ever want to see you really mad."

"What?" She looked up at him. "Oh. Sorry."

The memory stick she'd hidden around her neck nestled between her breasts, a cold reminder of her mission, a reminder that she had no business talking to this man, let alone agreeing to coffee and dessert.

"No, not for you. Just trying to dump some stuff."

They sat down. "Whew. That's a relief. Does the guy you were thinking about still have any balls left?"

He thought she'd been jilted. As good an excuse as any. She tossed him an evil grin and replied, "I heard it took several days before he got out of the hospital."

"TMI," he replied, with a mock shudder. "I'll file that intel away for later."

"Intel?" A frisson of fear ran up her spine.

He gave her a sheepish look. "Sorry. I was in the army. Sometimes the slang slips out."

"Ahhh." She handed his jacket back, feeling her trust radar slip back into place. "Let me go and grab a coat from my car. I'll be right back."

"Promise?"

She bit her lip with indecision. She wanted to so badly she could taste it. No one would know. Would they?

Her next thought was to get in her car and drive far, far away, because that was the right thing to do. He gazed back at her without judgment. Maybe he knew. Maybe he understood she was all about integrity.

Did she dare?

"Friend of the bride or friend of the groom?" he asked softly.

"Neither," she replied, her lips twitching. He raised a brow, and the dimples did her in. "Friend of Jack."

EVEN IN THE DEEPENING TWILIGHT, SHE COULD SEE THE doubt in his gaze as she returned. He inhaled and blew out a deep breath. "I'm flattered you came back."

"You should be," she replied, her mouth curling into a smile.

He sat down as if he owned the chair. "Well, well, well, a battle of the sexes, eh? I have no objection to playing rough. If that's what you like."

Rough? Hot and hard filled her being for a second. God, what was she doing? "Battle?" She paused and sat as well. "Ahhh, ex-Army. You would say that. Mating shouldn't be a battle. Mating should be about romance. Did you know that the male peacock does everything in his power to prove that he's desirable to the female? He struts his plumage in front of her, trying his hardest to entice her. There's no battle, only seduction, which she has the right to accept or decline. I rather like that idea."

"Ahh. But you forgot something. If she toys with him too long, he can find another female."

Was she toying with him? Morgan didn't think so, but if she was, she was dead wrong to do so. She had no right to play games with him.

Sometimes, a moment of truth comes to us when we least expect it. For one autumn night in a quiet shore town, he was asking her to pretend the world didn't exist. Ten minutes later, she found herself staring at a fresh pot of coffee along with a piece of decadent-looking chocolate cake.

"Don't even try to say no. There's absolutely nothing wrong with your hips."

She smiled. "You noticed."

"I wasn't supposed to?"

Morgan raised a playful hand to swat at him. She stopped mid-swing, letting her hand fall with regret. "Sure you were."

He handed her a cup of coffee, and she added some milk. He took his black as sin. They ate in silence except for the music serenading them in the distance and the sound of the waves adding serenity to the chorus.

"Want to go jump in? Might be a little cold but a helluva ride."

She smiled over the rim of her cup. "You're crazy."

"Crazy enough to ask if you want to skip the ocean and go upstairs?"

His gaze deepened, became alluring, nearly undeniable. She was positive he was thinking of what it would feel like to be skin on skin, with no barriers at all, dancing the oldest dance of all, her moist, wet heat wrapping around him.

Morgan shivered. "You don't give up, do you?"

"Never."

Damn the man. He leaned back and his head rested against the back of the chair, his eyes were closed, and a look of sheer bliss covered his face. Suddenly, he reached out his hand to caress the skin of her arm. Tiny shivers ran up and down her spine. Her mind jumped to thoughts of what could happen if she simply let go, thoughts of how he could take her up those stairs and have his way with her right up against the door.

God, what would he do if he knew what she was thinking?

"I'm not going to, either," he added with determination.

Damn him, she was already slated for the fire. "Even if I say no?"

"You don't really want to do that," he countered, his gaze heating. "You haven't even seen my plumage yet. It really is enticing."

"Really," she drawled, need filling her core. "In public?"

"Dare me," he breathed.

Morgan melted under the breathy whisper. But a sharp, swift kick to the libido stopped that right in its tracks. Scared to death for herself and for him as well, she started lifting the drawbridge, forcing the walls around her to thicken.

He must have felt her change of heart. "You don't have to answer." He sighed. "As much as I hate already knowing, I understand."

"You don't." She rose, the night and the fairy tale at an end.

"No, I don't," he admitted. "However, I know how to bow and cut my losses." He stood, lifted her hand like a courtier, and kissed the back. She stared at that hand for a long time, forcing him to lift her chin to look into his eyes.

"My mother always told me there were reasons for why things happen," he continued. "We'll meet again. I'm certain of it."

Tears filled her eyes.

She blinked and they were gone. Along with her chance to renege, tell him to stay, throw caution to the wind, anything that would keep her next to him. Without knowing why but knowing the fires of the underworld were licking at her skin in anticipation, Morgan lifted her face to his. Her eyes closed. He leaned down and kissed her forehead. Her whole being centered on the spot he'd kissed.

Her breath hitched. Morgan had never felt anything more erotic in her entire life.

Her eyes snapped open. She exhaled and the world started turning again. "Ah, hell."

Morgan couldn't let the moment end. She couldn't tear herself away from him no matter how much she knew she should. As soon as he realized that, he grinned. "Damn the torpedoes?"

"Full speed ahead," she answered, grinning in reply.

"Are you sure?"

"Very. Although I hope everyone at the wedding is too drunk to notice."

"Awesome. Come on then. Let's go."

Knowing she was making the biggest mistake of her life, Morgan grabbed his hand, and they ran down the steps together to go jump in the ocean.

SHE HAD TO BE CRAZY. NO, SHE WAS ALREADY DAMNED AND absolutely freaking nuts. She started laughing and couldn't stop. Jack had a hold of her hand, and they ran halfway into the water before they both stopped. Gasping for breath, she looked over to see him doubled over with laughter.

Now Morgan knew why make-believe was so much fun.

"Didn't think I had it in me, did ya'?" he shouted. "Certainly didn't think you'd go for it."

Morgan lifted back to look into his eyes. "No, I certainly didn't."

He grinned, pulling her into his arms and nipping her ear. *Damn those dimples.* "You do realize what this means, don't you? That we're going back to my suite and making mad passionate love until the sun rises."

Her heart skipped several beats. "And then what, Jack? What happens in the morning?"

His grin deepened, became even more alluring. "We make mad passionate love all day."

She smiled, bitter and sweet, blending to make a fine dark chocolate in her body. "Even you're not that good."

"I'm not? Says who?" he replied, his voice growing lower, sexier, just above a growl.

Morgan sighed. "The sun rises in the morning, Jack. You want to create a fairy tale, damn the torpedoes, full speed ahead. You don't want to think about the future, but despite all our wishes, the enchanted evening has to end. I can't. The more I taste, the more I'm going to want. You want a one-night stand. That's not my style. It would be less painful if it ended now."

"You could make it your style—if you really wanted to."

Morgan pulled away. "I can't, Jack."

He winced. "And I can't let you go. Not yet. No one, and I mean no one, has ever dared to jump in the ocean with me."

"I know." The water turned icy, and she shivered, the fire and the excitement but a memory. "You can't keep me here, either."

His shoulders slumped. He looked down at his wet clothes and then at her, at her straggly hair and rumpled suit. "You're right." He reached out for her elbow to help her up out of the water. "Come on, I'll walk you back."

They headed back to the deck in silence. The night was exactly that again, just a damp, chilly autumn evening. The waves continued rolling in jumbled abandon. The music from the wedding continued to play. The party went on.

He escorted her into the hotel and to the elevator. Her stomach knotted with the truth. She wanted him. She wanted everything he was offering. She had no right to take it.

He reached into his pocket and gave her the key to her room, then he turned to her and sighed, lifting the back of her hand and caressing her skin with his thumb. He kissed the back and let go. "Good night, Mac. Thank you for the best night of my life."

The best night? Morgan's heart ached. However, she knew she was doing the right thing. "Good night, Jack." The elevator doors opened, and she walked through them. She lifted her shoulders, carrying the memories of this night, and she turned. He grinned, that uptick of the side of his mouth that she'd never forget. That smile, those dimples, would haunt her for a long time.

Morgan tore herself away. Sometimes, you're damned if you do. *Don't turn back. Don't turn back.* The elevator doors closed. Her heart wrenched. She bit down hard as her stomach hollowed and she started walking down the hallway to her room. Morgan was damned because she couldn't. Someday, there would be a reckoning.

CHAPTER THREE

MORGAN OPENED THE DOOR TO HER ROOM AND SHOOK HER head. Her suitcase was still in the car. With a gentle laugh, she shut the door and trudged back to the elevator again. A spike of adrenaline surged as the elevator doors opened, the hope of seeing him one last time. A time that wasn't meant to be.

She went out to the parking lot and stared at the car door, wondering if it wouldn't be better to climb inside and continue on, find a small dive motel, and spend the night sleeping in a chair. Okay, that would be stupid, wouldn't it? After all, she had a nice, clean hotel room right here.

And the chance to perhaps see him one last time.

No. Not happening. She would have to be gone before the sun rose.

Morgan grabbed her suitcase from the back seat and rolled it back to the elevator. Shivering with cold inside and out, all she wanted was a hot shower and a night of sleep she might not get. She opened the door to her room and heard shower water running. Her heart leapt in her chest as she told herself she'd better start breathing again. The knowledge of him being there hit her square in the solar plexus. She looked down at her soaked clothes and wondered...did she dare join him? Nah, that would be a bit too much, wouldn't it? Suddenly, the bathroom door opened. Funny, she hadn't even realized the water had stopped running.

Whatever words were about to come out, they skidded to a halt. Her jaw simply dropped. Funny, she'd expected him to smile or maybe give her that patented little grin of his. He didn't. He knew. The moment meant too much to both of them.

His gaze caught hers. She answered with a thousand unspoken questions, the last one asking if she was doing the right thing.

A slight nod affirmed he wouldn't judge nor let her down.

Morgan swallowed hard as her gaze drank in every detail. A white cotton towel slung low over his hips. Smooth tanned skin stretched taut over sculpted muscles. A thin line of hair disappeared beneath the white cotton.

"Do I pass?"

She started. "Pass what?"

He grinned. She melted. "Inspection."

"I wasn't trying to—"

Swift strides closed the space between them. "I wasn't complaining."

Caught in a trap of her own making, Morgan couldn't move. She couldn't breathe as he captured both her hands in his and, closing his eyes, kissed each one. She melted again.

"Been a while?" he asked, grazing his cheek softly against her skin.

"Yes," she strangled out.

He lifted back up. "Like riding a bike, you know."

"Easy for you to say," she replied, trying to breathe and failing miserably.

"That's where you're wrong."

He let go of her hands and feathered his fingertips up her arms, her skin rippling beneath his touch. Every cell in her body woke up, hungry for sensation after a long dormancy. She shivered as his hands roamed up the sides of her neck, cupping her cheeks to lift her chin. She drank in his breath, tasting his desire.

Her hands rolled over his chest, pure delight racing through her veins. But a dam can only hold back the inevitable for so long. She locked her fingers behind his neck to draw his head closer… closer. He devoured her mouth with the same *joie de vivre* he'd shown while dancing. She'd never made love to a man like this before.

A fire ignited inside her belly, and she opened her mouth wider as he took full advantage. Morgan knew she edged perilously close to the point of no return. She broke the kiss, gasping, trying to bring her heart rate down from infinity.

Damn that grin of his. "Let's try losing the jacket first."

She'd forgotten she was still wearing a suit. Hell, she'd forgotten she was still wet from their escapade in the ocean.

He slid the cloth from her shoulders, and she shivered as his hands skimmed down her arms. He tossed the offending garment over the back of a chair and then reached out to lift her turtleneck over her head.

"Jack," she whispered. "Wait. Let me rinse off at least." Her breath caught and held each time his fingers grazed her skin. Her nipples beaded inside her bra, begging for his touch, her heart pounding with an insane rhythm beneath his knuckles.

"I like the taste of salt," he growled. He bent his head to swipe his tongue across the line of her jaw.

"Please," she begged. "I'm all sticky."

He reached around to slide his palms up the skin of her back. Then next thing she knew, he had her bra unsnapped and was pulling her ever closer to his body. His gaze roamed her face, the banked desire in his eyes bursting into flames. He started to hum and sway with her in his arms as he grazed his lips against her forehead, rimming his tongue along the shell of her ear, and the dance took on a whole new meaning.

He pressed his hard length against her belly.

She closed her eyes, her head falling to his chest as his heart beat out of control beneath her. She couldn't help herself. Morgan pressed light kisses all over his chest, stopping to nip at his nipple. He jumped. Jack couldn't help *him*self. His hold tightened, tucking her into his body as if she belonged there. The dance being long over, neither one of them moved, but the fuel continued firing inside her veins.

And then she froze. The data stick was ready to fall and would be so very hard to explain.

Morgan shrugged out of his grasp. He looked down at her in surprise. She hurried toward the bathroom. Once inside, she reached in and grabbed the stick and stuck it inside the tissue dispenser. Then, she shucked her clothes and rinsed off, toweling dry in minutes.

Morgan opened the door, inhaling deeply. She checked the towel to make sure she was covered and walked back into the room. He sauntered up to her, no longer grinning. Indeed, his gaze couldn't have been more serious. Could this evening mean more to him than just sex? Had he been telling her the truth or at least his version of it? Morgan hesitated. Jack shook his head and deepened his grin, turning naughty, as he closed the space between them. He slipped his forefinger inside the towel between her breasts and started working at the knot, daring her to stop him. She felt a slough against her shins from the cloth of his towel and then felt hers puddle at her feet.

"Now, we're even."

Not exactly. Neither one had taken that next step to go past the point of no return. He stared down at her, blue diamond lights firing in his gaze, daring her. Morgan licked her lips in anticipation.

Funny how she'd forgotten how to be sexy. Jack gave her a whole new meaning for the word. Did she dare?

A thrill ran through her. The men she'd known in the past were all about themselves. Not Jack. Morgan watched as his hands slid over the skin of her chest. Her breath caught with each touch. His gaze darkened as he refused to look down. He didn't need to. He reached out to cup her breasts with unerring accuracy. His thumbs brushed back and forth over her nipples. Pleasure raced through her veins and ended in her core.

God, she wanted him.

He brushed his thumbs over her nipples again. She moaned and her knees started to cave. He smiled, knowing full well what he was doing. He drew her closer and bent his head. *A kiss is not always just a kiss.*

Morgan let go. For better or worse, she put her body and her life in the hands of a stranger who was a stranger no more.

He started as he tasted her full response and then plunged into the depths with her, wild heat radiating between them, tongues dancing, lips melding, lighting a fire only one act could quell.

Morgan wanted him. All of him.

She closed her hand around his hard length. He moaned, breaking the kiss. His hand fell on top of hers.

"Easy, kitten. I'm not Superman, you know."

Morgan returned his grin ten-fold. He laughed softly, dipping down to feast on her breasts. Each nip, each lick, made her heart race. Her core went nova as she ground her hips against his. However, there was still one last barrier to remove.

With a quick push on his shoulders, Morgan broke away. A lift of his brow seemed to ask why and then a slight twitch of his lips told her he had the answer. His gaze flared as he approached.

Lathing each nipple with his tongue, Morgan shifted, so he'd begin the journey with the valley between her breasts. He let his fingers take over, shooting jolts of pleasure through her as he tweaked her nipples. All the while he moved steadily lower until he could go no further.

He rose, lifted her in his arms, and carried her over to the bed. Her head curled into his chest as if the spot belonged to her and her alone. He let her go and she found the back of her legs up against the mattress. Morgan didn't think, she simply fell, opening her core to him. He licked her belly and the crown of each hip before halting at the top of her hairline. His fingers teased, rimming the edges of her folds, opening them inch by torturous inch. If he touched her, no, even *breathed* on her, she'd explode.

He seemed to sense that, urging her to lift her hips. So, he shifted instead, continuing to nip and lick at the skin just above her mound. Morgan struggled to rise. She sat up and found her mouth level with his erection. All her life she'd thought men weren't made to be beautiful. They were made to be functional. *What changed that,* she wondered, as her tongue licked at his tip.

He'd explored her body with care. Now, it was her turn.

Morgan nipped her way up and down his shaft before swallowing him whole. Her reward was a groan of sheer pleasure that came from the depths of his being. She drew back again and then sucked him deep into her throat. She cupped his balls, rolling them lightly. He shuddered and pushed her off, drawing in a huge breath of air until he regained his control.

He answered her wicked grin with one of his own, sheathing himself is less than a moment. Morgan fell back onto the bed, spread her arms wide, every nerve aware of the rough texture of the bedspread, the chill in the air, and the scent of spice and masculine heat. Jack knelt, spread her legs, and returned the favor by licking his way up her core. Then, he flicked her nub as she moaned in surrender. Morgan thought she'd die from the pleasure. Could anything in the world compare to this moment?

"Jack," she strangled out, pulling at his shoulders.

Morgan would never ever forget his smile, naughty, serious, filled with desire, telling her that an end was only a beginning. He lifted her hips and plunged deep inside.

She gasped. *Sweet, sweet heaven.*

There would be no long, slow, drawn-out lovemaking tonight. They both knew that. Morgan locked her legs around his back, drawing him deeper and deeper inside.

He plunged his tongue into her mouth, sealing her fate with a kiss. He told her exactly how he felt with his kiss, told her that he was going to take everything she had to give. Deep inside she felt a promise, the promise that he was going to give her everything back and more.

In that moment, as he pushed her higher and higher toward release, Morgan realized what yearning and desire were all about, and that she couldn't stop him, wouldn't stop him. She wanted the moment to go on and on and on.

He ripped his mouth from hers, leaning back and bracing his weight on his elbows to drive deeper inside her core. He pulled all the way out, thrust all the way in, grinding against her. Her breath hitched. His caught. Their eyes opened at the exact same moment. Morgan screamed, and she exploded.

How he didn't follow amazed her. But he didn't. He froze, swallowing hard. He clenched his jaw and sweat beaded his chest.

"I—," he gasped. "I wanted to watch you come."

Morgan kissed him, biting his lip, already feeling herself rise again. He could too. He worked his hips so the base of his cock rested right on her nub.

"That's it," he growled, biting her lip in return. "Fly with me."

He started moving again, slowly, savoring the pleasure of each thrust. Morgan slid her hands slid down his shoulders to his chest and tweaked his nipples. He shivered, thrusting even harder. She groaned.

Leaning down, he nipped his way along her neck, spreading her legs even further apart with his hand. She'd never felt so filled and so fulfilled, the thought sending her climbing to the top of the mountain once again.

He kept on thrusting and Morgan could feel his control snap as he rammed into her, once, twice, three times before he toppled over the edge. When his breath caught and he cried out in completion, she found herself following a moment later, straining to hold on to every sensation. Time and motion ceased to exist.

One minute she was thinking about him, the next she exploded, bucking and heaving against him, the earthquakes inside her refusing to stop.

His head dropped to her neck, his heart beating wildly atop hers, his breath warming her as aftershocks pulsed through her body. Long minutes passed before he moved. She didn't want to let him go. Her arms tightened around him, feeling bereft as he slipped out of her body. He held on, arms wrapped around her, a haven for her uncertain world.

He brushed her forehead with his lips. "Stay with me tonight."

If she did, she wouldn't get much sleep.

Another kiss. "Please."

Most men wouldn't ask. However, Jack wasn't most men. Her arms tightened around his shoulders. Her mind, that ever-practical organ, shouted warning after warning. Her ears refused to listen.

One enchanted evening. One fairy tale night.

She lifted her chin, and he leaned down to kiss her gently. When he let go, she was done. Toast. *Damn that grin of his.* There was no use fighting the inevitable.

Pulling his head down to hers, she figured, *what the hell.* She had only one life to live.

A sharp pain pulled Morgan out of a deep sleep. She tried to move and found her hair caught beneath a casually thrown arm on the bed. A casually thrown *what*?

Memory flooded her. Heat filled her cheeks. And between her legs? Oh no, better not to even go *near* there. Morgan rolled over, wincing as reality slipped a stiletto between her third and fourth ribs. Everyone had the right to indulge in a fantasy, and Jack was the best fantasy she'd ever had, but not any longer, not when reality waited right outside his door.

How could she have been so stupid?

On the one hand, she'd fallen into the mantrap and thought things through with the lower half of her body. On the other hand, if doing Jack really were stupid, she'd stay a dunce for the rest of her life. Her only regret was the hurt she was going to cause him.

Sure, last night was all about the sex. But unless she was totally brain dead, she got the message that he cared enough to make sure she was going to have to crawl out of this hotel room and not walk.

Damn, damn, damn, damn, damn. Why now?

Because it's better to have lived and made love than not to have made love at all.

Morgan rolled over and began easing herself out of the bed so as not to awaken him. Even in his sleep, he didn't seem to want to let her go. He finally turned on his side and freed her so she could slip out of the bed. She picked up her clothes, piece by piece, and tucked her memories deep inside her heart. She would pull them out later. If there was a later.

Luckily, her clothes were at least semi damp so she could slip them on without making a racket. She crept back out of the room and stared at the bed as the door shut slowly, branding him in her mind. As quietly as she could, she let the lock click into place, leaning her forehead against the wood once the latch closed. There would never be another night like this. Ever.

Morgan rolled her suitcase down the hall and went down to the lobby. She used the main bathroom to clean up, the water washing away his scent, his mark on her, but it could never wash away the stain of her mark on him. Remorse was an emotion she wasn't allowed. Another reason why the seeds of vindication were going to grow into the fruits of justice. Once those fruits ripened, they were going to taste really, really good.

Thirty minutes later she was dressed and ready to leave. She glanced toward the hotel from the parking lot. *Goodbye, Jack. Thank you.*

She imagined, when he woke up, he wouldn't return the sentiment.

THE MAN IN QUESTION, HOWEVER, HAD BEEN UP FROM THE moment she awoke. As soon as her door closed, he jumped out of bed. Jack paced back and forth like a caged tiger begging to be set free. However, freedom is a relative term. One neither of them, he imagined, would be able to enjoy. He picked up his phone and hit speed dial.

"Damn it, Sam," he muttered as his phone rang and rang. "Pick up."

"Hello?"

At last. "Where the hell have you been?" Jack bit out.

"Fuck you."

"The feeling's mutual. I have about ten seconds. The ferry. Lewes, Delaware."

Dead silence greeted him, but he knew his partner was already sitting up on the edge of his bed wide-awake. "You sure?"

"Yeah, I'm sure. I've got her."

CHAPTER FOUR

THE CHILL IN THE AIR MATCHED JACK'S INTERNAL temperature. The discordant swish of the breeze through the trees seemed to be dying the same death as his emotions under the weight of the early morning fog.

Right's right and wrong's wrong. Nothing could be simpler than that. *Oh really?*

She stepped up to the car and opened the back door, looking more like an angel than a criminal. But Jack had been fooled before. He sat on the pavers that lined the parking lot behind a car where she wouldn't see him. Play it straight with her...or don't.

Jack rose and cleared his throat. "Going somewhere?"

She spun around to stare at him, and even in the dim light of the impending dawn, Jack could read the guilt running through her face.

Her throat worked as she tried to swallow. "What are you doing here?" she strangled out.

A tiny shard of pain reached under his skin, just enough to bother him. Morgan Mackenzie was anything but stupid; however, her question seemed superfluous.

"I'd have thought that was obvious."

Her shoulders sagged for a moment and then she drew in a breath and locked them back in place. Jack wasn't one to admire another's fortitude, having had few examples worth admiring. However, the way she stood before him, proud despite her guilt, open just enough to allow him to read her inner angst, he almost felt a kinship with her.

They were both caught in the game with no way out.

Jack walked around the car in his way, shoving his hands into his pockets to keep from touching her. Under the aura of the artificial lights, and with the dampness in the air, Jack could have sworn he saw a halo form around her head.

Impossible. Thieves are thieves. They don't get halos. They get Jack. And justice.

"Is it?" he replied, making sure his tone resonated with hurt. "I'm not so sure. I didn't take you for a coward."

She looked as if she had to stave off every word. Even now he itched to tear away her armor and bury himself deep inside her, where neither of them could feel anything but the panacea of making love.

She winced, picking up her bag. "Do you really want the truth?" she cried. "Do you really want me to go there?"

"Yes," he whispered, knowing he deserved any punishment she could dish out and then some.

"All right. When a lady leaves in the middle of the night, it means the sex was hot but you're not. Goodbye."

She turned to leave, and Jack's instincts kicked in. Despite breaking every rule he'd ever made for himself, Jack still had a job to do. And by God, he was going to do it come...

Yep, no doubt about it now, he was going to burn in hell. So, hell didn't matter. High water didn't matter. None of it mattered. Because there was right, and there was wrong. She'd started it and he was going to finish it. Pain be damned. Pride be damned. Jack be damned.

Yeah, well, he'd deal with that little problem later.

He walked up to her, wondering how someone so right could have done something so wrong. And how a night in her arms could have been so right when it should have been wrong.

Love ‘em and turn ‘em in, Jack?

Okay, so the taste in his mouth wasn’t exactly sweet.

Her scent reached him, fresh, clean and untouched by the world he lived in. He drew in a deep breath. He unclenched his hands and pulled them out of his pockets. Looking deep into her eyes, he thought he read fear. But the air sparked and sizzled, and he knew that any fear she felt was from this insane desire igniting between them.

His arms reached out to close around her. “No, Jack.”

Even though they hadn’t touched, she broke away as if bound to him, yanking and jerking, stumbling backward. She turned and hurried around the car to the driver’s side. He followed and caught her halfway there, trying very hard not to remember how he’d felt the last time he’d touched her.

“No, Jack,” she repeated. “This is wrong.”

He pulled her close. “No, Mac. It’s right.”

He couldn’t help himself. He was the one who gave in to his desire while she followed. He’d led her in the mating dance. He’d dazzled her with his plumage. How could he have expected anything less?

With one arm around her waist, he reached out to tuck her hair behind her ear. Her skin rippled beneath his fingertip. Jack had never realized how seductive seduction could be.

“Stay with me. Just a little longer. I’ll find a way to explain another charge on my card.” Was he really begging? Was he really that pitiful?

No, he told himself. It’s part of the con. Make her feel safe with you. Get her to talk some more. Get your rocks off at her expense. Real pain knifed through him. Oh, this was not good, this was *so* not good. Remorse had no place here.

Jack donned his persona like a second skin.

Reading her indecision, he pressed his advantage. "You know you want to..." he growled softly, just above a whisper. "I can feel the heat coming off you in waves. Come on. We'll go upstairs. We'll go back to your room. Better yet, let's try my suite." He let the words he didn't have to say hang between them like a prize waiting to be seized.

She hesitated. He slid one hand around the back of her neck. He engulfed her mouth with his, plundering and punishing with his tongue, trying to erase his mission. He didn't stop until she sagged against him, her body betraying her desperate resolve. Then and only then did he tear his mouth from hers.

"Jack." One whispered word held all the anguish in her heart and then some.

His cheek grazed her chin, her temple, until it came to rest against her forehead. His arms banded around her, pulling her close to his body, his heart beating way too fast in his ears.

He leaned back and lifted her chin. "Did you think I'd ever let you leave without saying goodbye?"

"I was trying to avoid a scene."

He cocked his head, letting his eyes fill with hurt and the questions she didn't want asked. "At whose expense? Yours or mine?"

"Both," she admitted.

"My choice. So was last night."

Morgan buried her head in his chest. "Don't do this, Jack. Please."

As if he could stop himself now. "You see, I have this problem," he began, kissing the hair on top of her head. The artificial light glittered off the red and gold streaks, making him think of the fire inside her and his insane desire to ignite it once again.

She didn't answer. Maybe she couldn't. "I didn't sleep at all last night," he continued, a touch of awe in his tone. "I've never done that before. Because all I wanted to do was hold you in my arms."

The funny part was the words were coming too easily to his lips, which told him way more than he wanted to know.

He leaned back and watched Morgan's face turn to stone. She tried to shrug her way out of his arms. He wouldn't let her go. "Generally, men take the hint when a lady leaves without saying goodbye. One night. That's all it was. One night."

"Liar."

She frowned. "I am? What? Are you really Kreskin now? You can read minds?"

Jack didn't need to. She was a thief, and that was all he needed to know. He had to keep her close. He turned up the heat another notch. "Look me dead in the eyes and tell me that."

"I'm not lying, Jack."

He feathered his lips across her brow, letting her scent invade his senses. "Yes, you are."

She shuddered once then stilled in his arms. "And you seem to require a baseball bat over the head." She lifted her gaze and locked onto his. "We had a little fun. You're outrageous, a good dancer, and jumping in the ocean was a hoot."

Jack didn't let her finish. He bent down and engulfed her mouth with his. She started to give in and then tore her mouth away. "Okay, so you're great in bed," she gasped. "There, I admitted it. Now I have to leave."

He laughed. Not a pretty sound. He hated the game he was forced to play because right now, he realized he wasn't playing. He clenched his jaw. Letting go was hard. "I wasn't interested in having my ego stroked. I just wanted to know why you chose to crush it in the first place. Or didn't you think that would happen when I listened to you shut your bedroom door?"

"Leave me alone, Jack. We shared one night. That's it."

Morgan broke out of his embrace and threw open the car door. He followed. Without another word, he reached out to grab her arm. She stopped. So did he. Only the sound of their breaths, rapid as if they'd run for miles, broke the silence of the early morning.

Jack stood there, letting his hand fall away, so close he could feel the heat radiating off her skin, offering to make the world go away if she would let go and take him up on it.

"Which way are you headed?"

She frowned. "Why?"

He stuck his fists into his pockets again and hunched his shoulders against the morning damp. "Let me tag along. I'm not committed to going anywhere right now. Besides, it's Sunday. And even God..."

"I know. He rested on Sunday."

He watched her fight with herself. He was beginning to know that fight very well. She started to cave. She bit her lip and her gaze flipped from him to the car door and back to him again. He moved next to her as if his body could make up her mind for her, trying to make her craving for him drown the fear. Then, she lashed out. At herself, he figured, as much as him. "This was supposed to be a one-night stand, not a relationship."

He stiffened, shoulders rising. He lifted his chin. The spikes she hammered into him were only making them both bleed more. "I know," he agreed. "But I've enjoyed every moment I've spent with you. You can't blame me for not wanting it to end."

"Can I blame you when I get fired?"

He frowned. "It's Sunday. You have to travel. Play hooky with me for a little while. You're going to take the ferry, right?"

"Yes..." she hesitated.

"Come on," he said, threading his voice with excitement. "We'll take the ferry and then I'll buy you lunch. I know a wonderful little bar and restaurant..."

"Bad idea. Very, very bad."

He let his expression fall, hoping to twist at her heartstrings. "Why?"

"Because it's just putting off the inevitable. I'm still going to have to go my way and you're still going to have to go yours."

His gaze grew serious, and he sighed. "All right. I know. But let's not end things like this. A ferry ride and lunch. That's all I'm asking for."

"You promise you'll be able to say goodbye without the drama?"

"I promise."

In celebration or perhaps in retaliation, Jack would never know, but she thumbed her nose at the world as she grinned back at him. He watched as she pushed away reality, turned off her mind, and let a very bruised psyche win the day. Two very bruised psyches.

She tilted her head up to look at him and said, "I'm starving. How about we start with breakfast?"

He grinned back at her. "How do you like your eggs?"

"Over easy with a hint of heat."

Seriously, she didn't say that, did she? God, he was so damned.

CHAPTER FIVE

FOOL. FOOL. A THOUSAND TIMES A FOOL.

Dr. Morgan Mackenzie looked out at the water meeting the horizon as the Lewes ferry sped along toward Delaware and hung her head, wondering how and where she'd lost control of the situation.

"I fell in love with you the moment you turned the corner," Jackson Kent told her, his tone way too sincere, and his gaze way too hot to handle.

To hide her surprise, she laughed, unable to suppress the heat filling her cheeks. But inside her stomach was doing flips.

"Jack, really. Be serious."

Morgan made the mistake of looking down and watched the water slap and roll against the hull of the ferry. She'd taken this as an alternate route from Cape May, New Jersey, thinking it would be less easily followed. Both the ferry and her predicament caused her stomach to clench.

"I am."

Could she believe him? They'd only met last night.

You need to go to the police.

No, I need to get as far away from this as possible.

Morgan pulled her coat closed and shivered. BioClin wasn't stupid. They had to have somebody looking for her.

You need to go to the police.

And what? Hand them everything? How would that prove my innocence? Only my name and my notebook notes are connected to that poor woman's death.

Her shiver turned to a shudder. *And to top it all off, there's no body to prove that someone's died.*

"Jack, look. What we shared was—"

"The most incredible night I've ever spent with anyone," he answered, cutting her off. A lock of hair fell onto his forehead, giving his face a look of boyish earnestness as he reached out and clasped her hands in his.

But there was nothing childlike about the heat simmering in his eyes or the intent in his gaze. Thank goodness he couldn't see the liquid fire answering in the pit of her belly.

The ferry rolled. Her stomach clenched again, just the bucket of cold water she needed to counteract him. He was a drug she couldn't afford to take.

Damned motion sickness.

Any worse than the sickness in your head? What the hell were you thinking when you walked into that man's hotel room?

Thinking?

Morgan shook her head to clear it. Was it really that simple? Had she given into his charms simply because she wanted to taste the unattainable?

She drew in a deep breath. There was something insanely exquisite about the man, just the right combination for her taste. He was beautiful, almost pretty, but all male. Her fingertips had explored every hill and crevice of his chest and biceps, so she knew.

The fresh air helped her stomach, but there wasn't anything she could think of that would save her from this man. Jack.

Despite the hard consonants, his name simply rolled off her tongue. Jackson Kent. The one luxury she couldn't afford.

Eventually, the people who were after her would pick up her trail. The proprietor of the hotel would remember her and probably be able to identify Morgan even though she'd changed her appearance. No one would ever know she and Jack had any contact other than being guests at the establishment at the same time.

Her logic helped ease the sickness that had leached from her stomach to her head to her heart. She didn't want to hurt him. She definitely didn't want him caught up in her problems.

"Hey, are you all right? You don't look so good."

Time to exit, stage left. "A soda would be great. Can you get me one from the snack bar?"

"My pleasure."

He was back before she could collect her wayward thoughts. Turning her head from the horizon, Morgan watched him approach. God, he was beautiful. The kind of man you figured just had to be a player.

Morgan knew firsthand exactly how good he really was.

"Morgan," he growled, handing her the bottle. "You sooo don't want to look at me that way."

"What way?" she asked, her tone full of innocence.

He grinned, lifting his hand so that his thumb grazed her cheek. His touch shivered all the way down her spine. "The way you looked last night. When you were naked in my arms. After our second time. Or was it third?"

Morgan choked despite herself, "I *am* not."

He cocked his head, his tone teasing. "Oh, no? As a matter of fact," he answered back, his tone low and full of promise. "I believe you're daring me."

"Daring you?" Morgan opened the bottle with shaking fingers and drank. "Jack. Stop. Behave this instant."

"Oh no, darling," he replied, pressing against her with a dangerous look. "That's not what you want. And I know it."

Damn, damn, damn. Incorrigible. Impossible. Not only had he made her ditch her better judgment, but he'd also made her forget who she really was.

He was seducing her all over again. Sayonara, backbone. In fact, there wasn't a bone in her body that stayed solid when he looked at her like that.

In the interest of self-preservation, Morgan dragged her gaze away from him. She stared at the horizon again, trying to quell the heat inside. Talk about a losing battle.

"So, what are you?" she asked, her attempt to change the conversation a pitiful one. "What do you do? I didn't really have time to ask last night."

She made the mistake of turning her head to look at him, and he grinned, that very special kind of half quirk, half smile that reached right down to her toes. "I own my own business. Which allows for..." He reached out, grabbed her shoulder, and forced her to pivot toward him, his gaze turning incendiary. "Diversions."

This insanity had to end. "Jack. This is a public place. It's a ferry, for crying out loud. People. Cars. Workers."

He stared at her, looking way too innocent for his own good. "It was the only way I could capture you."

Morgan blanched inside until she read the sexy, on-the-prowl promise on his face. "I tried to tell you before. I can't be captured."

He punched his chest with his fist. "Me, Jack. Hunter. You, prize."

"Seriously," she snarked back at him.

His head dipped, his gaze acknowledging that he was getting rather carried away. "The problem is you don't see yourself as one."

She snorted, taking his words at face value. "Jack, be honest. I'm not a model."

He didn't let her continue, placing his finger on her lips. "Beauty's only skin deep."

She nipped at his fingertip, appreciating that he was trying to make her feel better.

"Brains and this," he told her, moving his finger to point at her heart. "Make for the real prize."

"You're a fool."

"And yet..." He trailed off and pulled her to him so that their bodies nearly touched. "You make the world go away."

That was the amazing part of all of this. It did for her too.

He took the bottle out of her hands and placed it on the railing of the ferry and then reached around her to draw her close. The breeze, once cold, was now refreshing as it counteracted his heat. A strand of hair blew across her cheek, and he brushed it aside before cupping her cheeks with his palms.

He lowered his head, and Morgan could feel herself reaching up to meet him. Then, she realized where they were. "No, Jack. Not here."

His head shifted slowly from side to side. "Oh, no," she cried, putting her arms in between them and pushing at his chest.

Those sturdy limbs refused to budge an inch. "You wouldn't dare."

"Try me," he challenged, still not budging.

"No, no, no, no, no. Public place. If we get caught, we could go to jail."

His gaze told her he was too far gone to listen to reason. "Then, we don't get caught."

His grin faded. He turned serious, scaring her even more than she was already. He couldn't know what getting caught by the authorities would mean for her. And she couldn't tell him. "Where there's a will, there's a way. Come on."

He began pulling her away from the railing. "No, Jack. And you can't make me."

"I can't?" he asked, his tone low and sexy, barely above a growl.

They fought for every inch of ground until he let out a roar of aggravation and swung her up against his body. He'd finally reached the breaking point where it didn't seem to matter anymore that they were in a public area. He was going to do exactly as he implied.

If he did, she'd let him.

Mortified by her own willingness to throw away her pride, her principles, *and* her fear, Morgan stared up at him. She came as close to begging as she could. "Jack. Not like this."

He stilled, sanity returning to his eyes. He swallowed before he whispered, "I guess now you understand."

She did. She had the ability to make him forget everything because he was doing the same thing to her.

"I could take you right here, right now," he told her, his gaze sobering. "And you'd let me."

"God help me—I think I would."

She dropped her gaze, to look him in the eyes was like looking in a mirror, something she wasn't too sure she wanted to see.

Oh no, you don't. Morgan Mackenzie is not a coward.

She forced her head upward. The breeze ruffled a few strands of his hair. His face grew taut with desire, telling her exactly what his intentions were. But his eyes. Oh, heaven, his eyes. Those killer blues had softened. They'd gone from sapphire chips to the color of swirled marble, filled with confusion and heat. Funny, he didn't seem to be able to understand this thing growing between them. Theirs was an insane passion, a fool's passion, one she couldn't begin to understand either.

Letting her see inside, though, made up her mind. There was no way to stop what was about to explode between them. He bent his head closer to hers. Her chin tilted upward to meet his. One touch would reignite the fire that would probably get them both locked up for certain.

His lips closed over hers, his tongue sweeping into her mouth before he let go, his breath going staccato as he leaned his forehead against hers.

"Jack," she whispered, panting, her heart thundering, "all right."

He grabbed her arm, pulling to where a steel beam met the sidewall of the ferry and created a tiny private corner.

Trembling fingers cupped her cheeks. Molten fire scorched her skin as his gaze roamed over her face. One enchanted evening had morphed into pure need. And that frightened her more than anything else. His head drew closer, and Morgan fell back into the wall, finding the cold metal strangely comforting, solid in a sea of emotions she could neither accept nor deny.

He dragged his lips across her forehead, her skin burning under their trace, and then tasted her brows and cheeks as if touch could imprint her features. He drew in short, helpless breaths. His hard length pressed against her belly. How had everything gotten so out of control?

"Jack," she choked out once more, trying desperately for one last bid at sanity. He stilled. His arms tightened around her back. His head dipped and his lips devoured hers.

So much for the word *no*.

Perhaps he tasted her inner struggle. Perhaps he tasted her fear, and not just the fear about getting caught making love on a ferry. Whatever the cause, his kiss gentled, coaxed. Their tongues tasted and mated, giving and taking. And that frightened her most of all. It wasn't just about sex anymore. It was about sharing.

Jack tore his mouth away and leaned his forehead on top of hers. Neither of them could breathe. Two hearts beating out of control. They were both a hairbreadth from exploding.

It was all so wrong.

And so right.

He opened her jacket and pulled her blouse out, his hand sliding up her belly as she sucked in a breath. His fingers captured her breast, tweaking her nipple until her knees buckled against him. He caught her, pressing her into the wall of the ferry.

"I need to be inside of you," he choked. "*Now.*"

"Jack…" she mewled, making one last feeble protest.

A slow, sly grin grew on his face. His hand slipped from her breast to reach into his back pocket. He pulled out a pocketknife.

A knife! "What are you—"

His grin went beyond wicked. He simply nodded.

"No," she whispered, a most delicious tingle rising up from her toes. "You can't be thinking—"

"The same thing as you?" he answered.

"Oh no, you're not," she cried, trying to deny what she wanted more than anything else.

"Watch me." He yanked her to him, spread her legs, and sliced open the seam at her crotch, letting the cold metal graze the skin of her inner thigh.

Her heart thumped wildly in her chest. "You're crazy!"

"Yes," he said, his tone devilishly wild. "Now open your legs. All the way."

He shoved her panties to one side with the knife handle as the metal brushed her core. Morgan shivered, gasping.

His gaze burned right through to her soul, sinfully delicious. "You like that, don't you?"

Her answer was to pull his head down and grind her mouth against his. The knife clattered to the deck as his hands spread her wider. One finger. Two. His mouth covered hers just in time, her scream reverberating down his throat.

He gripped her legs and lifted her up, shoving deep inside her. He tore his mouth away, waves of heat rolling through her, forcing her up against the wall as he thrust in and out, little moans escaping his lips.

Maybe it was the realization of *getting caught,* that they could get caught. Maybe it was the realization that she really didn't know anything about him. Maybe it was the knowledge that she knew more about him in that moment than some people know in a lifetime. Whatever it was, once Jack's lips touched hers, once his tongue entwined with hers, Morgan lost it. Totally. Her arms reached around his shoulders, her hands clawing at his back. Her legs tightened around his waist. She growled, biting and sucking, finally begging for more. "Jack—oh, Jack! Please don't stop—oh *Jack...*"

She could feel his arms and legs trembling. His hard length filled her to overflowing. Each time he pulled out, he took a piece of her with him. Each time he thrust deeper, he gave a piece of himself in return.

Then suddenly, he stopped.

As his breath caught all at once, hers let go, and with one final thrust, Jack cried out in release. She covered his mouth with hers and swallowed his cries, her insides imploding, exploding.

Reality returned in pieces. The metal wall digging into her back, the difficulty breathing, his hard length still deep inside her.

"Jack," she barely whispered.

He didn't answer.

"*Jack.*"

His head lifted from her neck. "That—that was amazing."

She kissed him, wanting to linger, knowing they couldn't. "I know."

She waited for him to withdraw. When he didn't, she said, "Please. Someone might come."

He grinned. "Obviously, someone just did."

He lifted her legs and pulled out, yet still, he held on. Which was a good thing, Morgan figured, for even with the wall behind her she wasn't sure she could stand. He nuzzled his head into the crook of her neck, his soft sighs reminding her of what could never be.

"I think you got the better part of the deal," she whispered.

"Yeah, I guess I did."

She kissed him, unable to keep from grinning against his mouth. "You owe me a suit."

"I'll buy you one when we dock."

"Not really fair when I asked for this, but it's a deal."

She shivered as a gust of wind whipped around them and glanced down, realizing why he'd been waiting. He was still half-erect.

Jack gave her a slightly bewildered, slightly naughty, a tad embarrassed grin. Morgan started laughing, but when he joined in, she was certain she was going to cry. She swallowed hard, bending to pick up the knife.

"I like the way you use your tools," she said, closing and handing it back to him.

He threw back his head and roared, before he lifted her chin, his face sobering. "Yours, too."

Morgan desperately needed some space between them. She pulled away. "I have to change."

There was that grin again. "I guess you do."

Banked embers in his gaze flared hot before he shrugged. He fixed his clothes, and she fixed hers. He leaned down, his palms cupping the sides of her cheek to bring her lips to his. A kiss for them both to savor.

When Morgan finally tore her mouth away, she saw they were approaching land. The fairy tale had to be over once they docked. She had to get away from him. Gentleman that he was, though, Jack escorted her to her car. Morgan shuffled through her luggage until she found the clothes she wanted. They went up to the main cabin of the ferry, stopping at a hallway ladies' room.

He kissed her once. Hard. "Go ahead. I'll be out here when you're done."

Jack would never know how innocently he was wounding her. "Will you?"

He kissed her again, deeper this time. "Absolutely," he reiterated, letting go.

Morgan went into the ladies' room, changed in a stall, then went to the sink, catching her reflection in the mirror.

"Friend of the bride or friend of the groom?" he'd asked her.

All at once, she crumbled. For that moment, she let the pain consume her.

Walking into his hotel room, Morgan convinced herself she could have one enchanted evening. How ironic was it to meet someone so right at the absolute worst time of her life?

She clenched the edge of the sink.

God help her, she was *so* in trouble.

CHAPTER SIX

JACK BE NIMBLE, JACK BE QUICK. HEY, JACK, DON'T GET caught by that candlestick. Because you really ought to burn for this one.

Jack followed Morgan to her car. They were about to dock, and he knew this was going to be the diciest part of all.

Right and wrong. That's the way it has to be.

He just wished it didn't have to be so hard.

Every time he touched her. Even now, just following her, he had no control. Over his feelings or where they were going. He couldn't understand the insane power she had over him. Because it was wrong. It meant he cared. And he couldn't. She was just another name on a list.

And he had to turn her in.

Jack reached out and caught her by the shoulder, swinging her around to face him just as they reached her car. His was a couple of cars behind hers. He advanced like the predator he was. She retreated until she couldn't back up anymore. He gazed down at her, wishing circumstances could have been different. But that didn't stop him from wanting her. So, he turned off his feelings and turned on the charm.

"I'll be right behind you," he whispered in her ear.

She shivered against him. "You just won't give up, will you?"

He shook his head and nipped at her earlobe. "Never."

Moving back, he watched her smile up at him, wounded by her trust. Jack banished his conscience. The searing guilt in his guts had no place in this play.

He had to stop.

He couldn't.

Knowing the fires of the underworld were licking at his skin in anticipation, Jack lifted her face to his. Her eyes closed. He leaned down and tried very hard not to ravage her mouth. Instead, he gave her the lightest of kisses while his whole being centered on that kiss. They both came down to earth slowly.

"You'll wait for me to park my car in the lot?" he asked.

Her eyelids shuttered. The moment died a slow death, and a shot of pain accompanied the anger that scorched through his belly. So, she *had* been thinking about ditching him. "Yes."

"You promise?"

"Yes." Her slight hesitation made him certain she was lying, and the pain only got worse. Jack knew he had to take control of the situation, and he knew exactly how. He rubbed against her, letting her feel her full effect on him.

"Mmmm."

He covered her lips with his, kissing her until she sagged against him. "Besides, I owe you a suit," he added, tearing himself away.

Her head tilted upward, and her mouth reached for his, answering with a kiss. It seemed like she was fighting the same losing battle, disobeying what he figured had to be a direct order from her brain. He didn't care. He wanted her, disobeying his own direct orders. The world stopped turning every time their lips met, making him realize that the thought of control was merely a facade.

You've really blown it this time.

Yeah, well, the one thing he wasn't going to blow was his assignment. No matter how right she felt in his arms, no matter how good she was with her hands, he was going to give her to the authorities and let the law decide.

Because right's right, and wrong's wrong.

Jack tore his mouth away, breathing hard, wondering how his lower extremities could be so disloyal. "If we could," he growled softly in her ear. "I'd show you a few more tricks."

Her body began to shake with laughter. "I'm certain you could."

He smiled. "Lunch, then. And a suit."

He rimmed the shell of her ear as a reminder, and she shivered. "I already said yes."

"I know. But now I'm going for gold. How about a Holiday Inn?"

She leaned back to stare at him, her smile fading. Caution warred with a hint of despair in her gaze. "I thought we agreed—"

He put a finger to her lips and gave her a sheepish grin. "Can't blame a guy for trying, can you?"

Her face fell. "Just don't blame me because I can't."

He nodded and sighed, not having to make his disappointment real. Mentally, he slapped himself. She was going to bolt the minute she got off the ferry, and he had to be ready for that. He leaned in once and kissed her forehead, then opened her car door for her. She sat down in the driver's seat.

"I'll follow you and park my car. We'll take yours and go have lunch. I'm starving."

They both knew why.

She smiled and nodded but Jack could tell she'd already retreated to a place where he wouldn't be able to touch her. He smiled back anyway.

One enchanted evening, he thought, closing the door. And he knew he'd never be the same again.

THE FERRY STOPPED AND THE CONGA LINE BEGAN. SINCE her's and Jack's cars were toward the back, Morgan knew she was going to have to sit for a while. She drummed her fingers on the steering wheel impatiently, trying to figure out the best way to get out of the mess she was in. Even trying to bury herself in Jack hadn't completely erased the horror that filled her soul.

She swallowed, knowing she'd never forget the taste her discovery had left behind. She'd stumbled upon the file as she was going through her data. It certainly wasn't hers and just thinking about it left her whole body numb. Despite Jack's heat, she was certain she'd never get warm again. The day seemed as if it had happened only moments ago.

Day one. Subject: female. Morbidly obese. Weight: 398 pounds. Blood pressure now: 189 over 95 without medication. Glucose without medication: 512 mg/dL. Cholesterol: 325 mg/dL. Enzymes slightly elevated. Subject in excellent spirits. Excited to be accepted into the program.

Program? What program?

Morgan remembered her consternation as she exited out of the file and clicked on another. How did these files get here? No one had access to her personal database.

Day eight. Weight: 370 pounds. Blood pressure: slightly lower now. 180 over 90. Glucose down to 375 mg/dL, a marked improvement. Cholesterol not changing as rapidly. Enzymes still slightly elevated. Subject feeling much better. Very happy with results.

Results? A hollowness had filled her being. Bewildered, she'd asked herself, *What the hell's going on? What is this experiment?*

Day fifteen. Weight 350 pounds. Blood pressure not changing. Still at 180 over 90. Blood chemistries not changing but this is to be expected as the body needs to catch up with itself in regard to the rapid weight loss.

Rapid weight loss? Was this an additional experiment that BioClin was conducting while she was working on her project?

Total comprehension eluded her as Morgan skipped a couple of file folders and went to one marked a month later.

Day 32. Weight dropping too quickly. Patient now at 300 lbs. Blood pressure spiking again at 198/100. Began administering beta-blockers again as a precaution. Glucose at 225 mg/dL. Enzyme levels still elevated. CRP level very high, indicating inflammation within the body. Patient has begun to run a low-grade fever and exhibits general malaise. Advised this might be a reaction to the extremely rapid weight loss.

Suddenly, the notations began to sink in and she remembered her heart beginning to pound. The journal read much like the notebook she'd kept on Pinky and Louie. Someone had stolen her process. Not only that, but whoever stole it, had used it on a human test subject.

With trembling fingers, she'd opened another folder down in the series.

Day 50. Subject deteriorating rapidly even though all therapy halted fifteen days ago. Weight at 250 lbs. Blood pressure still spiking even with beta-blockers. Liver enzymes have climbed to near-critical levels. CRP levels extreme. Muscle and skeletal mass decreasing at an alarming rate. Debating hospitalization at this point. Patient exhibiting bodily stress akin to acute starvation. Patient on constant nutrient drip. Hypothesis: the more nutrients consumed, the more the body is burning. Considering halting all nutrients to see if metabolism slows down.

Morgan hadn't wanted to read any more. She'd taken the same steps with her test mice. Once the metabolic rate reached a certain stage, it couldn't be turned off, even if the subject starved.

Murderer.

Her mind had refused to accept sentence. She'd begun working on weight loss theories and drugs to save lives, not take them.

Murderer.

MORGAN SHOOK HER HEAD AS ANGER IGNITED ONCE AGAIN in her belly. What that "who" didn't realize was Morgan was part pit bull. She was going to find out who killed this woman if it was the last thing she did.

And that meant no more Jack.

With a shiver and a swift shake of her head, she reined in her libido and tried to think. Her priority was to get away from him. Maybe she could lose him as they shopped. Maybe she could use the excuse of the ladies' room in the restaurant he wanted to go to and leave through the back door.

Knowing her luck, they wouldn't have a back door. For a moment, her mind flashed on what they could do with a back door. *Damn you, Jack,* she thought, wishing his arms held her tight once more. When they did, reality disappeared.

Morgan inched the car forward and pulled off the ferry. She glanced in the rearview mirror to see Jack hadn't pulled out of line yet. She snorted. He didn't trust her. But at least now they were in the parking lot, and the line was moving faster.

The car in front of her pulled forward. Morgan was so engrossed in trying to figure out what to do that she didn't follow right away. This allowed a uniformed guard to walk in front of her car.

What the—?

Morgan's grip tightened on the steering wheel. Why was a guard standing in front of her car, signaling to her? Her heart shot to her throat. This wasn't good. This wasn't good at all.

The guard motioned for her to pull out of line to her left. She bit her lip. She couldn't run him over, and she didn't dare pull out.

She flipped her head to the left and then to the right. Wait a minute. If she pulled out, she could go around the traffic and get out of the parking lot through the entrance instead of the exit. She just had to get around the guard first.

She frowned and nodded at the guard as if she didn't understand what was going on. She hit the automatic button for the window to bring it down and get the guard to walk around the car to come and speak with her.

As he moved, the car in front of her pulled forward. She pulled the steering wheel to the left and edged around in between the other car and the guard. She was just about to step on the gas pedal when another man stepped in front of her car.

Sandy-brown hair, dark glasses, and a black suit. All she could think of now was the police, the FBI. Her heart slammed into overdrive as fight or flight took over. She jerked the wheel hard around him. Out of the corner of her eye, she saw another car approach, trying to cut her off from the left.

Pulling back hard to the right, Morgan clipped the other car with her front fender, just enough to bounce off of and steady her car so she could peel rubber out of the entranceway.

Without another thought, without knowing how she managed to miss the guy, Morgan drove. She saw a sign that said 'exit' and followed it blindly, having no clue where she was going. Then, she noticed she was on some kind of long access road and to her left was the highway. She hit the gas.

Long moments followed before she got the courage to look in the rearview mirror. She expected a line of police cars to be after her.

All she saw was Jack's car.

Jack?

What the hell was he doing following her?

The man had to be insane—it was the only logical reason.

He held his own as she sped down the highway. She took several deep breaths, told her heart to cut it out before she had a heart attack, and loosened her grip on the steering wheel. She looked down at the speedometer and realized she had to slow down. The last thing she could afford was an accident. She certainly didn't want anyone to get hurt.

Then, it hit her. What was she going to do about Jack?

Lose him.

How? She had no formal Double-O-Seven training. Tell him the truth? Out of the question. Wouldn't that make him an accessory after the fact? Morgan wasn't positive. She was a scientist, not a lawyer.

No, she had to get rid of him, get him off her tail. Fast. But first she had to figure out what direction she was headed in. She didn't have time to waste doubling back.

Finally, a highway sign came into view. She breathed a huge sigh of relief. By some miracle, she was headed south, exactly as she needed to be.

Morgan finally had time to check her rearview mirror again. Jack was flashing his high beams at her. She couldn't really see his face, but she had a pretty good idea that he was rather confused and a lot concerned at the moment. Probably mad as hell too.

He started tapping on his horn and Morgan knew she had to do something. Anything. He was drawing too much attention and was becoming a liability instead of an asset.

Just as she was about to pull into the center lane and weave her way through traffic to get rid of him, Morgan watched him pull out and come alongside her. He was signaling frantically for her to follow him.

She couldn't. But she had to to lose him. Maybe she could make believe she was parking, wait for him to get out of his car, and then pull away.

She nodded to herself and began to slow, seeing a large outlet mall up ahead. She watched Jack nod. He slowed down with her, then pulled behind her again, waiting to follow.

As Morgan pulled into the outlet mall, a strange thought struck her. Something had glinted in the late-morning sun, catching her attention, causing her to look over at his car.

And what she witnessed begged the question...why was Jack shouting and making angry gestures with his hand?

CHAPTER SEVEN

"WHAT THE FUCK WERE YOU THINKING, SAM?" JACK yelled into his car, a lead ball taking up residence in his stomach. "That had to be the sloppiest setup I've ever seen."

"Public place."

Jack rolled his eyes. He almost laughed. Almost. "We've done this in public places before. What the hell is the matter with you? I just served her up on a silver platter for you, and you blew it."

"You've still got her, don't you?"

Smug bastard. "Of course."

But as he said the words, something started bothering Jack. The lead ball became a lead weight. Then, it hit him. Where were the authorities? The police? The state troopers? Someone in law enforcement?

"Sam?"

"Yeah?"

"What's going on?" he asked, his tone even.

"What do you mean?" Sam replied, *his* tone too innocent.

Confusion rang through at the end of the question, enough for Jack to shrug off his fear. After all, it was Sam. But that didn't stop him from asking, "Where are the authorities, Sam?"

"Authorities?" Sam repeated.

Was that bewilderment he heard, or was bewilderment what he wanted to hear? "Uh, you know, uniforms? Black suits? Those guys?"

"No time."

Jack snorted. At best, Sam was a bad liar. "Bullshit. You had plenty of time."

"I swear to God, Jack. They wanted to make sure their i's were dotted and their t's were crossed. I figured I had to try it alone first."

Jack frowned. It all sounded logical on the surface, so why was his gut screaming at him? "Next time let me take care of the details. You suck at it."

Sam laughed. Was that relief he heard or self-deprecation? "No problem."

"So, what now?" he asked, not quite sure how to rectify the mess Sam'd made.

"Pick a place," Sam replied. "I'm in a car tailing you about five or six deep. We'll converge, and I won't blow it again."

Jack shook his head. Somehow, Sam didn't make him feel reassured. Then again, Sam wasn't the guy to go to for exact plans. He had "people" for that. "We've got two ways to go on this," Jack answered. "Get her out of the car or get us both down to one car. Stay back until I get this fixed without you fucking things up again."

"No need to get testy."

Now, Jack had every need. Especially when Sam didn't volunteer the rest of the information, forcing him to reiterate, "This will give you time to bring in the good guys."

"You got it."

Jack sighed, glad his buddy agreed. "Hey, Sam?"

"Yeah?"

"Why do I always end up saving your ass?"

He listened to Sam roar, wishing he felt like laughing. "Just lucky, I guess."

Jack hung up knowing luck had absolutely nothing to do with it. Jack had been trained to find people, people who didn't want to be found. Criminals who deserved to be punished.

And that made him wonder. Why did it feel as if he was in the middle of a role reversal? Why was his gut telling him something that couldn't possibly be true? That Sam might be lying to him, and Morgan might not?

MORGAN EASED HER FOOT DOWN ON THE BRAKES. SHE glanced at the rearview mirror, and a sharp sear of acid burned a hole in her stomach.

When things go south, they really go south.

She pulled her car into the outlet parking lot. She didn't have to look. Jack was right behind her. While one part of her mind wondered if things could get any worse, the other cleared and took note of how many cars were in the lot and where they were parked.

Morgan pulled into a row, making sure no car was in front of her. This would force Jack, at the very least, to get out and walk around to talk to her.

So why wasn't he getting out of his car?

She watched a black sedan pull into the row opposite her car. She started to wonder about that when Jack was suddenly standing next to her door, a world of hurt in his gaze.

Trapped as much by Jack as by circumstance, she rolled down her window. "You could have let me say goodbye."

"Jack, I—"

He leaned forward to grip the metal above her car door. "Are you that much of a coward that you wanted to get someone killed back there?"

Yes, she wanted to scream. *Yes.* Instead, she answered as calmly as she could. “Jack, I’m sorry.”

One of his hands released the metal as if it burned and raked through his hair, his weight shifting from one foot to the other. Then, it fell with a heartfelt sigh. “Not half as sorry as I am.”

“Let me go, Jack. Please.”

“I’m sorry, kitten. I can’t.”

Morgan’s insides twisted at the raw ache in his voice. “I have to go. Now.”

She watched him lift his head and scan the area with a deep frown creasing his forehead. “I owe you lunch.”

She shook her head. “No, you don’t. Goodbye, Jack.”

He stepped up against the car, leaned into the open space of the window, and got as close to her as he could. "Aww, hell, kitten,” he whispered in that sexy way of his. “What’ve you got to lose?”

My life?

“Half an hour,” he cajoled, deepening his tone the same way he did in bed, giving her that patented grin of his. “Thirty minutes.”

Morgan knew firsthand what the man could do with thirty minutes. “No, Jack. I can’t.”

“C’mon, Morgan. Please,” he begged. “At least let me settle up with you. I can’t let you go, now. It’s a matter of honor.”

Was that why he’d followed her?

She scanned the area. Nothing seemed amiss. Maybe she’d lost her pursuers. Her main problem, now, seemed only to be Jack.

She shook her head. “I’m sorry, Jack. I need to leave. You promised. No scene.”

“Phone number?” he asked, surprising her that he really wasn’t letting go. “E-mail addy?”

She shook her head again.

“How about one last kiss?”

He ducked, lifted his head, and stepped back so she could open the door and stand. She opened the door, calling herself all kinds of a fool, but left the engine running to make sure he got the point.

Before she could settle her weight on both her feet, he hauled her up against his body. Funny how he had the ability to make the world go away with a simple touch.

He held her for what seemed forever before bending down to kiss her. His tongue tasted everywhere inside her mouth as if he could brand her in his memory. She couldn't believe how safe she felt in his arms.

For a moment, the earth stood still.

"I'm sorry," he whispered as he broke the kiss.

"Jack!" she cried, realization crashing. Her gaze shot past him as two men barreled toward her from the black sedan directly across from them. One was the same sandy-haired man she'd seen at the ferry, the other looked like a linebacker.

Even as her stomach fell, Morgan knew she had to protect him. She'd created this problem, now she had to fix it.

"Jack," she whispered urgently "you need to get out of here. *Now*!"

He started looking at her as if seeing her for the first time. "What are you talking about?" he said, holding her closer.

"Let go of me and go. Get out of here!" she yelled.

"I don't understand."

"*Go*!"

Morgan pushed him away, turning to climb into the car but his hand clamped her arm, refusing to let go. God, what a fool she was. The man was going to play knight in shining armor when all she needed to do was escape. Now. Before it was too late.

And then all at once, it was too late.

"Good morning, Dr. Mackenzie," said the sandy-haired man.

Her gaze flew to Jack. "Jack...?" He looked like he'd been punched in the gut. "Jack...?" This time, in a whisper.

"I'm sorry," he said again.

Morgan wrenched her arm free, throwing herself into the car, but Jack held fast to the door, gripping it like a man in shock. She thought she was going to be sick, her whole body shaking, when all at once she saw her only option.

Run!

She slammed the car into gear, her hand yanking at the door when suddenly the sandy-haired man grabbed it. “I wouldn’t do that if I were you, Dr. Mackenzie.”

She slapped at his hand. “You can’t hold me!” she screeched.

“Kitten, please,” Jack said soothingly, his hand covering hers as she looked up into his eyes. Confusion, shock, hurt, and anger all roiled inside his gaze. “Wait.”

“Wait?” she cried, still tugging at the door. “Wait for *what*?”

Was Jack trying to help her? But if he did, that would put him in the same danger she was in. She shook her head violently. “No!” There was no way she’d let him help her.

He grinned at her, trying to reassure, a sadness filling his features now that had nothing to do with the situation they were in. Or did it?

“Do we have a problem here?” he asked the sandy-haired man.

“I don’t know,” the man said. “Do we?”

Jack let go of the door. *Finally*. But now the burly-looking man was standing in front of her car, arms crossed over his chest as if he could stop the car by himself.

“What the hell is going on?” Jack asked, his tone as hard as steel.

The bull of a man advanced. “Nothing,” he said.

But Morgan knew better. She slammed the door closed just as the sandy-haired man lunged. Jack tripped him and sent him sprawling. Then, all at once, Jack swiveled around to the bull and knocked him aside like a running back. He ran around the front of the car, threw open the passenger side door, and jumped in beside her.

“Drive!” he ordered.

Morgan threw the car into reverse and cut the wheel, hitting the gas and whipping the car around before she was out of the parking lot.

"Slow down," he said. "Last thing we need now is the cops."

"Okay," she said, her heart still pounding in her ears.

"Pull out onto the highway. Get around as many cars as you can."

"Why?" She stole a glance at him. "Why are you telling me what to do? Why are you here?"

He ignored her, straining against the seat belt he'd finally put on, his hand braced against the dashboard. "Up ahead. The car wash. Pull in."

All right, this was starting to freak her out. And she had only a slim thread keeping her sanity together at the moment.

"Why?"

"Just do what I tell you!" he barked.

"Why?" she cried, "I don't understand!"

He glared at her. "Just do as I say, goddammit! Now, turn!"

Her heart in her throat, she slowed down and pulled into the driveway as he ordered.

"Good. Now go around back and shut the car off. They'll pass us first and have to double back."

How the hell did he know all this?

She was just about to ask when he turned, his gaze filled with regret. "Kitten," he said, "we have to talk."

And that was when the lightbulb clicked on inside her head. Jack wasn't her knight in shining armor. He wasn't even the cowboy on the white horse. He was part of the posse.

CHAPTER EIGHT

RAW VENOM CLAWED ITS WAY UP HER THROAT. "BASTARD!"

He didn't answer.

Ice invaded her limbs, then her heart as she threw the car into park. Morgan started shaking. "You freaking bastard."

She flew at him, her fists finding any contact they could make. He let her hit him a couple of times before he corralled both her wrists.

"Yes."

"Liar!" she spit out.

"Yes."

Her insides turned to stone, falling to the ground with a heavy thud. "Who are you really?"

He shrugged, not answering this time. Eyes filled with sapphire flakes stared back at her, colder than ice. "A tracker."

"How could you?" she cried, all her pain wrapped into those three little words.

"Part of the job, kitten," he answered, letting her go with absolutely no expression on his face. Except for the little twitch above his cheek and the muscles in it that now stood out like the Bas-relief sculpture technique.

He knew who she was. He'd known all along. A thousand knives sliced her guts open and let them bleed. With one mighty swing, she slapped his cheek as hard as she could. She didn't even acknowledge the pain in her hand. His surprised expression turned to one of pain.

"Do you always sleep with your intended target?" she hissed.

His eyes widened slightly, but he didn't answer right away. Instead, he rubbed his abused cheek.

"No."

His gaze caught hers. They stared at each other for a long moment. Even the agony of her shredded insides couldn't douse the spark between them. That made him more dangerous than ever.

"Fine. Just get out."

Morgan reached over to start the car again when Jack's hand closed over hers. She ripped her hand away as if burned. He frowned as he got the message. "I don't think so, kitten. Not yet. I need to know what's going on here first."

"Don't you dare call me that!" she cried.

He shrugged, showing her that if this was what she wanted, it was okay with him. "I need to know what's going on," he repeated, his tone steely.

His gaze never left hers, and they continued to stare at each other, locked in a power struggle that didn't want to end. "No, you don't. And I'm not going to tell you. You betrayed me," Morgan answered.

The tension between them thickened. He'd sold her out. He'd been willing to give her over to someone he obviously knew very well.

"I did what I thought I had to do."

"Fine." As if that justified everything. Morgan slammed her hand down on the steering wheel, her anger already at its breaking point. "Just get out of the car and have a nice life. Goodbye, Jack."

"You won't last one day," he sneered.

His words penetrated her anger. It was the first truth she'd heard in the last twenty-four hours. He was right.

Morgan clenched her fists so hard her nails bit into the skin of her palms. But the pain helped her focus, helped her not to cry. Crying would be a sign of weakness, and she would never be weak in front of this man again. "Okay. You're right. I won't. So, what now?"

He twisted, looking in the back seat. "Take anything you can carry and throw it in that canvas bag. You have thirty seconds."

She hesitated. He recaptured her gaze. His face could've been carved in stone for all the emotion he showed, except that his fingers tapped on his thigh, a sign of impatience.

Reaction set in and her body started trembling again. But she leaned over the seat, threw open her suitcase, grabbed her jeans, a sweatshirt, underwear, and her makeup. Then she complied with his command and threw the rest of what she could carry into the canvas bag.

"Good. We're going to go through the car wash. You're going to change clothes. Do you have sneakers?"

She nodded. "Those too. As soon as you pay the man approaching us, you're going to start. You'll be finished by the time the car is done. Got that?"

She didn't answer. She couldn't. A ball of anger burned in the middle of her throat.

"You can haul off and hit me again later if it'll make you feel better. But right now, I'm your best shot at survival. So, make up your mind."

She nodded. "Good," he replied. "We're going to take the car when the car wash stops and pull it around to the back again. These parking lots look like they're connected, and we won't be seen from the highway. I could swear I saw a limo company about three or four buildings back."

She didn't ask what would follow. She didn't have to. If Jack really were a tracker, then he'd know how to get them out of danger.

He didn't watch her undress. He simply stared at the water sheeting the front windshield. But when she looked up, she could feel his anger. Hers matched his.

Funny how things come full circle.

"How much cash do you have?"

"That's none of your business!" she cried.

He barked out a laugh. "I'm only going to tell you this one more time. I'm your best shot at survival. Don't question me. I know what I'm doing and how to do it. So, make up your mind. Either I stay in the car, or I get out. If I get out, I'll disappear."

"Do you really expect me to believe that? After what you've done? What's stopping you from going back and turning me into that man who tried to kidnap me?" she spat back at him.

"His name is Sam." A tick flared in his cheek as his jaw tightened. Several moments passed before he replied, "And no, I won't."

"Why? I don't get it. Betraying me didn't seem to bother you one bit even while we were on the ferry."

At least he had the grace to look a little ashamed. "We don't have time to get this out in the open. Make a decision. I stay, or I go. We can knife each other to death later."

"Who says there's going to be a later?" she shot back.

He didn't answer for a long moment. "If I stay, you're stuck with me for the duration. No in between and no halfway. If I'm going to be a Benedict Arnold, then I'm going to be a Benedict Arnold. Got that?"

Flabbergasted, Morgan started laughing. "You expect me to trust you? After what you've done?"

"I expect you to trust *my abilities*. I found you. I can lose you just as easily."

An empty hollow formed in the pit of her stomach. "God, I feel like a freaking package."

"Up until about ten minutes ago, that's all you were."

"Sonofabitch!" Morgan hauled off and slapped his face again.

He swung his head around to glare at her, then grabbed her arm and pulled her as close to his body as he could. "The first one, I deserved. The second one was for your pride. Don't even think of going for three, got that?"

"Never!" she spat back at him. "If I had a knife right now, I'd cut your balls off."

He smiled. "No, you wouldn't, kitten. You'd have nothing to play with then."

Furious, Morgan couldn't even think straight. "You freaking son of a bitch!"

"Yes."

"Damn you to hell and back again."

"Welcome to my world."

Morgan really wanted to cry. Then she wanted to hurt him. And keep on hurting him until he felt the same way she did. But that wouldn't save her, and right now, all the hurt in the world would be in vain if she got caught.

"All right, you win," she said finally. "We do this your way. I go along for the ride. But, baby, watch out when we get there, because I'm going to spend my every waking moment thinking of ways to pay you back. We're going to have a reckoning. Remember that."

He sighed as if he already knew what he was facing. Then he motioned for her to drive the car out of the car wash and over to the limousine service.

"Yes, we will."

As he waited for her to pull back over to the limousine service, Jack had a reckoning with himself. He'd become emotionally involved with the target and committed a cardinal sin.

He'd been powerless to stop himself. He'd fallen right into their enchanted evening.

The problem was, he hadn't slept during the night. And when the door to his room closed, well, all of a sudden, he felt empty inside. Hurt and empty. But that hadn't stopped him from making his phone call. And now he was paying for the mistake of the century.

Bewildered, Jack couldn't begin to fathom what was going on. The kind of fire that erupted between the two of them happened to a man, if he was lucky, once in his life.

He'd gotten one enchanted evening. Plus.

A grin spread across his face, and Jack turned his head away so she wouldn't see. He remembered her expressions against the bulkhead on the ferry, especially when he'd used the knife. He'd nearly exploded right then and there.

Then, he remembered the world of hurt in her eyes as he and Sam greeted each other. His grin faded.

Jack had honed his tracking skills as an Army Ranger. Korea and Afghanistan weren't the only thorns in America's side. There were others. Little by little, Jack began to excel at his job. He fed off the challenge.

The harder the jobs became, the more he enjoyed them. Until it occurred to him that in finding these people, he might be setting them up, possibly for extermination. And that still wouldn't have been a problem. They were the enemy. Until a couple of kids got mixed in. Then, he started questioning motives, and he didn't like what he saw. He served his term and played good little soldier until his last tour was up.

The Army hadn't wanted to let him go.

Jack didn't give them a choice. He disappeared in exchange for an honorable discharge and waited a long time before re-surfacing. Sam gave him his life back, let him do what he did best—find people—without them getting killed.

Until now.

Which didn't make sense. Sam wouldn't just give up his soul for a bunch of zeroes on a check.

Would he?

If Jack could ask himself that question, the possibility existed. The Sam he knew ten years ago was long gone. And the number of zeros might have been an offer Sam couldn't refuse.

So, whatever she'd stolen had to be something important. Really important. Or else someone was a really good liar. Because Sam wasn't stupid, and he didn't get snowed very easily.

And he certainly wasn't about to throw away his honor for nothing.

Which left him and Morgan drowning in a sinkhole filled with raw sewage. And the only way Jack knew to get out of a sinkhole, even one that smelled as bad as this, was to dig. And keep on digging. Until he found the truth.

Truth? Wasn't that being a bit two-faced?

Jack frowned, acknowledging she had every right to hate him. Now, he had every reason to protect her. Last but not very least, he owed Morgan a debt for finding her and betraying her. He needed to get to the bottom of this sinkhole. He turned his head to stare at her profile.

What the hell did you do, Morgan?

CHAPTER NINE

AS THEY CLIMBED INTO THE BACK OF THE LIMOUSINE, Morgan realized that between the bursts of anger and the surreal feeling surrounding her, she was exhausted. Silent tears, the tears she'd tried to hold back, now dripped down her cheeks. She would wipe them away, but they would keep coming.

When he zeroed in on her face, he muttered a curse. And even though he'd hurt her, he took a long moment to break the connection. Her features hardened. She willed her heart not to feel. She turned off the sickness in her stomach and she smiled.

"Is your name really Jackson Kent?" Morgan asked, needing answers.

"Yes. Andrew Jackson Kent."

She almost laughed. "And you're a tracker. Like a bounty hunter?"

He scowled at her as if she'd called him a dirty name. He *was* lower than dirt. "I find people. But I'm not a bounty hunter. I don't turn them in for money."

Time for some payback. Painful payback. "You don't? Obviously your 'partner' does. So, I guess it's a matter of semantics."

His jaw tightened and he didn't answer.

"So, exactly what is the connection between you and your, ah, friend?" she continued.

He winced at her dig. "We were in the Army together."

That was interesting, and explained some of his loyalty. But nothing could ever explain his betrayal. "Did he tell you why he was looking for me?"

"No. And I didn't ask."

"I guess I can understand that. It's easier that way. Isn't it?"

Again, he didn't reply. "Isn't it?"

"Yes," he bit out.

Poor bastard, she thought, even though not an ounce of her felt any remorse. He had no idea what was going on. "So, he never explained to you that I'm one of the good guys?"

"Good guys?" he exploded. "How can that be? You're a thief."

She frowned. "I guess that's a matter of semantics. Like the word 'trust'."

"What do you mean?"

Morgan sighed. "The work I stole was mine."

"Seriously?"

Morgan started laughing at the shocked look on his face. Oh, the deliciously sad irony of it all. Or as they say, one good turn deserves another. He'd screwed her over, then gotten screwed over by his buddy.

So, Jack didn't know why his partner, Sam, was looking for her. That meant he also didn't know what was in the journals on her thumb drive.

"Information, Jack," she sneered. "One tiny piece of the equation can change the entire outcome." When Jack didn't answer, she added, "He didn't tell you that on purpose."

She watched him frown, that same deep frown from the parking lot, as he considered the truth of her words. *Okay, now, Jack. Here comes the important question.* "Would you have taken the job if he had?"

"No."

Score one for you. "You could just be saying that."

He winced, a sadness stealing his countenance. "If you believe that after what we shared—"

Believe? How could she believe anything right now? Exactly how many betrayals was she expected to handle?

"Don't even go there!" she cried as her insides filled with pain. "You have no right."

His jaw clenched again, but he had good sense not to speak. This was her show for the moment, and he was going to bleed.

"At the hotel when I walked in looking for a room. Why did you make contact with me? You'd already found me. There was no need."

When he didn't answer, Morgan watched the tick in his cheek with morbid fascination. A desire to knife out his emotions and make them spill out like life's blood filled her. But Morgan was first and foremost a scientist. Satisfaction wouldn't get her the information she needed, so she fell back onto her most trusted belief—her belief in logic. And she thought out loud.

"All you had to do was....oh, I get it. You wanted to keep me close by, didn't you? You didn't want me to get away, so you'd have to track me down again."

"Yes."

"But not that close."

"No." He scowled at her as her words drove the truth home with precision.

"You took a pretty big risk," she continued. "One wrong word would have jeopardized your entire mission. On the other hand, closing the quote unquote surveillance gap kept me from bolting, didn't it?"

"Yes."

"Was the sex part of the facade?"

He winced. Good. Causing him pain helped ease the ache in

her heart. Yet, there was a hollow emptiness to this pleasure. Morgan decided asking why would be best left for later.

"An hour ago, you wouldn't have asked that question."

"An hour ago, I wouldn't have had to," she spit out. "Are you going to answer?"

He shook his head. "You already know what the answer is."

Did she?

"So, does it matter? That I'm not a thief?"

"I don't know," he answered, his tone a touch perplexed. "I'm still not sure of the truth. Corporate espionage is stealing in my book. I have your word against your employer's on that one."

"And my word against Sam's," she shot back at him, her gaze narrowing. "Gives you a warm and fuzzy feeling inside, doesn't it?"

He glared at her, and the tick really began to jump in his cheek. Morgan simply smiled back at him.

Ding, ding, ding. Round one to you, girlfriend. "That brings us full circle, Jack. Because you've been exceptionally consistent up until now."

He raised a brow at her. "What are you talking about?"

"Once a bastard, always a bastard," she spat back at him.

He inclined his head. "Touché."

She inclined her head back at him. "So, I'm going to ask. Even though I know I shouldn't." Morgan paused just long enough to make her point. "Why were you willing to help me get away?"

He blew out a short, sharp breath. "I'd have thought that was obvious."

"Oh, no, darling. Enlighten me. Say it. I dare you."

He caught her gaze, allowing her to see what he was feeling. "I care."

Morgan shook her head, anger flaring, burning hot inside her belly. *Oh really?* "You care so much about me that you were willing to screw me over? Even after you screwed me?"

"I—I didn't screw you." His gaze held onto hers. "I made love to you."

Even now she could feel his touch on her body. "You betrayed me. Despite—" She didn't finish. She couldn't.

His eyes widened as realization cut into him. She almost felt sorry for him, because there weren't enough words in the world to apologize for what he'd done to her.

Morgan shuddered, keeping a very tight lid on the floodgates before they got out of control. And that brought *her* full circle.

"There was another reason, wasn't there?"

He nodded. "I gave you to Sam on a silver platter. But when we docked, there were no police cars. I called Sam to find out why. He told me there wasn't time. It sounded lame but I accepted it."

Morgan thought about that for a moment. It all came down to trust. Jack had trusted his partner. Poor fool.

"And it never occurred to you to question his methods?" she replied, her tone half question half statement.

"No."

Now this was where the ugly part came in. Because Morgan was the only one that knew she was innocent. On both the theft and the murder.

"He didn't call the police because *technically* I didn't do anything wrong," she insisted. "The data was mine. My work. My project."

He shook his head. "I don't make judgments," he insisted. "And that's a matter of interpretation."

She snorted in disbelief. "Then you're a fool."

He shrugged. "More than you'll ever know."

Morgan doubted that. He'd done a pretty good job on her.

"I knew something was wrong as soon as I saw Sam's car in the outlet mall," he continued. "And still no police."

"No police?" she repeated. "I don't understand."

He shifted in his seat, as if he wanted to pace but couldn't because of the confines of the car. "We hand perpetrators over to the authorities, damn it! Sometimes I work with the police. Most of the time I don't. But we uphold the law. We don't break it." He raked his hand through his hair. "At least, I thought we did."

"So, you were doing this under the impression that there was some kind of warrant out for my arrest?" Which would have been impossible. BioClin wouldn't want *anyone* to know they'd lost their golden egg.

"No. He never said there was any kind of warrant. Sam told me you were wanted for questioning in connection with the theft of corporate property. Which meant handing you over to the police."

"And that's all he said to you?"

"Yes." She watched him lean forward and stare at his fingers as if he didn't know what to do with his hands, or himself, before he lifted his gaze to hers. "Don't you get it? I don't ask for more."

Morgan let that one go for the moment. She had to understand what she was up against so she could figure out her next steps.

"So much for friendship," she sighed. Jack's gaze skittered away in answer. But she asked anyway. "Now that he has a stake in this, Sam isn't going to stop until he finds me, is he?"

"No, not if he's personally involved."

All right, pit bull against pit bull. She could handle that. But she needed more information.

"Exactly how good is he?"

He gave her a halfhearted grin. "He hired me, didn't he?"

She didn't answer that.

"Now it's my turn to ask a question," he continued. "Because I really need to know." He took a deep breath, and she recognized the hurt in his gaze. "What the hell is going on?"

How much did she tell him? While her entire psyche wanted to pour itself out to him because of the sheer stress of the situation, he was still the enemy.

"It seems your friend betrayed you because of what I have in my possession," she answered.

"What are you trying to tell me?" Jack asked her, his tone low and filled with disbelief.

“That he’s going to try to retrieve it.”

“That’s his job,” he fired back at her.

Morgan nodded. “Yes. But there’s a flip side to that. He’s not going to care if you stand in the way.”

She watched him frown and rub his face with his hands. Then, he leaned back in his seat to look out the window. And no matter how good his discomfort felt now, it had no bearing on what was going to happen next. Because no matter which way she visualized the past, she was still a wanted woman on the run. And no matter which way she visualized the future, everything had just gone from bad to worse, allowing her to come up with only one result. Dr. Morgan McKenzie was a dead woman.

CHAPTER TEN

MORGAN SAT BOLT UPRIGHT IN THE SEAT, NOSTRILS flaring to catch each delectable pheromone he exuded. Exhausted, she must have dozed off for a moment. Then, she realized what woke her up.

She'd have to have a talk with her nose later.

He gave her a sort-of half smile, looking no worse for wear while she felt like she'd been run over by a Mack truck. He couldn't shutter his gaze fast enough though, and she saw the desire there. Half-awake and half-asleep, her body betrayed her, yearning for the fire, the incredible sensation of fulfillment. He'd awakened feelings deep inside, broken open a dam of reined-in emotions. As a scientist, Morgan wasn't allowed the luxury of feelings. She'd been taught to think, deduct, and reason.

Jack had changed all that.

Morgan didn't know whether to be grateful or furious. Could one enchanted evening really change a person that much?

Her mind filled with a picture she'd seen in a zoology text—a picture of a chrysalis—a caterpillar turning into a butterfly. He'd broken open her cocoon and given her the ability to fly free. That might, just might, keep him alive when they stopped.

"Easy, kitten."

Her gaze must have narrowed because his half smile fled, and her heartbeat soared from zero to sixty in less than three seconds, a new land-speed record. To hide her reaction to him, she turned away to look out at the landscape speeding by them. A new wave of motion sickness ruined what mood was left inside her.

"Call me Morgan. Better yet, make that Dr. Mackenzie. You have no right to call me kitten anymore."

"All right, Morgan. But this isn't about me, anymore. It's about you."

She snorted in disgust, hugging herself to keep from going after him again. "Nice of you to understand that."

"Not too long ago, I screwed over my best friend and partner to save your sorry ass. I even let you sleep. The least you could do is try to be a tiny bit grateful."

"Grateful? You want me to be grateful?" She tucked her hands tight and told him to go do something anatomically impossible.

Obviously, that got his nuts in an uproar. "Listen, Morgan. And listen well," he bit out. "You're going to have a hard time trying to explain to your employer why you're not a thief."

That was the least of her problems.

"They didn't hire Sam to play games."

No kidding.

"Now, Sam made it seem as if this job was on the up-and-up, but obviously it's not."

Tell me something I don't know.

"The people who want their property back obviously want this all on the hush-hush. That's why Sam didn't bring in the police."

Tell me something I really don't already know.

"But if they have to drag in the authorities, I'm getting a real bad feeling they will. Just remember it's not always innocent until proven guilty. So, taking your anger out on me is a waste of time."

If he was trying to scare her, he was doing a good job. But she'd be damned before she'd let him know that. Wait a minute. She was already damned. So, what the hell?

"All right, Jack. I want the truth."

"Ditto."

"I get to go first," she retorted, her tone icy cold.

He inclined his head.

"One of the things I don't understand is why you stopped me in the hotel."

His lips lifted into a self-deprecating smile. "Couldn't help myself."

Did she dare believe that? Suckers were born every day.

He pinned her with his gaze. Two could play this game very easily. "You know what I don't understand?" he asked. "I don't understand why you came to my room last night."

"Couldn't help myself," she replied, throwing his look and his smile right back at him.

A long silence grew between them. She tried to tamp down the well of anguish inside her belly, but as they stared at each other, it became part of the silence. His gaze told her he couldn't stop it from growing any more than he could make amends. But he could try.

"I know you won't believe me, but it wasn't just sex," he finally told her.

"You made love to me," she cried, clutching her body as her insides twisted.

"I know."

She watched him lean forward and balance his forearms on his thighs. "God." He laughed, the sound bitter but at the same time sweet. His gaze lifted, caught hers, and refused to let go. "I can't explain what happened except to say I stopped breathing the moment I saw you."

Oh, no.

"So, that made everything all right? Being 'in sex' with me made it all okay. You knew you were going to have to hand me over, you bastard. You knew, but that was just fine. Because you got your rocks off along the way."

He jumped up out of the seat and dropped to his knees in front of her. His posture begged.

Not to forgive him, for he seemed to understand the impossibility of that now. No, he dropped to his knees begging her to allow him an apology.

"I'm sorry. I had no right to do what I did."

He didn't try to excuse his behavior or his actions. "Thanks for making me the exception," she bit back at him.

He released a heartfelt sigh, which finally reached through her anger. "No problem."

His gaze darkened, catching hers, refusing to let go as they both remembered the ferry deck.

"You should never have come to my room," he told her.

"And if I hadn't?"

His smile hurt both of them. But the truth hurts sometimes. "I'd have come to yours."

"To keep me near you," she whispered, her tone bitter.

"Yes!" he exploded, her pain reaching him. "I couldn't let you go."

Did she dare believe him? That they both fell into the enchanted evening knowing they shouldn't? "Thanks for being honest."

Her tone let him know exactly how she felt. The South Pole would have been warmer.

His hand lifted to graze her cheek, then fell without making contact. "I know it's no consolation, but you stopped being a job the moment I danced with you."

That didn't help matters, although a small, secret part, deep inside her, felt better. "You gave me up."

"I had no choice." He raked his hands through his hair. "I had to find out why you were so special."

She frowned. "Special?"

Pride laced his tone. “I don’t get called out on a job unless it’s really important, kitten.”

She let his endearment slip by while she put on her snark. “Wow. I mean, gee. I’m a celebrity.”

His gaze hardened. Guess he didn’t like snide. Too bad.

With a deep, indrawn breath, he rose and sat back on the seat. “You need to tell me everything, Morgan,” he replied, his body language simply weary now. “Whoever is paying the bill, well, they mean business.”

No kidding.

Her heart sank, but she dared not let him in on the rest of her problems. She couldn’t. So, Morgan played this the way it needed to be played.

You’re a thief. Stay a thief. Act the part.

“All this time I’ve known I was in trouble, that I’d done something wrong. But to hear someone else say it—” She shivered. “I’m in a whole lot more trouble than I thought.”

“Not if I have anything to say about it,” he protested.

She shook her head. “Not your problem, Jack.”

“You don’t think so? Guess again. I’m up to my neck in this now whether you like it or not. And I don’t feel like giving up just yet. So, I need to know the truth.”

He took a deep breath and asked, “Just what the hell did you do?”

THE SIXTY-FOUR-THOUSAND-DOLLAR QUESTION.

Morgan knew she was just as guilty as BioClin. She’d accepted the job. But someday, the people at BioClin were going to know just what they’d done to her life. *Her* life?

Damn bastards.

There was a murderer lurking out there somewhere. And Morgan had no idea what to do about that.

She knew she would never be safe until the memory stick she carried made its way into reputable hands. The rest, she could only guess at. On the one hand, it made her a suspect, and on the other, a target.

Morgan needed help. Only one person could do that for her now, her old graduate advisor Dr. Huan Chuan Lee, the head of Molecular Biology at Emory University in Atlanta. An expert in the field of metabolic research, he'd contributed to research that went on to win a Nobel Prize. His safeguard was that he wasn't expendable, not without raising some serious questions.

Morgan needed time, time to find out who was behind the journal entries. She needed Dr. Lee's reputation and status as a shield. BioClin knew the process didn't work and now Dr. Lee would too. They wouldn't dare go public with anything if they knew he had the project in his possession.

But that would also put him in terrible danger.

Welcome to the reason she'd been running around the East Coast for the last week. And the reason Jack was able to track her.

Damn the man.

Could he help her buy that time? Could he help her get to Dr. Lee's in one piece?

Yes.

Did she dare trust him farther than that?

No.

Morgan examined her logic again. Silence in exchange for time.

God, she still couldn't believe it.

What she'd stumbled on—oh hell, even *she* couldn't begin to estimate the possibilities. They seemed endless. And the potential profit for BioClin? Astronomical.

All for a new diet drug.

She'd been hired to find a solution to the growing problem of obesity in America. All they had to do was come up with a method that worked. Morgan and her team decided to go after the triggers that stimulate metabolism. If the glycolytic rate inside the cell necessary to maintain cellular energy level could be forced to continue in excess, a person would burn more calories than they could take in and lose weight.

The problem was that the natural activation pathways were generally unknown. Her team found one. Then, all hell broke loose. At the height of promise, just as Morgan was about to prove their findings, top management leaked their results to the press, creating a flurry of expectation.

The bastards didn't wait. Damn them all to hell and back again.

BioClin knew she and her team weren't anywhere close to anything concrete yet. But they also needed money. Now they were going to do whatever they thought necessary to get their property back.

Morgan shook her head, trying to tame her emotions. Anger warred with fear. She would never understand why. Sure, her brain had figured it out. By letting the proverbial cat out of the bag, BioClin already had investors breaking down their doors. But ethically? They had to know there was a possibility something might go wrong, would go wrong.

Did go wrong.

Morgan shivered, trying not to let Jack see. She corralled her imagination before pictures started creeping into her head. No one else was going to be put in harm's way. No one else was going to die.

Whoever had done this despicable thing, well, they'd underestimated Dr. Morgan Mackenzie. She was going to make damned sure they paid. Big-time. Because Morgan Mackenzie was about saving lives, not taking them.

Maybe that was why she couldn't get Pinky and Louie out of her head.

She'd been a fool to name her test mice.

She'd been an even bigger fool to let herself get caught by a man. Now she was sitting in the back seat of a limousine headed toward freaking wonderland.

"I'm not exactly sure how to explain."

"Try English. I'm not stupid."

She smiled, enjoying his discomfort. Obviously, he was out of his element. "Testy, are we?"

He waved away her enjoyment. "I don't speak geek. Sue me."

Morgan laughed. "All right, all right. Take it easy." She sobered, then tried the easiest explanation she could give him. "You're aware of who I am?"

"Dr. Morgan Mackenzie," he quoted. "Bachelor of Science degree in Biochemistry."

"With a minor in Genetics," she added.

"A Master's in Molecular Biology," he continued.

"Just a steppingstone."

"A PhD in Cellular Kinetics."

"That one was hard."

She watched Jack's eyes widen with appreciation at the pride in her tone. "You think keeping you alive is going to be so easy? Guess again."

She thought about that for a long time. "I barely finished high school," he continued. "Doesn't make me stupid."

She nodded and her chin lifted. "All those degrees don't make me stupid either."

Point received and taken. "Agreed."

He sighed. "You didn't answer my question."

"Do you know who I work for?"

He shook his head. "No."

"I work for a company called BioClin. I found a process that would lead to the first diet drug that would work naturally with the body. All totaled, it could be worth billions."

She listened to him whistle. "Really? You're not playing with me?"

"No. No joke."

"Wow," he whispered. "No wonder—"

"Yeah—" Morgan nodded, her smile turning sad. "No wonder

Sam wanted to turn me in without any help. Probably would've earned one helluva bonus."

Jack's face tightened. "You don't mind if I reserve judgment on that, do you?"

"You can think whatever you want. I don't give a damn. All I need right now is to get my data into the hands of someone reputable, someone *my employer* will think twice about going after."

"And once that's done?"

Morgan's blood chilled but she answered honestly. "I'll face whatever consequences I have to."

Jack didn't reply, and she didn't continue. Morgan knew the ramifications of her actions. She wasn't about to change course now. Besides, no matter what anyone thought she had right on her side. Giving in, not following through, would make her wrong, and she wasn't about to let anyone or anything make wrong. Ever.

CHAPTER ELEVEN

JACK DIALED A NUMBER HE KNEW TOO WELL ON HIS prepaid cell, not surprised when the phone picked up after the first ring.

"Not bright, Andy," Sam chided.

God, he hated that name. But, right at this moment, he was a fool. Because getting screwed always came when you least expected it. From the last person on earth you thought would betray you.

Across from him, sound asleep, Morgan half sat, half lay against the inside of the limo, looking all kinds of innocent.

"You know I hate that name."

Sam laughed. "Very dramatic. You also know I'll find her."

"Probably," Jack replied, realizing the inevitable. "But not on my watch. And not until I know the truth."

Could what she had in her possession really make Sam turn traitor to everything they fought for, everything they believed in?

"No can do," Sam answered. And Jack could have sworn there was a hint of regret in his tone before the voice on the other end of the line turned cold. "Need to know only."

Jack frowned. Sam was lying to him. Why? Damn it all, none of this made any sense.

What you did to her makes no sense.

He looked at the long lashes resting on Morgan's cheeks, her face innocent in repose, and knew he'd made a whopper of a mistake.

"We don't do the dirty jobs, old buddy. Remember? We work for the good guys. You can't tell me that you'd give up your honor for a bunch of zeroes on a check."

A long silence greeted him. "I needed the money, Jack. We took a bad hit. I made investments that...well... coulda, shoulda, woulda. I haven't been able to recover."

Jack didn't want to believe it. There had to be more behind those words. So, he probed. "Blood money?"

He listened to the man he thought of as his best friend sigh. "Yes! Blood Money!"

Jack couldn't believe how bad that hurt. "All right. No one said you couldn't lose your honor. But did you have to drag mine into the sewer with you?"

He listened to Sam snort. "You were just supposed to find her. That's all."

"And what? Turn my brain off? Do I look fucking stupid to you?"

Jack finally reached his last straw. First, he'd betrayed Morgan, believing he was doing the right thing and then he found out his best friend and partner, the man whose life he'd saved, had betrayed him.

Life did go around full circle, didn't it? Very painfully, he acknowledged bitterly.

"Why, Sam?" he tried, one last time. "Come clean now. Don't make me find out the hard way."

"I wish I could, old buddy. But I can't."

Nah, that just meant he didn't want to. "I'll go to the authorities. Don't think for a moment I won't."

Sam laughed. The sound brought reality home to him. "You don't have the balls."

Oh really?

Without thought, he told Sam what he could do with himself and hung up. He'd never be able to make things right with Morgan. But that didn't mean he couldn't try.

As for the rest, Jack was going to find out the truth. Not only had Sam challenged him, but he also knew only exceptional circumstances would have brought about their telephone conversation. So that meant Jack would have to get Morgan to trust him again. How? Well, he was going to have to get her to forgive him. Jack would have smiled except that his decision might be an exercise in futility.

Oh, well.

First, he was going to have to apologize. If she let him, and he doubted very much that she would. Then, he was going to have to get her to tell him what was going on. And finally, he was going to have to keep her safe until he knew what to do with the truth.

This last decision was going to take all the skills he possessed.

MORGAN AWOKE AGAIN, CRACKING HER NECK ONE PAINFUL inch at a time. Just one more strike in a list of strikes against him. His eyes were closed, his breathing even. He'd fallen asleep too. But the moment she lifted from the seat to get comfortable, his eyes popped open. Heat flared in his gaze. His lids lowered. Her gaze flicked from his crotch to his face. He had the audacity not to be bothered by his reaction to her.

She ignored him completely and asked, "Where are we going?"

He gave her one of his patented little grins and ignored her question. "I'm going to assume you haven't told me everything that's going on. Which could be very dangerous for both of us. So,

I'm going to ask once. Is there anymore that you're not telling me?"

Did he really think an apology equated to trust? "You were doing fine with your telepathic abilities, so I think I'll let you figure it out."

He frowned at her snide tone but answered, "I'm good, kitten but not that good."

She caught both meanings. "Not funny, Jack."

His tone turned serious as he replied, "Wasn't trying to be." He raised a brow, studying her. "Are you going to answer my question?"

"No. Are you going to answer mine?"

He smiled. "That's my girl. Stubborn to the end."

Girl? Did he just call me a girl? "Where are we going, Jack?" she repeated, her tone hard and exasperated.

"I figure by now Sam's got a bunch of guys looking for us but he's not sure what direction we're headed in."

"That sounds like a good thing."

Jack smiled as if he were enjoying the conversation. "Ah, but you see, kitten, there are always the percentages. A tracker never leaves any stone unturned. So, Sam has no choice. He'll have someone follow every direction."

That didn't sound so good. "I see."

"Not quite. What you don't understand is that Sam has manpower. That's his advantage. So, he'll follow every direct route out of Delaware. Eventually, he'll find the car and know we're clean." At her questioning frown, he clarified his meaning. "He'll know we're using hard to trace transportation."

"Oh."

"In the meantime, he'll cover all possibilities by using time and distance. He'll create a search circle, then tighten it. He'll assume you'll sleep, he'll know I won't."

Despite her misgivings, Morgan said, "But that means we'll have to slip past his net somehow."

"All I need is a direction, kitten."

She sighed. "He'll find us."

Jack smiled. "I'm counting on it. Eventually."

"You might end up in jail too."

He gave her that patented grin of his again. "Not a chance. I'm the best at what I do. I'm going to save your, um, derriere, whether you want me to or not."

"Why?"

"I happen to like your derriere. Very tight. Round. Bitable—"

"Not funny," she spat at him despite the flare of heat in her veins.

He shrugged. "Right now, we're headed for Virginia Beach. I gave the driver a few hundred and told him to take us as far south as he could. That's probably about as far as he'll go. So, are you going to tell me or do I guess?"

Just to be bitchy she said, "Guess."

"Really? Are you sure you want to play the game that way? I mean, I have a stake in this up to a point."

"What do you mean?"

"That I can decide to play along for a while because of Sam, or I can turn you in and let the authorities figure out the whole mess. Which I'm inclined to do right now so don't press your luck."

She thought about that for a moment. "What's stopping you? Sam or me?"

He didn't answer. Which gave her a real warm and fuzzy feeling inside.

"Now back to question number one," he continued. "I made the first step. You make the next. That's how it works from now on, kitten."

She frowned, wishing he'd stop calling her that—then wishing he wouldn't. God, she was such a mess right now.

"I really need to know what's going on," he insisted.

Damn the man, he was throwing the ball back into her court.

He wouldn't be satisfied until she told him the truth. But if she did that, there'd be no going back.

"If I do, you're in this up to your eyeballs."

"I am already. Give."

Morgan sighed. He was such a bulldog. "It would be easier to show you."

"What do you mean?"

"I need a computer."

He frowned. "I don't have enough cash to buy one and that would be a waste of money anyway. A public library would have access plus that would give me a way to search for some wheels."

Morgan considered their dilemma. "I've got a better idea," she said. "Most hotels have business centers. Less conspicuous."

She watched him lower the window. He told the driver to find the name of a national hotel chain and then closed the window again. "We've got another hour or so. Why don't you try to rest some more?"

"Only if you tell me why you're trying to be nice."

"Ouch! I guess I deserved that. You'll have to let me know when I get out of the doghouse."

She gave him an evil smile. "You mean Chateau Bow-wow? It's like Hotel California. Once you check in, you can never check out."

He grimaced. "I'll remember that."

STARING AT HER WAS BECOMING A HARD HABIT TO BREAK. And Jack knew that if he wasn't careful, he wouldn't just be teetering on the edge of a cliff, he would end up falling for her.

Time to play the game his way. He was a master at seduction. He also knew how to do whatever he had to do to find the truth. Truth, justice, and the Andrew Jackson way.

He turned his grimace into a deliberate smile, showing her he could be unfazed by her attitude.

"What will you do when you can't hate me anymore?"

She sighed. She looked weary. They were both tired. "I don't hate you, Jack."

"Good to know, but I'm being serious. BioClin feels they have every right to press charges. You work for them. The property is theirs. But you believe the work is yours. Did you sign a contract? Was there a nondisclosure agreement?"

She gave him a long-pointed look. "Why are you asking?"

"Just curious."

Of course, he was lying, and they both knew that. He was more than curious.

She answered after what felt like hours. "The nondisclosure agreement was regarding leaking information to a competitor. It didn't say anything about not letting anyone have it at all."

He sighed. She had a point. "So, you're basing your freedom and your career on semantics? Not a good idea."

"Sue me."

"Now there's a thought I'm sure your employer has thought of."

"Too much bad publicity. They won't." She grinned, not a nice sight. "And you can stop the third degree. It won't work. I'll let you know when I'm damned good and ready."

That was great. Just wonderful. Because without answers, he was blind. With a sigh, he said, "Get some sleep, kitten."

"Don't call me kitten."

She settled back into the corner furthest away from him, which made him sad for a moment, and then made him realize he was going to have to work harder. To get to the truth, since she wouldn't answer him any other way, he was going to have to seduce her. Not an arduous task at all, just dangerous.

"What would you like me to call you, then?" he asked, trying hard to be patient. After all, they were both at fault.

"Nothing. So, stop being annoying."

Funny, but her anger only made him more determined. Because if there was anything Jack hated, it was falling into someone else's cesspool. But what really got to him was the thread of raw hurt underneath.

"Who are you, Jackson Kent?"

Obviously, she didn't realize she'd actually whispered the question out loud until she heard the words reverberate through the silence in the limousine.

Jack reached out without realizing. A little too much too soon? To cover the action he answered, "A friend. More than a friend, I hope."

"You've got to be kidding me," she cried in disbelief.

He gave her a what-can-I-tell-you look. He hoped it would seem genuine. Most of it was. "It's not just going to go away, you know."

"Touch me, and I'll break your fingers."

Jack threw back his head and laughed. "Damn. I like you feisty."

"I don't like you at all."

His chest shook with suppressed laughter. She was lying and they both knew it. "By the way, just so you know, the driver thinks you're cheating on your husband and that's why the ride's on the QT."

"You didn't," she whispered, her tone scandalized.

He laughed out loud. "We really shouldn't disappoint him, you know."

Shocked, she cried, "You're nuts!"

And yet, he watched her struggle to maintain her composure. Good. She sat up in the seat, trying her damnedest to look neutral, and stared out the window. "Where are we?"

Obviously, she was trying to change the subject. "We should be arriving at our destination very soon."

Jack knew he was her best shot at survival. So did she. Yeah, he'd made a mistake. And yeah, he was going to pay for it. But so had she. Guess that made them even.

He started laughing softly. He tilted his head to look at her. "Just for the record, it's not going to go away."

"What's not going to go away?"

They both knew damned well. The reason she kept shifting in her seat and the reason his pants felt like jail.

"Whatever is between us."

The afternoon sun created a frame for her hair, sparking tiny flames around her head. So, Jack turned up the heat. "Just feel. Live in the moment. You know you want to."

"Go to hell."

He let his gaze skim over her skin, making it hard for both of them to breathe, let alone think. "Let your hair down," he insisted.

"Never. Not after what you did to me."

"Broken record. Ditch the anger. You don't need to hide behind it anymore."

He grinned, letting his gaze soften, letting her see his marbled blue eyes weren't the only part of his body that swirled with heat.

"Unlock the door," he cajoled. "Feel. Just feel."

Despite her anger, he watched her shiver. She shifted in her seat again and he knew he'd won the first battle. The spark between them was far from dead. But that also made him realize that playing with fire usually got a body burned.

"And forget what happened a couple of hours ago?"

He nodded. Her jaw clenched. She was fighting herself all the way. "You're freaking crazy."

"Maybe. But I'll never give up. You can bet your life on that."

As a matter of fact, I'm betting both our lives on it.

CHAPTER TWELVE

SAM ORMOND SAT AT HIS DESK, FUMING. JACK HAD vanished. Not without a trace, but damned close to it. He had men canvassing the area for a rental car and stationed at the outlet mall to make sure Jack didn't double back to get his car. He didn't think Jack would be that stupid, but he might assume—

Jack Kent wouldn't assume anything.

The sound of mortar fire rang inside his head, and he could feel the spray of sand biting into his skin as one exploded way too close to them. Sam remembered lifting his head and trying to see the direction the shells were coming from only to catch sight of Jack skirting a perimeter and lobbing a grenade before ducking behind a dune. One more tick and the entire squad would've been toast.

Sam shrugged and turned off the memories.

Instead, he went over his painfully thin dossier on Dr. Morgan Mackenzie one more time. She was a straight arrow. Not even a parking ticket. Spent most of her life, so far, in school or in a lab doing research.

A real geek.

Her mother and father, both older when she was born, were

dead. Her mother from breast cancer, her father a few months later. No siblings. A couple of cousins but obviously not real close. When he'd contacted them, they said they hadn't talked to her in years. Her parents had been professors at a small college in Connecticut, but Dr. Mackenzie had started her academic career at Boston College and finished her doctorate at Columbia University.

You would think that going to school in two major cities would open a lead or two.

Not.

She couldn't be this clean. It was...boring.

Sam threw the file on his desk and leaned back in his chair, raking his hands through his hair in frustration. It might not look like there was a crack in the wall, but there had to be one. There always was. And Sam knew he'd better find it. He was in this up to his eyeballs with no way to turn back now.

Suddenly, his cell phone buzzed on his desk. He snapped forward in his chair. "This had better be what I want to hear."

"It is, boss. It is. We checked every taxi and limo service just like you said. He paid a guy on the sly. Said he was with a married woman."

Sam's heart started to pound. He took a deep breath, then let the air out slowly. "Where?"

"Virginia Beach."

"Are you sure?"

"Yes, sir. Very sure."

Sam didn't respond right away. "Three hundred miles. All directions. Especially south."

"Sorry, sir. Why south?"

"Because Jackson Kent is the best tracker I've ever known. And my first inclination is to double back and go north."

"But I don't understand, sir. If you think he's going to double back north, why don't we concentrate our efforts to the north?"

Sam smiled. "Because he's also the most unpredictable son of a bitch on the face of the earth, that's why. And you'd better hope that he doesn't double back north, because that means he's going to slip right past you."

"No, he won't, sir, you can count on me."

"Oh, I am, Mr. Anderson. I am. Because you know how I feel about failure."

"Yes, sir." A thread of fear reverberated through the line and Sam smiled.

"Keep me posted."

"Will do."

Sam broke the connection. His next step would involve finding an ace in the hole. But for now, the information refreshed him. But he had another call to make. One that darkened his mood immediately.

He punched in a number and put the phone up to his ear with a frown. "Hello?"

"We're closing in."

"That's what you told me yesterday. And the day before." Sam heard the exasperation in his client's tone, and a slow burn began to simmer in his belly.

"And I told you Jack Kent is the best there is," he snapped back. "Now, do you want to do this my way, or lose him altogether?"

He listened to his benefactor sigh. "Good," he continued. "What do you know about Dr. Mackenzie?"

"Why?"

"Because she's going to run to a safety net, someone in her past. Someone you would know a whole lot easier than I would."

"Why would you assume that?"

"Because she's too clean and too boring not to."

Sam waited while his patron assessed the situation. "I'm not certain," the voice on the other end of the line replied in a thoughtful tone. "But I'll get back to you on it."

"The sooner the better," Sam replied, his tone sour. "And you'd better make sure I see a deposit in my account by morning. This whole fiasco is costing me a fortune."

"Understood. As long as you do the same. I'm running out of patience."

The phone went dead, and Sam stared at it. His hand tightened around the plastic as the burn erupted. One of these days he was going to be able to stop taking orders.

Until then he was going to have to settle.

MORGAN AND JACK REACHED THE HOTEL IN VIRGINIA Beach in the afternoon. As they approached the front desk, Morgan realized she was going to have to share a room with him. The thought must have occurred to them at the same time because he simply looked at her and smiled, daring her to request a second room. And while she wanted nothing more than a long hot soak, a seven, no eight, course meal, and a nine-hour nap, Jack, it seemed, had other ideas.

"Do you want to rest?" he asked her, his tongue shoved deep into his cheek as he stared at the bed in the hotel room.

Bastard. "No. I mean, yes."

He roared at her discomfort. "Well, I'm going to take a shower." She didn't answer. "You sure you don't want to join me?" He grinned, pointing at the bathroom. "A nice hot shower would do wonders for that disposition of yours."

"Don't get started on my disposition, Jack. My psyche would rather I hurt you again."

"I could make it worth your while," he continued as if she hadn't said a word. "A nice massage. Starting at your shoulders. Down your back."

Morgan shivered despite herself. "You certainly have a pair, Jack. I'll give that to you. So, if you don't want said items tied up in a knot, very tightly, I suggest you go into the bathroom and forget all about what you're thinking right now."

She watched him shudder. "Heaven forbid. Does that mean the honeymoon's over?"

"Yes," she bit out.

"You know, I'm not averse to having other parts of my anatomy tied up. You know, like wrists, ankles...not too tight, of course."

"Jack!" she screamed.

"I'm going. I'm going."

She listened to the door close and wondered how she wasn't on the floor rolling. God, he was outrageous.

That's what you like about him.

"I don't like him at all," she muttered under her breath.

You like how he makes you feel.

"Yeah, when he's not betraying said derriere."

"Do you always talk to yourself like that?" he asked with a slight smile on his face.

She started, looking up. She hadn't realized he was still in the room. "No. I thought you were taking a shower."

"I am. I will. As soon as we get one thing straight."

"Oh? What's that?"

"This."

He pulled her hard against him and covered her mouth with his. She fought against him but fought against herself more. Her body knew what she wanted better than her mind. Still, there was always pride.

He let go as swiftly as he'd snared her. "You think about that while I'm in the shower. And remember something."

She didn't answer. She couldn't.

"It won't simply go away because you want it to."

She listened to the water run, knowing he was right. But she didn't know how to reconcile her emotions. She certainly didn't know how to separate them. She wanted Jack with every fiber of her being. He was an addiction. He was the dream she had no right to dream.

On the other hand, she was still furious with him for his

betrayal. The only thing that saved his balls from becoming as blue as his eyes was his timely rescue. And Morgan wasn't secure enough in her own skin to believe Jack couldn't help himself.

She sat down on the bed feeling hurt and angry and confused. He'd asked her to simply feel. But her feelings were tied up tighter than the knots she'd dreamed about tying in the limo.

"I understand, kitten."

Morgan looked up to see him standing in front of her, a towel slung low over his hips. She couldn't swallow any better now than the first time she'd seen him this way.

"No, you don't," she bit out.

His brow lifted. His head cocked as if to ask, *oh, no*?

"Better yet, I don't Jack. That's the problem. I don't understand. You let me down." He nodded, his arms widening as if to say, *I can't change that.* "And what you don't and what you never will understand is how many times in my life that's happened to me. All I've ever wanted was the cowboy and the white horse."

His features tightened as her knife speared his guts with razor-like accuracy. But to his credit, he simply inhaled and raked his hand through his hair. "Sorry, kitten," he told her, expelling that breath. "Wrong guy. I flunked hero school."

"I figured that out," she replied with a derisive smile.

He didn't answer at first. He just sat down on the bed next to her. "I really do care about you, Morgan. Give me some time. I'll prove it to you."

Morgan kept on speaking, deciding not to listen to a word he said. "You know what hurts the most? I mean, I know this might not seem true after what happened to us, but it is. I don't just fall into bed with men."

He picked up her hand, gently rubbing the back with his thumb. "I believe you. Do you think you could start believing me too?"

"I'm trying, Jack. I really am."

"Try harder."

"That is soooo easier said than done. Every time I open the gates on my feelings, they get trampled. You're smooth, Jack. Almost too smooth. Don't you get it? I'm really tired of being hurt."

He grinned, rose, and then gave her a swift peck on the cheek. "Guess I'm going to have to convince you the hard way. Go take your bath. By the time you're finished, room service will be here."

Morgan shook her head. Jack was Jack. She rose and shrugged. He wasn't about to give up, but neither was she.

Nearly an hour later and feeling more human, Morgan stepped out of the bathroom. The aroma of dinner made her mouth water. Were those mushrooms she smelled? Some kind of gravy? He'd even ordered a bottle of wine.

"I thought we were on a budget," she said, before her tone turned nasty. Was her desire to be bitchy because she was afraid of what would happen if she allowed him to be nice?

"We are. I kept it simple. I could have spent a lot more." He opened the bottle, pulling out the cork with way more force than necessary. "Do you want a glass or not?"

Morgan frowned. Her emotions were already riding a colossal roller coaster, he didn't have to add to her angst. Or maybe that was his way of retaliating. "I don't get it. A few moments ago, you were being nice. Now you're not. Are you doing the good-cop, bad-cop thing?"

"No. I just got testy. I really am trying."

"Try harder."

She watched his jaw clench, but he had good sense not to answer, which made her feel better.

"I'm hungry," he stated, placing dishes and cutlery on the small table. "How about we eat first, fight later?"

"Sounds like a plan."

"Then, we can have makeup sex," he added with a wink. Jack's moods seemed mercurial and about as stable as her own.

Morgan threw him a look, sat down at the table, and lifted the cover to her dish. She inhaled. "Heavenly." The chicken, covered in sauce and mushrooms, looked delicious. And asparagus, green and seemingly cooked to perfection. She lifted her wineglass after he poured.

"What shall we drink to?" he asked. "Us, perhaps?"

"No. Let's drink to the truth."

He stared at her as if to say she needed to learn that one as much as he did. However, he lifted his glass and replied, "Truth it is."

They ate in near silence, both of them starving. Then, Jack cleared away the dishes. Once he'd placed the tray in the hallway and come back into the room she asked, "Do you want to go downstairs now and let me show you the data stick?"

"No, I have a better idea." His gaze lasered into her, bypassing hot, hotter, and hottest all the way to supernova. "I'll show you my stick first."

He didn't give her a chance to say no. He rose, walked around the table, lifted her out of her seat, and simply pulled her tight against his body. Even though Morgan had known he would try, she hadn't expected immediate capitulation. *Oh, pride? Hello? Are you there?*

Talk about being betrayed. By her own body, no less. It knew exactly what it wanted and refused to accept no for an answer. He feathered kisses over her forehead, down her cheek, grazing her lips with his, making delicate shivers wrack her muscles. Her hands clenched at her sides. She willed them not to move. She refused to give him an inch.

He took a mile. He lifted her up and threw her onto the middle of the bed. "All right, kitten. We'll play this your way. I already know you're hotter than a furnace for me right now but if you want me to prove it, then I guess I'll just have to prove it."

He pounced on her, covering her body with his. At first, he simply kissed her. And kissed her. And kissed her. Until she knew she was going to go insane if he didn't play with the other parts of her body.

She squirmed, trying to get her hips against his.

He finally came up for air with a soft laugh. “Oh no, kitten. I’m not going to do this with clothes on. So, you make up your mind right now. Yes or no?”

Was he kidding?

Morgan found her pride cowering in a corner in the face of desire. God, she was going to hate herself in the morning. Or was she? A thought entered her head that wouldn’t leave. Did she dare? Not one scruple stopped her from taking his hand and placing it square on top of her breast.

His head bent down, and he lowered his mouth to hers again and all sane thought ceased. He pumped his hips, just as a reminder, and flames shot through her core. He’d wanted this to be his show, so Morgan let him drive. He reached under her shirt to play with her breast as requested. The next thing she knew, he decided her shirt had to go, and she found her buttons had been unbuttoned and his fingers were pulling on her nipples inside her bra.

She gasped, unconsciously riding him. “Fly with me,” he whispered.

But before she could, his lips locked on hers again. His tongue tasted everywhere inside her mouth. Hers entwined his as pure heat filled her body.

This getting dressed, getting undressed, business would have to go. He flipped over onto his back. “The jeans,” he choked out as he bit and sucked his way down her neck.

Morgan scooted to the side a little and unsnapped them. He let out a heartfelt sigh of relief when the denim folds parted. She rubbed her hand up and down the hard length of him through his boxers and he shook his head. It was her turn to grin.

He fell back against the bed. There couldn’t possibly be anything sexy about trying to help a man struggle out of tight jeans with a hard-on, but his eyes glittered as if she were the sexiest, most beautiful creature on earth.

Morgan stopped, aware perhaps for the first time in her life of being a woman with innate power. She'd always wondered why they called it a battle of the sexes, finding now that lovemaking could distill down to one-upmanship. But then she realized, as he watched her remove her clothes and his gaze darkened and filled with raw desire, that she was wrong. The give and take between a man and a woman was exactly that. And without balance, it meant nothing. She knew what she had to do.

She straddled his legs again, lying down on top of as much of his body as she could. "You want me," she exhaled in awe.

"So bad, I think I might die in a second. If we don't—you know—"

She slid back and pulled his boxers down to his thighs. As much as she wanted to inhale him right then and there, she knew better. She rose on her knees and inched her way back up to his chest so he could feast on her breasts.

He would never know how good that felt.

Then, she slid back a little so that the tip of his erection grazed the outer edges of her core. He swallowed. Hard. Sweat beaded his brow. "Umm. I thought this was going to be my show."

"It was. It still is." She grazed his tip again. "You need to get off in a minute," he choked. "In my back pocket—"

She slid back a little further and smiled. "Not just yet."

He gasped and closed his eyes. "It'll help if you think of complex chemical equations the way I am, " she teased.

He burst out laughing. "Wouldn't know one of those if they bit me in the ass."

She shifted her hips, licked her lips, and lifted a brow. "Well?"

They both knew he was unprotected. After a moment of shocked silence he replied, "You sure?"

She slid back even farther and rotated, making his erection strain even harder toward her core. Yet, Morgan refused the prize. "What do you think?"

"Oh God, Morgan," he cried. "You know, a man in this position might say anything to get what he wanted."

"That's the point."

"I'm clean. I'm clean," he told her.

"Are you?" she asked as she lifted off the bed and walked away to go into the bathroom. The door slammed and then the lock clicked.

CHAPTER THIRTEEN

JACK WAITED FOR HER TO COME BACK. AND WAITED. AND waited. Until he figured out, she wasn't coming back. And that was when he realized how much he'd hurt her. Trust was a terrible thing to kill, so she'd gotten even with him. Inside her there wasn't just a door that needed to be opened, there was a castle wall that would need to be breached.

Her point made with crystal clarity, Jack tried not to let her hurt him. With his cock still yearning for her touch, only one thought beat like a live wire inside his brain. He wanted her.

Had she known he was trying to seduce her for his own means? Was this her way of showing him that backhanded tactics weren't acceptable?

Were they?

Jack wanted to put his fist through a wall. He wanted to yank on his crank so his balls would stop hurting. He wanted to know how things had gone from bad to worse.

He already knew. He'd decided to use her again. Instead of simply believing her, he'd figured sex would get the truth out of her. Instead, she'd turned the tables on him and shown him a boatload of integrity in the process.

Not to mention killing his lower extremities.

He jumped out of the bed and stormed over to the bathroom door, pounding on the wood. "You made your point. I get it already."

"Do you?" she yelled back. Even through the wood he could tell she was crying.

"I need the truth, Morgan."

"Morgan?"

"Yeah, Morgan. Real names, real people, real situations. Starting from the beginning. So that we both deal on the same playing field from now on."

"Why should I do that?"

"Because if you don't, all we'll do is keep on hurting each other. I need to understand. I want to believe you. I have to know what happened."

"Are you sure?"

Jack leaned his forehead against the door. The wood felt cool, not enough to cool the fire in his gut, but soothing. "I betrayed you. I can't take that back. I used a night like I've never spent with anyone else in the world believing I was doing the right thing. I was wrong."

She didn't answer right away. "At least now you sound like you're telling the truth. But I had to slap you in the face to get that out of you."

He sighed. "You're right. And I deserved every second. I'm still paying for it, if that's any consolation."

"You are?"

It sounded like she was licking her lips with satisfaction. Damn her.

"Yes."

"Good."

"Morgan, listen to me. I'm only going to say this once. I want you. I'm in agony because of that. But I won't touch you until *you* want me to. All right? And along the way, I'm going to help you get out of this mess."

"Why?"

"The truth?"

"Yes."

"Swear to God. Because I believe you're not a thief," he insisted

"You do? Why?" she cried.

"Because I couldn't want you as badly as I do without knowing your integrity."

"So, it's just about the sex?" she bit out, her words filled with hurt. "And you don't make mistakes?"

Jeez. Does she ever give up? "If that's what you think, then I'll leave. You've got the room for the night. And I've got some cash left. I'll leave it on the table."

Jack turned from the door, his stomach hollowing. He started to get dressed, his desire surrounded by a strange empty feeling. Funny how now that he had to go, he didn't want to.

He was just tucking his shirt into his pants when the bathroom door opened. She'd obviously washed her face but that hadn't taken care of the redness rimming her eyes. He tried not to let her distress reach him. He tried not to let her nudity reach him even more.

"There's still some wine left," she told him in a quiet voice.

"You can enjoy it after I'm gone." He grinned. "At least I paid for the meal this time."

Her mouth quirked but only sadness poured out of her gaze. "I still need to run."

He shrugged and put on his jacket. "I know. If you can at least trust one thing, trust this: I'll disappear for a while. Sam won't find me. At least that will give you a head start."

"You'd do that for me?"

He nodded, hoping that she could read the honesty he was trying to convey. "I owe you that much at the very least."

"True." She mulled that over as she walked toward her clothes.

He tried not to watch. "You'd walk away not knowing why I'm doing what I'm doing?"

Jack knew there was only one answer to give. "Yes."

Her bitter smile cut him to the quick. "Because I'm not giving you a choice?"

He shook his head. "No. Because I care."

"You probably won't after I explain." She sighed.

Jack sat down at the little table in the room. "Try me."

"After I get some clothes on."

He sighed. "If you insist."

THE SAME PLAYING FIELD. MORGAN DOUBTED WITH ALL her heart that would ever be possible. Not with his raw beauty. But he'd been right about dealing with one another. She'd needed to prove to him she was smarter than he ever expected. And honorable.

As she dressed, Morgan began to explain. "At first, I thought I was going crazy. But I've just spent a week in a bunch of hotel rooms with nothing to do but think. First and foremost, I'm a scientist. And like most of my contemporaries, a little too specific with my requirements. It's kind of, well part of, the job."

He smiled at her. "I guess attention to detail is important."

"It is," she replied. "Well, I would go back to my desk after being in my lab all day and I could swear someone had been there and touched my things. Items on my desk were out of place. Not by a lot but enough for me to notice."

Morgan shook her head. "Like most normal people, I denied reality. I dismissed it. It was impossible. There was no logical reason for anyone to be snooping around my desk. Then, someone got into my lab notebook. It's a journal of my experiments. Someone must have been reading it."

"How can you be sure?"

"Because it's a hard-bound book and pages open when you write in it. It would open automatically to a page well before the one I was writing on, as if someone had broken the binding in that spot."

"That's hardly life threatening, you know."

Morgan smiled. "I know. And, after denying everything, I thought I was simply being paranoid. But it happened more than once."

"Someone was spying on you?"

"Science is just as competitive as everything else, you know. Someone was reading my work and maybe threatening my career. I wanted to go to my boss and tell him. But without proof, with just feelings, he'd start looking at me sideways. And I didn't want anything—anything—jeopardizing my project."

"And?" Jack encouraged, pouring them both the last of the wine.

Morgan realized she needed some. She took a sip and nodded her thanks.

"I never dreamed someone was going to give me a reason for being paranoid. One day we all went out for Rebecca's birthday."

"Rebecca?"

Morgan smiled inside. One of the sweetest young women she'd ever met, and with so much to offer. One of the people that Morgan was sweating bullets trying to cure. Because underneath the excess weight was a heart of gold.

"My admin. Well, all the heads of the departments shared her." She gave him a wry smile. "Not a lot of common sense with a bunch of PhDs."

He half-laughed. "I get it."

"Anyway, when we got back from her birthday lunch, I could swear my desk had been searched. Everyone knew we were taking her out. But I chalked it up to professional paranoia again. Then, I found a couple of creases in my lab notebook. Whoever had been reading my lab notebook had made copies of pages. I had no idea why except that I thought someone wanted to steal my thunder. God, I wish that was all that happened."

She watched Jack lift a curious brow.

She waved at him to tell him she'd get there eventually. "They took the project away from me."

Morgan closed her eyes, remembering the hurt and betrayal. "So, you played the game and lost," he replied. "I'm sure that happens more often than not in your business."

"Not nice but probably true. And if losing my job was the only problem, I would never have done what I did."

"Okay. So why did you steal the data?"

"BioClin made an announcement about my findings so they could get funding for the project. They had no right to do that. They knew there was no way my work would be finished in time to satisfy any bankers so either someone told them they could finish the job, or they decided to use the investment capital to jack the stock price, make a killing, and let everything die."

"Any idea who that someone might be?"

"Dr. Anton Dvorak. Sleaze ball extraordinaire."

He frowned at her. "Sorry. Personal opinions aside, he's a molecular biologist and was my direct competitor within the company. He was always trying to impress everyone with how great he was."

"So, you think he was responsible?"

Morgan started laughing. "Anton? He's not that smart," she added with disdain. "All show, trust me."

"Then he had help."

"That's what I've been thinking for the past few weeks."

She watched Jack nod. So far, everything she'd told him made sense. "So, why did you run?"

"We need to go downstairs for that."

SINCE IT WAS RATHER LATE, NO ONE ELSE WAS IN THE business center, for which Morgan was grateful. She walked over to one of the computers on the desk then dug into her pocket and pulled out the memory stick.

"This is what Sam wants and what BioClin wants back even more."

She turned and watched Jack take a deep breath, then let the air out slowly, gesturing for her to sit in front of the computer while he stood behind her.

"You might want to explain a little before you continue."

"All right," she replied, returning her focus to the computer. "I'll try to remember you're not a colleague."

Jack started to chuckle, but the sound faded. "We're in this together now, Morgan. Got that?"

She sat down and he gave her shoulders a reassuring squeeze.

"I'm trying," she answered.

Morgan booted up the stick and began clicking on file folders. The entire screen was filled with them. But she knew exactly which one she was looking for—the presentation she'd given at the project meeting—goodness, was it only a few weeks ago?

"I guess I'd better give you a little background. BioClin isn't quite biotech, not quite pharmaceutical, sort of in between with a little clinical thrown in for good measure. We have several branches—Biochemistry, Clinical Chemistry, Molecular Biology, and my specialty: Cellular Kinetics."

He squeezed her shoulders to get her to stop and gave her a bit of a sheepish grin as she looked up at him. "Remember, I barely finished high school. I don't speak geek, okay?"

Morgan smiled back at him but then reality started closing in and she forced herself to lock her shoulders in place.

"You're not alone, kitten. I promised to help you."

Morgan nodded. She took a deep breath and continued. "A while ago but not that long ago, the new paradigm in the scientific community was genetics and gene mapping. Aside from not wanting to follow the crowd, the development of a new scientific process can cost millions of dollars.

"And there has to be enough return on the investment in a reasonable enough amount of time to substantiate that cost. BioClin simply wasn't big enough to play with the big boys and so they had to find something new. Something no one had thought of yet. Their marketing department decided to target the weight-loss industry. I'll bet you didn't know people spend upward of two hundred billion dollars a year on weight-loss and weight-loss products."

"You're kidding, right?"

"No joke, Jack."

"Wow. I had no idea."

"Exactly."

"But I don't understand. Where do you come in?"

"The idea was presented to me as a challenge. Find the pathway that triggers the glycolytic rate inside a cell. Find a way to stimulate that rate, keep it going, and then the metabolism inside the cell would use more calories than could be taken in. Even you know that if you burn more calories than you take in, you'll lose weight.

"The problem was that the pathways were unknown. Trust me, if someone had figured them out already, they would have come up with the ultimate diet drug way before now."

"I see." She turned to watch him stare at the computer screen, his face serious and his gaze filled with concern. "Something tells me you found a pathway."

Morgan smiled. "By accident, of course. Then, it took a while to recreate the experiment, but I was able to do it."

"And?"

"I made the biggest mistake of my life. I presented my findings during a project meeting and BioClin leaked my findings to a bunch of bankers."

"I don't understand. You recreated one experiment, right? That's not a whole lot to bank on."

She winced at the pun. "True. But think of it for a moment. Think of the investment capital that could be offered just to continue. All of which would make the company stock price soar. They're a small company. Everyone has stock options. It's part of the gamble. If the project you're working on succeeds, you win. Up until recently, BioClin's stock wasn't worth that much."

"I see."

Morgan sighed. "I guess I could have lived with their greed. After all, companies are in business to make money. And the officers of small biotech companies don't always get a chance to make a boatload of money on their stock options."

"You don't have to be nice, you know."

She nodded. "I know. Funny thing is, from the company dynamic, I also thought they were looking for the prestige and the glory—the ability to thumb their nose at the huge pharmaceutical companies and their enormous research-and-development departments. It's a small community out there. Everyone knows everyone else. Being able to beat the big boys is a huge feather in a company's cap."

He smiled. "Follow the dollar. Works every time. By the way you're talking, though, I'm figuring there's a huge 'but' in there."

Tears filled her eyes and then anger filled her belly. "They jumped the gun, Jack. I couldn't get it to work."

He looked down at her, thoroughly confused. "But I thought you just said you *did* get it to work."

Morgan shook her head. "You can't understand the excitement, Jack. But you also have to understand that years of careful research go into getting a drug on the market. I was able to recreate one experiment."

"Okay, kitten. I get the point. But you said you were able to do it successfully. I'm going to assume that means more than once."

Morgan sighed. "Yes, you're right. I did what I set out to do, all right."

She closed the presentation file and found the file that would haunt her for a long, long time. She clicked on it, and a picture filled the screen. Pinky and Louie. Her test mice. God, every time she looked at this picture she felt evil inside for their poor little bodies that were lying on the bottom of a cage, emaciated, grotesquely twisted, and totally lifeless.

"I found the trigger, all right. I found out how to turn the metabolic process on, Jack. There was only one small problem. I couldn't figure out how to turn it off."

CHAPTER FOURTEEN

JACK DIDN'T SAY ANYTHING, AND THE SILENCE STRETCHED out for several long, cold minutes. Her heart sank. Morgan knew what she was. The picture on the computer screen only brought that home with startling clarity.

Dr. Morgan Mackenzie. Murderer.

She hated that she'd killed those mice. If they'd gone in the name of science, she could have lived with that. But somewhere, somehow, she'd let her ego get in the way. Science and ego never mixed well. Hadn't Dr. Lee told her that?

"Morgan?"

She turned from him as shame flooded her body. "This is all my fault, Jack."

He wouldn't let her run away, swiveling around the chair until she faced him once again. "Hey," he said, his voice soft with understanding. "Don't do this to yourself."

"Why not?"

"Because you made a mistake."

"Mistake?" she asked with a bitter laugh. "Sorry to disappoint. They died because of my pride. I got cocky. I started believing the hype. Look at me, I'm the great Dr. Morgan Mackenzie. I did something no one's ever been able to do. Oh, and by the way, forget that I figured it out—by accident."

"Gee," he snorted right back at her. "You were human. Fancy that."

Morgan pushed at his arms, wanting to get up so he would leave her alone. "I'm not allowed to be human. I can't be human. Not when lives are at stake."

He stared at her until her words sunk in. "And I'm different... how?"

He had a point. "I've never doubted myself until now," she continued. "Science has always been straightforward, clean, razor sharp. No gray areas. Experiments work or they don't. And failure teaches better than success. I could have accepted that. Except—"

He reached out to lift her chin. His smile filled with pride. "Except what, kitten?"

"My world turned dirty on me. Okay, I admit it. I'm a geek. My work was my world. And when you're a scientist, you live by a code of honesty and integrity."

She turned and stared at Pinky and Louie for a long time, then closed the picture. "They deserved better. But damn it, so did I."

He frowned. "What do you mean?"

"Twenty-four-seven. For two years. Each step building on the next, with each failure knocking me back down and making me even more determined to succeed."

"And you did."

"Sort of." Morgan remembered the hurt well. "They didn't even have the decency to tell me what they planned to do."

"Okay, so they screwed you. So what?"

She threw him a look. "Jack—"

He cocked his head at her. "Look. Drama's not your style."

"Don't be too sure about that," she answered with a laugh. "You should have seen me. I went ballistic on them after I found out about the bankers."

He kind of smiled at her then, part disbelief, part pride.

Morgan wondered about that smile, and then she dismissed it. She couldn't believe he'd be proud of what she'd done. After all, she'd failed. Miserably. "Forget the sweat. Forget the tears. No one was going to take this project away from me until I could make things right."

Anger still burned in her gut that they didn't want her to. "I owed that to Pinky and Louie."

She watched the light bulb finally go off in his brain. "That's why you didn't destroy the data."

She nodded. "Well, there's also theft of company property, destruction of said property, broken confidentiality agreements, and a slew of other legal things, I'm sure."

He grinned. "You thinking what I'm thinking?

"Probably. Busted confidentiality agreements are the least of my problems right now."

"*Our* problems."

She closed her eyes, realizing how much that meant. Opening them, she said, "Thank you."

The look he gave her said she was welcome—anytime.

"Jack, I swear to you. I never thought things would get to this point. Honest. I'm not a thief."

"Technically, you are," he teased.

Morgan wanted to smile but didn't have the heart. "I'm not a criminal. I want to finish the project. I want to make things right. I don't want anyone to get hurt."

She reached out, and he covered her hand with both of his. Amazed, she realized he cared. "Sure, my pride's involved. And I'm arrogant. I have to be. But BioClin jumped the gun. They want their property back so they can finish the project and make a ton of money without making sure that the process can be fixed. You've seen what happened to my test mice. They know about this. I reported it at my last project meeting. I couldn't let anyone get hurt," she repeated.

Anyone else.

Did she dare tell him that? No, not yet. Not until she was totally sure he was on her side.

"They were going to fire me to keep me quiet. They were going to make it known that I was a sore loser because I couldn't fulfill my contract. They were going to use my professional pride to make sure everyone in the business knew so I'd never get more than an entry-level scientist job again."

"Wow. That's low."

Morgan sighed. He brought her hand up to his lips and kissed the backs of her fingers, giving her a hard squeeze before letting go. Aside from the thrill his touch garnered, she couldn't get over how much his acceptance of her story meant.

"Part of me didn't want to believe it, but I've been running under the supposition that they'll do whatever is necessary to get this data back. Hell, they hired you and Sam, didn't they?"

His mouth quirked in acknowledgment. "And if they're willing to go to these lengths, what happens next?" he asked out loud.

"That's the question, now, isn't it?"

He nodded. "Supposing the next person to work on this project gets pressured to cut a corner or decides that the one little tweak that fudges some data won't be found. If these experiments aren't completed correctly, someone might die like those mice."

Oh, and by the way, should I mention already did?

"I couldn't live with that. I'd rather be the target than put anyone else at risk. That included you until you convinced me you can take care of yourself."

He gave her a "duh" smile. "I can."

Morgan watched him turn away and pace as he processed. Funny, she was like that too. She thought better when she was moving.

"Does this happen very often in your business?"

"No, of course not. The FDA won't allow it. Start to finish, getting a drug to market takes upward of five to seven years, usually longer. The pressure is to make sure the process works and make sure it keeps working. That's the hedge against the bet. Make sure the drug works. Then, the investment isn't in vain."

He stopped pacing for a moment and rubbed his chin, deep in thought. "What if it doesn't? I mean, what happens if the whole project is a flop?"

"Companies cut their losses. People like me lose their jobs. Nice try but it just can't be done. At least no one dies."

"BioClin is different?"

"I don't think so. They probably thought I was all glory and no guts—that I wanted my name on the scientific papers and in the newspapers, and that I'd roll over and let them take the project away from me. Don't forget what I'm working on is huge. So big I've been trying to wrap my head around all the implications since I started running. Just think Jack. A new diet pill. One that triggers the body's own metabolism to function. I mean hell, got a hot date on Friday? Take a pill from Monday through Thursday and lose five pounds."

"Wasn't that the idea?"

"No!" she exploded. "The idea was to save lives!" She lowered her voice and added, "When I started this project, my personal stake was Rebecca. I wanted to find a way to help the morbidly obese, the people who just can't lose weight by themselves."

When Jack didn't answer, Morgan sighed once more. "Sorry. I'll get off the soapbox now."

"Hey, I'm with you all the way," he told her, his tone full of commiseration.

She turned, rose, and he opened his arms. Morgan ran into them. Her head fell against his chest, listening to the strong thump-thump of his heart beneath her ear. His arms banded around her, and he kissed the top of her head.

How long they stayed together, Morgan didn't know. She didn't care. Being in his arms at that moment was so right, so necessary, she didn't want to move. Funny, he seemed to sense that because he didn't answer. He just held her. And waited.

Eventually, Morgan lifted her head. "So, what happens now? I don't think I'm going to be able to pass my fugitive final exam without some tutoring."

He laughed. "Sam has manpower and resources on his side. You have me."

"I'll take that deal any day of the week," she replied with a smile. "The limo was a good idea."

His arms tightened around her for a moment. "We've been lucky so far."

"I wouldn't say that," she told him, laughing softly at the irony that she was defending him. "You've got skills."

A wry lift of his lips told her he understood her laughter. "Which will only get us so far."

"You think Sam will find us."

"Eventually, yes. I think he's counting on you to run to a safe haven, or a person in your background who'll help you."

"He'll set a trap?"

"Sure. So would I." Morgan released her hold on him. He gave her one of his patented grins. "But, of course, now that I'm with you, he'll have to cover all his bases. Because I know better. He'll never really be sure what I'm going to do next."

"You're not thinking of asking me to feel sorry for him, are you?"

Jack snorted. "No. But he was—is—my best friend. We go back a long way."

"And I put you smack in the middle, didn't I?" she asked, leaning back to look at him.

"No, *I* put me smack in the middle. Got that?"

She gave him a mock salute. "Yes, sir."

The serious look on his face hinted that not all was well in Whoville. "How far are you willing to go?"

She frowned. "I don't understand."

"Well, compromise is always an option. Give them back the data stick but cover yourself by making a copy and leaving that copy in the hands of a neutral party. You won't be able to work on the project anymore but BioClin would have to be very careful about what they do in the future. One misstep and the neutral party makes the data public."

Her stomach fell. "I'm not going to be able to have my cake and eat it too, am I?"

"It may come to that, you never know," he answered, his tone trying to soften the blow.

She let go of him and began to process out loud. "You would think that BioClin would've realized I would call their bluff. Then again, I'm a scientist not a spy."

His features tightened, filling with concern. "They probably should have. Yes."

Now the poor organ sank completely. "But you don't think that's my only problem, do you?"

He shook his head. "No, kitten, I don't. I'm too expensive to waste. Any PI would have found you eventually. Something else is going on and I don't think you know what that is."

"No, Jack. I don't," she lied.

SHE WAS LYING. JACK KNEW IT. BUT INSTEAD OF BEING angry, he recognized her reasoning. She still didn't trust him. And now that he knew most of the truth, he couldn't blame her.

"If you want to hate me now, it's okay," he said.

"Hate you?" Her face registered surprise. "I don't want to hate you."

"I'd deserve it though."

She bit out a brief laugh. "No doubt about that."

"Then I've got my work cut out for me."

"That you do."

Was there a double meaning behind her words or was he

reading into them? He wished he knew. "What was your original plan?"

She hesitated, which sucked for finding an answer. Then, she said, "I thought if I gave the data stick to my old mentor and advisor, BioClin could be coerced into doing the right thing—finishing the project the right way. Dr. Lee has way too much clout to ever be called a liar. They'd have a ton of trouble trying to discredit him. If BioClin decided to go public too soon, he'd call their bluff. On the flip side of that, BioClin would get the expertise of a Nobel Prize winner."

"How's that?"

"Once Dr. Lee saw what I was working on, he'd want in. I'm certain of it."

Jack nodded. "Not a bad plan, kitten."

"I know. But I've been in such a quandary," she replied, her tone worried. "I don't want to put him at risk."

"Sounds like he can take care of himself," Jack answered.

He watched her face fall. "I hear a 'but' in there."

He gave her a what-can-I-tell-you shrug. "Like I said, not a bad plan but Sam's going to figure out Dr. Lee soon enough."

"Damn," she muttered. "Can we beat him there? Once Dr. Lee hides the stick, Sam won't be able to do anything, will he?"

Jack honestly didn't know. His best friend had been willing to kidnap Morgan. Well, that might be construed as a gray area too. But even so, if you broke the law once, what was once more?

"I'm not sure. I'll have to think about it."

He watched her remove the data stick and shut down the computer. When she turned to him, she hesitated. "We've known each other for all of twenty-four hours. In that time, we've made mad, passionate love and cut each other to the quick. You betrayed me because you thought you were doing the right thing. I'm a wanted woman for trying to do the right thing. There's a common thread here."

"True," he answered, wondering where she was going with her speech.

"Here," she said, holding out her hand. Inside rested the data stick. "Do the right thing. You take this to Dr. Lee. I'll keep running in the opposite direction. If we split up, we'll have more chance at success."

Stunned, Jack didn't know what to say. His heart leaped into his throat at her trust. Then he realized she didn't trust *him,* she trusted him to *do the right thing*. There was a huge difference.

He grinned, closing her fist around the data stick. "Hotel California, eh?"

She laughed softly and shrugged. "I'm only human."

He lifted her fingers and pressed tiny kisses against her flesh. "Does this mean I get a chance to redeem myself?"

Her gaze darkened as he licked each knuckle. "Maybe."

"You won't stop in the middle again, will you?" he asked with a terrified shudder. "A certain part of my anatomy wouldn't be able to withstand another blow like that."

She guffawed, sobering slowly. "You deserved more."

"Perhaps. But you owe me an honest answer. You do that again, and I might not be able to walk for a week."

"You keep looking at me like that and we might not get out of bed for a week," she countered.

He grinned. "Works for me. But who needs a bed?"

"Oh no, Jack. You can't be serious."

He pulled her close, nuzzling the soft skin of her neck. "Dare me."

She reared back, a look of total disbelief on her face. "No, Jack. We're on the run. Why risk being hauled into jail on an indecent exposure charge?"

"Because with you, I can't wait."

He let go of her hand, bent his head, and crushed her against his body. His cock hardened into steel. They'd been at this juncture before, not too long ago.

"Jack, don't. Stop. Someone might come in."

He let go of her and grinned. Walking as best he could in his condition, Jack turned out the lights and started backing her up into the farthest corner of the room.

"You *must* have a thing about doing it in public," she said as he advanced, and she retreated.

"I'll admit, you're the first person to tempt me this way. But I'm also rather pragmatic. I'm not into coitus interruptus. So, we're going to get over this hurdle now. Before I get another bathroom door slammed in my face."

"I—" He didn't give her a chance to continue. He had her jeans unsnapped and his finger deep inside her core before she could get her next word out. She grunted and sucked in her breath.

"God, you're hot."

She didn't answer. Couldn't answer. Not right at the moment. She was busy nipping and biting his neck. Hard as steel? Try titanium.

"Ah, God," he said, releasing a low growl of pleasure as her fingers clawed at his fly. Once the material parted, he breathed a huge sigh of relief.

Until her hand started working up and down on his erection.

"I know I'm not totally out of Chateau Bow-wow yet," he choked out, pushing her pants down to her ankles. "But I would never lie about being clean."

She lifted back. "You were in a rather compromised situation."

"Yeah, I was. So...are you?"

She smiled. "Geek PhD? Of course."

Jack thanked his lucky stars. He lifted her up onto the computer table, pulled her legs apart, and didn't give her a chance to say no.

CHAPTER FIFTEEN

"God," he whispered into her neck. "You're so hot I think I'm gonna burn."

She smiled. "That was the idea."

Morgan reached up and initiated her first real kiss. Sure, she'd kissed other men, and she'd made love to them too. But those few experiences paled in comparison to this. Like precursors, lessons learned, they led her down a path she no longer wanted to cease taking.

She could feel every inch of him inside her. His arms tightened, and he slid so he was lying full on top of her. With long and slow strokes, his tongue explored every crevice of her mouth. He didn't move his hips. Just made her realize she'd never joined with a man like this before.

He lifted back up and grinned that so very Jack grin. Morgan couldn't believe how deeply he nestled inside her. His hands knew exactly where she wanted them, tweaking her nipples and sending sparks of desire shooting through her veins.

"Jack," she strangled out. "I can't move. So, either you start, or I'm going to—"

She didn't have to say anything more. He thrust into her once.

Hard. He pulled all the way back out until she thought she would lose him and his hips slammed hard into her thighs. She watched his face tighten in an effort to hold back as he repeated the movement. He gritted his teeth.

He pinched and played with her nipples, and she was gone. Done. He started moving faster and faster, thrusting so deep at one point she thought he touched her womb.

Then, they both hit the precipice. His breath hitched. Hers caught. The world exploded between their locked bodies. Morgan thought she would never stop coming as he came with her. He collapsed on her chest, and the most amazing thing happened. He kept moving. As if he knew. And she reached the precipice again, jumping into the molten lava of sensation. She screamed—this orgasm more intense and incredible than the first, just as his mouth covered hers. Otherwise, they'd have ended up in deep trouble.

But that didn't stop her from giggling like a teenager or him from smiling at her as he slipped out of her body.

"Jack."

His head remained nestled between her breasts.

"Jack. The table."

"Hmm?"

He lifted back and pulled her arms up. She looped them around his neck, and he nuzzled her lips before giving her a last hard kiss. She stood and Morgan knew a woman's pride at making love. She'd never felt that before. "C'mon. Let's get dressed. Before we tempt fate to the utmost."

She grabbed his hand once they were finished dressing and pulled him out of the room. They practically ran to the elevator. Morgan couldn't believe she could let go of all her reservations like that. Whenever she was with him, just one touch, just one look, and her insides melted. He had the power to do anything, anywhere, with her and she'd let him.

"What are you thinking?" he asked, nuzzling her neck, his

warm breath sending shivers up and down her spine.

"That I'd like to try a bed someday."

He laughed and the doors opened. They raced down the hallway, and she noticed his fingers tremble slightly as he put the key card in the lock. She smiled and looked up at him. He smiled back, the banked fires in his gaze flaring as they both thought of the things they could do with one another.

Actions speak louder than words.

As soon as the door closed, Jack tried to embrace her. But she held his shoulders and shook her head. Swirling light touches up and down his arms, Morgan undid each button of his shirt with slow sensuality. His head cocked as if he didn't quite understand her game. But he did. It was the oldest game known to man.

She slid his shirt off and ran her fingertips up and down the hills and valleys of his chest. She paid special attention to his nipples watching them tighten and delighting in the way his chest muscles jumped each time she caressed them.

Of course, that wasn't the only muscle that was jumping.

Morgan undid his belt, opened his pants, and slid the zipper down, all the while drowning in the heat of his gaze. His lips parted slightly, and a thrill of promise shivered through her. Her fingers caressed his hips as she slipped his boxers down and her breath caught as he sprang free.

God, he was beautiful.

He stepped out of his clothes and cried out as her lips closed over his cock. His hands reached down to rest on the top of her head to tell her to hold on a moment. She waited, barely moving, until his hips began to flex, then she took him all the way into her mouth.

Sweet, salty, all male. She made love to him, paying special attention to every detail until he pulled away in desperation.

She grinned up at him. He lifted her to her feet, and had her clothes off in less than thirty seconds. He lifted her in his arms, staggered to the chair nearest them and fell into it. Morgan needed no other invitation. She twisted around and climbed up onto her knees, spreading her legs wide.

They both watched as she impaled herself on him. His fingers reached out to play with her nipples and his hands curled around her back to pull her forward so he could bring her breasts to his mouth. His hips strained upwards as she lifted and sat back down again. It took a moment to find a rhythm, but they did, and Morgan began to climb again.

She gazed down at Jack, falling into the depths of his desire, and began to ride him hard. His cheek tightened as he held on, but Jack was no match for Morgan. She milked him for all he was worth, and she let go just as she saw him give in. Her orgasm built and she climbed with him until they both fell. They cried out their pleasure in unison and Morgan collapsed on his shoulder, unable to catch her breath.

How long they stayed that way, she wasn't sure. Finally, he quipped, "We never made it to the bed."

She laughed softly. "I know."

Later that night, Morgan curled deeper into his body, awakening slowly. A tiny band of light from the street cast a gray shadow in the room. But it was enough for her to lift up and lean back so she could watch Jack sleep. God, he was beautiful. And she wondered why she'd been so lucky to "borrow" him.

After all, the geeks never get the captains of the football team.

With her body clock in complete disarray, Morgan knew she'd never go back to sleep right away. So, she contented herself with staring at him and creating happy endings in her mind. She daydreamed a lot when she was a child. Old habits, she supposed, never truly died.

Funny, she'd never been with a man who made her yearn to watch him sleep before.

Her fingers itched to trace the outline of his muscles. Not that he was a bodybuilder. Well maybe a cross between a linebacker and a tight end. He certainly carried a physique she'd never had the pleasure of pleasing before.

Morgan smiled. She had it bad.

Her smile faded slowly. She was going to have to tell him the truth. Sooner rather than later.

She knew that too.

And for a moment she stopped breathing as another thought occurred to her. She could get out of bed, get dressed, and leave.

Of course, she'd given her word that she wouldn't. But when balanced with the thought of his life, the scales tipped far in the favor of leaving. Only the picture of his face as he slept kept her in the bed. Morgan knew she couldn't do that to him again, no matter how much she wanted to.

His gaze burned into hers as he rolled over to face her. Just as she thought of *promethium tantalum*, his lips turned up at the corners. "Kinda hard, wasn't it?"

Her hand fell to the steel pipe poking her thigh. Would they really be able to burn up with the sun? "Yeah, I guess it still is."

He began to laugh. She didn't quite have the heart to do more than smile. At the very worst time in her life, she'd found someone worth making love to.

Instead of replying, he flipped her over on her back and started tickling her ribs. "Now you get tortured."

She cried out and started laughing. "Stop. Please. I'm really sensitive."

He sat back on his heels, half covered by the sheet, looking so delectable that she had to lock her hands into the mattress to keep from crawling all over him.

"I know."

"Jack, I—"

"Shh," he whispered, giving her the sweetest kiss imaginable.

Morgan broke the kiss, trying so very hard not to let the tears well in her eyes. "I don't want anything to happen to you. You can still walk away. Go. Now. Before it's too late."

He sat back again, a very disappointed look on his face. It seemed she had quite a few lessons to learn. But she'd always been an A student. "Do you really think I could do that?"

"Well, not right at this exact moment," she quipped, referring to his steel pipe.

"But—"

He shook his head at her as if she were acting like a child. Maybe she was. "You just haven't figured it out yet, have you?"

"Figured what out?"

"I really do care about you."

Could she believe that? After only one night? After what they'd been through? Done to each other?

"That's not how it works."

"How what works?" he asked, genuinely confused.

"It. Jocks don't fall for geeks."

"I left high school a long time ago, Morgan," he admonished. "I thought you did too."

She had. Sort of. But old lessons learned the hard way died hard.

"I'm a bad health risk."

He stretched back out on the bed, leaning nonchalantly on one elbow. "I thought we decided we were going to do this together. Did you decide something else now?"

"No, of course not," she exclaimed.

He smiled. "So, are you going to admit you like me too? Or make me stay in the Chateau for the rest of my life?"

"Jack, it's not that. Honest."

"I'll tickle you until you tell me," he threatened.

"I'd much rather lie in bed and ogle your buns. They really are nice. And very bitable."

"Morgan," he growled.

"Except that you're not getting anywhere near me for the next few hours. I can barely move."

He laughed and got out of bed to go to the bathroom. He really did have a nice ass. And while she wanted to do nothing more than admire his body, Morgan knew she was on a speeding train without any brakes, heading straight toward disaster.

Jack was about as pliable as a block of granite. In their own fashion, they both were. He was going to figure out she hadn't told him everything. He was going to want to know why.

He shrugged into his T-shirt and pulled on his boxers when he came back. "I need a kiss first."

She gave him one. A wet, sloppy one. Which made them both forget their primary objective for the moment. "Morgan?"

"Yeah?"

"Does this mean you forgive me?"

"Don't you ever take a break?" He shook his head, and she rose up on one elbow. "I'll let you know."

He sighed. "All right."

He climbed back in bed, and Morgan licked her lips in anticipation. Jack bent down and gave her a long, slow, thorough kiss. She finally broke away and rested her head against his chest. His heart beat fast and furious beneath her ear and she still couldn't believe she had the power to do that to him.

"Make me a believer, Jack."

His arms tightened around her. "You already are. I won't let you down. I promise."

"It's not me I'm worried about."

"We'll be all right, kitten."

She lifted her head to look at him, those pesky tears filling her eyes again. "I'm going to hold you to that."

JACK HADN'T HAD MANY WOMEN THAT WERE MORE THAN one or two nightstands. And, well, he wasn't proud of that period of his life, so lying in bed with Morgan was an unexpected treat. Despite their auspicious, inauspicious, beginning.

"You haven't told me much about yourself," she said, giving his hand a reassuring squeeze. "You know a whole lot more about me than I do about you."

Did he? He had to wonder about that.

"Not much to tell. I enlisted in the Army as soon as I got out of high school. I guess I displayed some talent, and I became a Ranger."

"You have an aptitude for detail."

"How'd you know?"

"The attention to each and every aspect of what you do. Takes one to know one."

Interesting. "Anyway, I loved the challenge of being a tracker. And, as far as I was concerned, the people I hunted down were enemies of the United States. They would get what they deserved."

"What happened to change your mind?"

"A couple of kids."

Jack tried to dismiss her swift, indrawn, breath. But he couldn't. Any more than he could dismiss the picture in his mind, still clear as day even in the pitch of night. The target's body draped protectively over them, riddled with bullets. Rolling him off them in horror. That cold, ugly, hollow ball forming in the pit of his stomach.

"They weren't supposed to be in the car. He wasn't supposed to put up a fight."

She squeezed his hand hard. "I'm sorry."

"I lost my taste for the hunt after that." He barked out a bitter laugh. "Lost my taste for everything."

"It wasn't your fault."

"Oh yes it was, kitten. That was my job, a job I screwed up. Royally."

She didn't answer and he was grateful. Any kind of judgment from her would end up hurting. Big time. "So, you left the Army. What happened after that?"

"I rolled around a while. Stayed low. Off the radar. Became a chauffeur for a while."

"Was she beautiful?"

How the hell had she figured that one out? Damn. "Yeah. But empty. Like me. I was in this, I don't know how to describe it other than calling it a fog. A funk. I couldn't feel anything, didn't care about anything. But she was good to me. And she did teach me."

"What?"

"About the other side of the tracks."

"Rich?"

"Yeah. And bored."

"What changed you? What brought you back?"

"To what?" he asked with a questioning frown.

"Double-edged question. To life and to the hunt."

She was really amazing. "So, you figured that out, did you?"

"We all have comfort zones, Jack. And we all have places where we belong. I'm not sure what I would be if I didn't have a Dr. in front of my name."

Jack lifted their clasped hands, kissing the back of hers. "Thank you for not judging."

She laughed. "Pure cowardice. You might do the same to me."

Giving her hand a hard squeeze, he let go. "I'm very good at what I do. So, when Sam found me, he threw out a proposal that was too good to pass up. No guns, no uglies, nothing deep. Only the high-end stuff. Embezzlers, corporate espionage, computer hackers, sometimes some dirt on a high muckety-muck. You'd be surprised how easy it really is."

"I guess I would." Despite his fear, his gaze caught hers, wondering if she thought less of him now. He certainly deserved her derision. "The emptiness went away, didn't it?"

He let go of the breath he was holding. She still wouldn't judge him. "Yeah."

Not far away, he was certain, a palm tree swayed lightly in the breeze. Waves crashed onto the shore. And a seagull flew high in the sky because that was what it knew how to do.

A peace descended on Jack that he'd never known before. He'd fought all his life, scraped and scrapped for what he'd wanted. And gotten more than he'd ever bargained for. But that was what life was all about.

He couldn't put into words what sharing this moment with her meant.

"What about now?" she asked.

Jack turned to look deep into her eyes. A strand of hair feathered across her face, and he reached up to move it away. He had no control over the hand that trailed, trembling fingers across her cheek. His heart beat high inside his chest.

He wasn't perfect. She knew that and accepted him as he was.

At the absolute worst time in his life, under the absolute worst conditions, Jack's heart filled again. The empty space, the hole, was gone. He wasn't sure why. He figured he'd better not try to find out. He'd trusted life and gotten burned in the process once before. He never, ever, wanted that to happen again.

His lips covered hers in the sweetest kiss imaginable. Because it was right.

"Friend of the bride or friend of the groom?" he whispered, letting go.

She didn't hesitate. She simply smiled up at him, the warmth of her gaze making sure the hole was sealed.

"Friend of Jack."

CHAPTER SIXTEEN

MORGAN WASN'T SURE WHERE ALL THE COURAGE WAS coming from, but she thought of that chrysalis again and realized the only limits were the ones she set for herself.

Jack's stomach had started to rumble, and Morgan knew they kept a twenty-four-hour coffee service with snacks down in the lobby. So, they threw on their clothes and he wrapped his arm around her waist as they left their room for a breath of fresh air. As they rode the elevator, Morgan couldn't get over how different she felt, how much stronger she'd become. In such a short time.

Because of him.

The lobby was quiet. Which was fine with her. They took their coffee and sat out on a small bench in front of the hotel. The night air was a bit chilly, but Jack's warmth more than made up for it. They didn't speak. They didn't have to.

Eventually, she got up and he followed. He turned to look at her and they shared the same thought, going back upstairs and living life to the fullest while they could.

God, she was insatiable. And for the first time in her life, not self-conscious of her desire. Somehow, some way, between the two of them, sex was just...right.

Which only made her want him more.

"Uh-oh, kitten. You don't want to look at me like that. 'Cause I may be a bit tired but I am *so* not dead yet."

Morgan laughed, amazed by her almost wanton behavior. The elevator doors opened and she looped her arm through his. They stepped inside, and as the doors closed, she said, "Dare you."

"You *are* kidding, right?"

He swung her into his arms, planted a hot wet one right on her lips, and slid his hand inside her pants and panties. His palm cupped her core and he slid his finger deep inside her moist heat. Her legs fell open, and Morgan couldn't believe she was ready again; however, sanity returned as the bell of the elevator rang, advising they'd reached their floor.

"Jack, please."

He pulled his hand out just as the doors opened. They stepped out and she watched Jack nod at a maintenance man standing in front of the elevator. As they passed, he licked at his finger. Mortified yet thrilled beyond imagination, Morgan started laughing. But when he swallowed that finger whole, she knew she was in trouble.

Jack opened the hotel-room door, pulled her inside, shoved her up against the door, and started making love to her. Again.

"I thought you said you were tired," she choked out as he nipped his way down the valley between her breasts.

"I lied," came his muffled reply.

The next thing she knew, her pants were puddled down by her ankles. He'd pushed her panties down with them, and his tongue had picked up right where his finger left off.

"Jack!"

In spite of the incredible soreness between her legs, Morgan felt her core open, ready and willing to receive all he offered. His mouth moved over her skin while his talented tongue licked everywhere but where she wanted it to go until, finally, he flicked at her nub. Her knees gave way and his hands gripped her hips, holding her upright as he spread tiny kisses all over her belly.

He took charge of the situation by helping her step out of her pants. He then unbelted and stepped out of his own before pulling her over to the table in the room.

"I've been dreaming about doing this ever since we met."

He turned her around so she faced the table and pushed on her back to bend her over. Morgan spread her legs, opening for him, ready to receive anything and everything he wanted to do to her.

He teased her with the head of his cock, sliding all around but never inside. "What do you want, kitten?"

"Damn you, Jack. Please."

"You can do better than that," he chided.

"Oh, please," she begged. "Don't play with me. Not now."

He teased her some more before thrusting deep inside her. "God, you feel good."

He pulled her legs even further apart with his hands so he could reach even deeper inside. Morgan had never understood the connection of two bodies before. Not really. Not until now.

Bending over her back, he undid her shirt and unsnapped her bra so that her breasts spilled into his waiting hands. He milked her creamy globes, sending sparks shooting through her veins, making her contract all around him.

"Ah, that feels really good."

He started moving, pulling all the way out until only the tip remained inside her and then he thrust all the way back inside. She moaned, and as sated as she thought she'd been, sought something even higher than before.

"Tell me what you want. Come on, kitten. Growl for me."

As he thrust deep into her, she did. Mewled, begged, and pleaded. She wanted him. All of him. And then she wanted more.

He didn't disappoint. His rhythm would slow, and he'd tease and then speed up until she wasn't sure where he ended and she began. Until, finally, his breath hitched. His fingers found her nub and started working furiously. He sped up, thrusting into her until he cried out in release. A moment later she followed him, shattering into a thousand pieces.

Jack collapsed onto her, his chest heaving against her back. If she hadn't been holding onto the table for dear life, she'd have collapsed.

"I could stay like this forever."

Morgan grinned. Her leg muscles were screaming and her ankles were shaking from the strain of standing upright. "*You* could."

He gave her a possessive nuzzle and her breasts a final tweak before lifting up. She watched with a soft smile as he stepped away, unconcerned by his state of undress. Or could it be he was so comfortable with her that he didn't care?

"I'm going to have to take another shower," he groused.

"Have fun," she told him.

"Um, kitten? Not without you."

"Oh, no. That's going to lead to something I can't finish. You go ahead," she said, pushing him away in earnest. "I'm just going to go lie down and try not to collapse."

The funny thing about best laid plans is they always seemed to go awry.

"RISE AND SHINE, SLEEPYHEAD."

A wisp of something tickled her cheek. Surrounded by warmth, the slightly musky scent of a man, and a hint of cologne, Morgan snuggled deeper into the bed.

"Morgan, it's time to get up. We need to go."

Fighting through layers of sleep, she mumbled, "Go away."

"Listen," a voice said from far away, now stern with a hint of concern. "We've stayed in one place long enough. You've got fifteen, no, thirteen minutes to get ready."

"Bite me."

"I would, kitten," came Jack's amused reply. "But that would only end up delaying us further. Now, no matter how appealing the idea, I don't want to get rough. Well, maybe I do, but we can save that for later."

Jack? Where the hell was she? A moment ago, she was dreaming they were on the beach, in a tight embrace, waves crashing over entwined legs.

She groaned. "What time is it?"

"Five o'clock."

"You're dead."

"Quite possibly. More certainly if you don't move. So how do we play this? The hard way or the easy way? Personally speaking, I'd prefer the hard way."

She bit out a physically impossible expletive, half opening one eye. "Coffee."

"On the nightstand," he answered, his laughter grating on her last nerve. "One shot. Almost espresso, if such a thing is possible out of this coffeemaker. Eleven minutes."

"Bastard."

He didn't seem fazed by her ire. "I could always tickle you, you know."

Her other eye popped open. "You wouldn't dare."

He raised a single brow. "I wouldn't?"

Morgan knew better. "I'm up," she answered with a tired sigh.

"You've got ten minutes. You can sleep in the car."

She lifted up onto one elbow. "Impossible. No way. I need a shower."

"All right. Fifteen. Or I come in and get you."

Morgan rose and swung her legs over the side of the bed. Every muscle in her body ached. Her psyche screamed for her to go back to bed.

"Car?" she asked, glad she wasn't totally brain-dead.

"You'll see."

She downed the coffee in two gulps and staggered to the bathroom. The shower helped immensely even though her stomach rebelled at the abuse of straight black espresso with no milk.

She'd aired out her clothes as best she could but wrinkled her nose as she put them back on. "I'm going to need fresh clothes."

"When we get to our next stop."

"All right."

She brushed out her hair and made a half-hearted attempt at putting on makeup. Then, she stood in front of him and waited. She stared at him, and he simply looked at her. Her brow furrowed.

"What are we waiting for?"

He laughed. "Directions. I have no idea where we're heading, remember?"

With a grin, she replied, "Yeah, I guess that would be a good idea. I think we still need to go south but we also need to head west. Atlanta."

He nodded. That he didn't judge simply amazed her. "All right."

A taxi took them near the airport and she liked that Jack chose the least obtrusive of the car rental companies. However, she watched in horror as he pulled out a license and credit card. His quick, sharp glance cautioned her to be careful and he explained once they were in the car.

"The ID is fake and the card is pre-paid under that name. But don't get any ideas about replacing the Ferragamos or buying a Louis Vuitton. The well has a bottom to it."

Morgan laughed and reached out to squeeze his hand. Damn bucket seats. But they would let her lie all the way back and take a nap.

"Why don't you try to get some rest?" he asked, his smile gentle.

"What about you?"

"I don't need much sleep. Old habits die hard. My norm is five or six at a clip so I'm good. I can still go twenty-four hours without full sleep when I need to."

Morgan realized that must have been from his Ranger days. But she didn't comment on it. The past was the past. End of story. "Then I'm going to take you up on your offer. I'm beat."

She lowered the back of the seat and settled in, but she couldn't fall asleep. Her mind wouldn't let her. So, she stepped back from the situation to process. Above all, she didn't want anyone to get hurt. She liked Jack's idea of using leverage to keep BioClin in check, but crunch time was fast approaching. Loosely formed thoughts of being rescued by Dr. Lee needed to be defined into a plan of action or she would put him—and, God forbid, his family —in danger.

The first step was to meet with him, preferably in some kind of neutral territory. The second step was to hide him from Sam until they could begin fixing her work. Her mind kicked into overdrive. Was there a way to do both? As she processed, she thought out loud.

"Jack, we need to get a hold of Dr. Lee and explain the situation first without Sam finding out. If he decides to help us, knowing the risks, then we also need to keep him safe."

He didn't answer right away, and she figured he was processing too. "Our first priority is a safe haven," he said. "Then BioClin needs to be told that 'someone' has the data but not who."

"But what if they find out?"

"Right now, bad publicity would be a good safety. We tell them if they continue to harass you or they 'fire' you, you're going to the press."

Morgan mulled on that for several mile markers. A deep pain welled inside her along with a full burst of anger. But once the anger started to simmer, Morgan realized she'd never had a choice. "You're right. I'd rather have the data lost forever than let it be misused."

"You're taking this really well, kitten. I'm impressed. I'd be spitting mad."

"I am, Jack. Believe me, I am. But I also learned my lesson the hard way. It can't be about the work or the science anymore. And certainly not my pride. Not when people's lives are at stake."

He smiled and nodded, and Morgan sat back, satisfied that if she couldn't have her cake, then no one else would. Her anger continued to simmer just below the surface and probably always would at the enormous waste of information and hard work. But more important were the benefits those patients would never utilize. That was the true crime of this whole mess.

All of a sudden, Morgan saw a road sign and sat bolt upright. Her heart started hammering double-time in her chest. "Where the hell are we going?"

"To Boston."

"Boston? Are you nuts? We need to go to Atlanta."

She threw him a hard look only to have it caught by a little boy grin. "We have some unfinished business to take care of first."

Morgan didn't understand. Confusion roiled in her belly, adding to her physical problem of being slightly carsick. "Whoa. Wait a minute, Jack. I've just spent the last two weeks running away from the lion's den. Now you want me to walk up to them and say 'hi, how are you?' I don't get it."

A slow smile grew on his face. "I was thinking of the SeaScape."

"Now I know you're crazy. We can do that anywhere. Already have, if memory serves me correctly."

He burst out laughing. "Sorry, I couldn't resist teasing you. You looked like you were about to freak out on me."

"I was. And I'm not in the mood for games. I get motion sick, as you should have remembered. All of which make my patience wear thin. So, I think you'd better explain. Pronto."

"First, a little misdirection," he replied, making a soothing gesture with one hand. At least he knew enough to keep the other on the steering wheel. "I'm betting Sam already knows about Dr. Lee and is expecting us to go directly to the good doctor. I'm thinking more of an end around."

Morgan shook her head at the reference to football, wondering if he knew she was a sports nut. Then again, there were a lot of things they didn't know about each other yet, things she wanted to learn. To do that, they both needed to stay alive.

"Wouldn't he think the same way you're thinking right now?"

"That's a chance we'll have to take, kitten. But I'm betting he's got his hands full. He's got BioClin on one side and me on the other."

She nodded, crossing her arms over her chest and thrusting her chin out. "Point taken. So why don't you explain what you plan on doing once we get to Boston? We've got a ways to go," she said decisively, her tone full of snark.

"All right. Here goes," he continued, ignoring her attitude. "So far, all BioClin knows is that you have all the data for your experiments and they don't. They hired Sam and then he sent me to track you down and bring you and the data back. But I'm the best there is."

"Egomaniac," she muttered with disdain.

He shook his head with a smile and she knew what he was thinking. "I think there's someone else in the company, or connected to the company, who has a whole lot more at stake in all of this than just missing data."

Morgan stiffened as she realized how close Jack was to the truth. "Think logically," he continued. "BioClin would never ransack your home. Violating a person's space is disturbing and very threatening on a personal level. And very illegal. Only someone with an intimate knowledge of what you do would have been reading your—that's right, notebook."

She shuddered a little. The murderer, perhaps? "Go on."

He took a deep breath and exhaled slowly. "My guess is that this particular someone started to orchestrate. He—or she—started sabotaging your image to the company and they bought it. As soon as they did, they gave this 'conductor' the freedom to work behind your back."

"I never saw any of it," she breathed, hurt and horror mixing with the sickness in her belly. The bastard who murdered that poor woman had tried to pin it on her.

He snorted. "You wouldn't. You were too busy trying to do the right thing—complete the project they'd asked you to complete—the right way."

"Talk about being naïve."

She watched him nod but his smile eased the sting caused by the truth. Without realizing, Morgan started thinking out loud. "I don't understand. Why would they back me into a corner?"

She was asking about a murderer, but Jack answered, thinking they were still discussing BioClin. "For that very reason. Because they wanted someone more pliable, someone easier to deal with, someone who knew what needed to be done and promised to do it."

"Including ransacking my house? Stealing my work?"

"This 'someone' wanted you out of the picture. They wanted you fired so they could take over your work."

Now that made sense. Only the murderer didn't want to take over her work, the fiend wanted to keep everyone else from finding out about what they did.

"They must have known BioClin could close their 'eyes' as long as everything worked out. And then you threw in the monkey wrench. You took the data, you wiped out the files, and you ran."

"So, they sent you to find me."

"But I'm the best there is, kitten. All ego aside. So, whoever's been orchestrating all of this will stop at nothing to get BioClin's property back. BioClin's not the real threat. This 'conductor' is. You were right when you decided to run."

"But I'm betting there's more," Jack continued. "I'm betting you know something this 'someone' doesn't want you to know. And the best way to find that out is to find out who's pulling your strings. I'm positive Sam knows. And I believe that whoever it is will be willing to make a trade—the data for your silence. Along with the threat of exposure if they try to hurt you. So, we're going back to where it all started and putting an end to the nonsense once and for all."

Morgan didn't answer. She didn't dare. Sooner than later she was going to have to tell him the truth. And that would make him an accessory to murder too.

CHAPTER SEVENTEEN

SAM ORMOND DID, INDEED, HAVE HIS HANDS FULL. BUT HIS mind wasn't on the task at hand. The huge mounds and dark aureoles should have been all-consuming, but lately one body had become the same as the next, until they were all a blur. Veronica, Tammy, jeez, he couldn't even remember the name of the woman he was in bed with. Wait a minute...Carol.

She had a certain amount of talent. He had to give her that. Her fingers and hot, greedy little mouth brought him to the brink. And she'd come once already. But his mind remained strangely detached. He could feel his lower half fill, grow heavy and ready to shoot his seed. Yet his thoughts were on Jack.

Maybe it was for the best that his dumb-ass partner had grown a conscience. Sam wasn't sure. All he knew was that he didn't like the way things were going and that maybe, just maybe, he'd gotten himself into something he might not get out of.

She was building again. And she smelled good. At least now he'd be able to get her off again before he came. He buried his face in her neck and nipped at her skin. Her staccato moans each time he thrust into her told him she was enjoying herself. He'd told himself he'd needed some hot, hard sex to clear his head. Maybe even help him relax.

It's funny what happened to the best-laid plans.

Sam pumped harder and nature finally took over. For a few bliss-filled moments, he was able to turn his mind off and focus on the task at hand. He pulled out of her core to the nether edge and then thrust deep inside. She screamed and convulsed all around him and that pushed him over the edge. With a resounding roar, Sam fell over the precipice and came with her, coming in mighty pulses. But he pulled out of her, strangely unfulfilled.

To his dismay, she turned out to be one of the clingy ones.

"You'll call?"

He sighed and sat up. "I said I would."

"You've got my number?"

He recited her phone number verbatim, knowing once he was out the door, he'd deliberately forget.

Her hand ran down the curve of his ass as he rose. He shivered, but the feeling wasn't from excitement. Obviously, he'd had enough of the bed-hopping routine.

Padding into the bathroom, he removed the condom and cleaned up. He dressed in minutes and stood by the door, ready to pay the price of indulgence with an awkward moment. Then, his phone buzzed.

He answered just as she approached and locked lips with him. He had to admit she had a talented mouth, but he broke the kiss saying, "I really have to go. Business."

She pouted, ran her finger down his chest, and stepped back.

"Yeah," he barked into the phone. "Just a minute."

He opened the door of the apartment and smiled, smelling freedom. She made a sign of a phone with her thumb and pinkie next to her cheek, and he nodded. As soon as the door closed; however, his face tightened.

"Did I interrupt something?"

Sam's heart sped up. "As a matter of fact, you did."

"I'm sure you'll find this much more important," the voice replied with haughty eagerness and a touch of what sounded like someone being interested in his sex life. Sam stared at his phone for a moment before placing the thing back against his ear. *The client is always right.*

"I'm sure I will too. What did you find out?"

"Dr. Lee, Dr. Mackenzie's graduate advisor. You'll find him at Emory University in Atlanta."

Sam frowned. His client had taken him at his word. Interesting. "What about him?"

"Dr. Mackenzie seems to have continued corresponding with him since she left school. In a recent email she sent him, she hinted at needing his help on a problem she was having."

"How'd you find that out?"

"She copied her boss on the e-mail."

"When?"

"About three weeks ago. Before she ran away."

"Did she send him the data?"

"From what I can tell, no. She was very vague. But he may be the one you've been talking about, the one she might be running to for help."

Very interesting. "Thanks. I'll put some men on him right away."

"Glad I could do your job for you."

That pissed him off and Sam felt the burn rise inside again. Only this time, his stomach didn't hurt. He was seriously getting tired of people pulling his strings.

"You're welcome."

He nearly threw his phone. *Not.*

Sam walked down the apartment building hallway, deep in thought. He punched the down button several times with impatience. Could Jack really be slipping this bad? Or maybe his partner didn't know.

Neither answer fit the man he knew like his own brother. That meant Jack knew about this Dr. Lee. But if he were Jack, he wouldn't go within ten thousand miles of the man, thinking it would be too obvious. Damn it. Now there were more players in this mess.

Sam stepped through the doors, catching a whiff of the woman's perfume lingering on his clothes. He frowned. It was time to take control of the situation. Before all hell broke loose. Before the hell that was certain to break loose got someone else killed.

Time to end this fiasco once and for all.

MORGAN STRETCHED, WONDERING IF HER NECK WOULD ever straighten again. She listened to the bones crack with a rueful grin. Eleven hours in a car with an hour for pit stops, a burger off the dollar menu, and only one other quick run-in for essentials, left her tired, cranky, and more than a little car sick.

"How are you feeling?" she asked Jack as they got out of the car.

"Tired. How about you?"

"You don't want to know. But probably better than you. I told you I would drive."

He gave her a halfhearted grin. "And I told you I was fine."

"Control freak."

"And that makes you—"

He reached out and captured her hand in his as they began walking toward the front entrance of an apartment type hotel, which Jack had chosen in case of budget constraints. She couldn't get over how his caring demeanor made her feel. In her other hand, swung a bag holding sweatshirts and tees from the rest stop they hit in New Jersey, along with some toiletries they purchased from a pharmacy chain in Massachusetts.

They checked in and Jack fell on the bed as soon as Morgan shut the door. She helped him peel off his shirt and told him to lie down on his stomach while she rubbed a thousand miles of driving out of his knotted muscles.

Morgan grinned when he purred. Then, she eased off the bed and sat in a chair by the window, watching him fall asleep. He really was beautiful, too beautiful for her. But for now, he was hers, and she was going to enjoy every moment they were together.

As soon as he woke up.

Morgan sat next to the window and watched the trees sway outside the hotel. A lingering essence of warmth from the sun brushed her face, even though the hotel was located on a side road off the main highway and she could hear traffic whizzing by in the distance.

Morgan started out thinking about her number one subject—Jack. He made her feel so alive, so secure within herself that, as she took a deep breath, Morgan felt invincible. He wanted her. He made her want him right back. And that was dangerous. Almost as dangerous as the predicament she was in.

At every turn, Jack had given her no choice but to trust him. And so far, he'd proven every word he'd said to her in the limo. Did she dare trust him with the rest?

Think. Deduct. Reason.

Being on the run had taught Morgan to look at as many sides of a decision as she could find. Morgan had every reason to believe that BioClin was being watched. On the one hand, there was only one true way to begin a murder investigation. And that was at the scene of the crime.

All right, that was the best-case scenario. Worst case, she would get caught. But neither Sam Ormond nor BioClin would know what she knew about the murder, only that she'd stolen her data.

Risk versus reward.

If Jack had taught her anything, he'd shown her that great risk equaled great reward. He'd convinced her to stay with him when every cell in her brain screamed at her to run. He'd done everything in his power to make her believe him and believe *in* him after realizing he was being used. And as a woman? Good Lord. What could make a human being more vulnerable than making love to them?

Hmm.

As much as she didn't want to put Jack at risk, she still needed his help. She had no idea how to start investigating a murder. Although investigating a scientific hypothesis had to work the same way, sometimes an experiment began with an idea, sometimes it began with a result. No matter what, forward or backward, she needed him.

Time to tell Jack the truth.

CHAPTER EIGHTEEN

JACK WOKE UP EXPECTING TO FIND A WONDERFULLY WARM, hopefully naked, body beside him. Instead, he got a pitch-black room and a pillow. He sat bolt upright wondering where the hell Morgan was.

Rubbing his face with his hands, his gaze flew to the clock. He'd been out for a couple of hours. His first thought was that Morgan had decided not to sit around and wait while he slept. His second thought was that she went down to use the gym or take a walk. Maybe she went to get them something to eat. His last thought had his stomach puddling somewhere between his knees. She'd flown the coop.

With his heart pounding, Jack jumped out of the bed. He threw on his shirt and shrugged into a sweatshirt. Each layer insulated him a little more, allowed him to detach and become the tracker he was. But not before he acknowledged the beating he was going to give her when he caught up with her.

Just as he was reaching for the door, it opened. "Where the hell were you?" he bit out, his tone tight.

He listened to her sigh and refused to let it reach him. "I went downstairs to find a place to eat. There's a decent restaurant within walking distance. So, I went to check it out. I didn't think you'd wake up so soon."

"Didn't it occur to you that maybe you should wait for me? Sam could have someone watching this hotel."

She raised a brow. "Interesting, especially when we walked right in through the front door a couple of hours ago. You weren't playing Double-O-Seven then, were you?"

"No," he conceded, hating that she was so damned smart.

Jack's temper ignited. All the fear for her safety, the anger at his own stupidity, and the bewilderment from feelings he'd never felt before, congealed into a knot inside his stomach. Without an outlet, he wrapped his hand around the back of her neck and pulled her face to his. He ground his mouth against hers, showing her what he was feeling. Their tongues twisted and turned. They didn't just fence, they went to war with each other. Then, nature took over. Their kiss softened and Jack let her glimpse the feelings she'd created. When he let go, he leaned his forehead against hers and gasped for breath.

"Do you know how scared I was?"

"No."

Her lips grazed his cheek and his eyes closed. He savored the feel of her against his skin. God, he was in so much trouble.

"You can't protect me all the time," she told him.

He nipped at her lips. "I can try."

He leaned back with a soft chuckle and wrapped his arms around her. "Don't ever do anything like that to me again. You understand?"

"No promises."

He grinned. "All right. Just as long as you remember that there are no promises back on your punishment."

"Hmm. Kinky. I might like that, you know."

With a shake of his head, Jack let go of her. "As tempted as I am with you right now, I need some food and a drink."

"All right." She let go of him and started pacing. "But before we do, we need to go down to the business center."

"The business center?"

"Yeah. There's something else I have to show you."

All of a sudden, a chill entered the room. "Show me?" he echoed.

"We can't do this alone any more, Jack."

He frowned. "I don't know what you mean."

THEY WALKED INTO THE BUSINESS CENTER AND MORGAN booted up the computer. "The data stick contains my files and my work, everything I've done for the past two years. But when BioClin threatened to pull the plug on me, I downloaded every file on the project into my home computer and then onto this data stick. Every file. Files from marketing, files from finance, all of them. I wanted to see what kind of profit-and-loss statements they'd come up with. And the research marketing performed in order to get approval for the project to begin."

"Go on."

His face shuttered and Morgan wondered at his tone. She sighed. He was going to be even more offended when she showed him everything. She hadn't trusted him either.

"In clinical research, one validation can have hundreds and hundreds of files attached to it. Everything has to be documented so that the FDA knows what you did, how you did it, and that what you did is beneficial not harmful."

"I see."

Morgan put the data stick in the drive and the screen filled with file folders. Most of them she knew by heart. But she was bound and determined to go through with this even if he hated her.

Morgan found the file folder with the notebook data. She'd

found it because it had a name that made no sense. She found it because it was stuck in a file folder with a bunch of profit projections based on current market trends.

Morgan remembered how odd it had been as she clicked on the first file. It was an Excel spreadsheet with two columns of graphs. She scanned it, but without knowing what she was looking at, numbers were simply numbers. She had guessed they were sales projections, but that was about it.

Then she clicked on a second file in the folder. This file also had a subset of folders. She clicked on the first sub folder and started to read out loud.

"Day one. Subject: female. Weight: 398 pounds. Blood pressure: now 189 over 95 without medication. Glucose without medication: 312 mg/dL. Cholesterol: 325 mg/dL. Enzymes: slightly elevated. Subject in excellent spirits. Excited to be accepted into program."

Morgan looked up from the screen to see Jack's face go stark white. More than a little alarmed, she wondered why. So she exited out of the file and clicked on the second file.

"So, you understand, these are journal entries. A cyber-notebook of an experiment," she explained.

"Day eight. Weight: 370 pounds. Blood pressure: slightly lower now. 180 over 90. Glucose: down to 275 mg/dL, a marked improvement. Cholesterol: not changing as rapidly. At 300 mg/dL. Enzymes: still slightly elevated. Puzzling. Subject feeling much better. Very happy with results."

She looked over her shoulder again to see his reaction and found he'd turned into a statue. A marble statue. *What the hell is going on? Is he that angry with her?*

"Day fifteen. Weight: 350 pounds. Blood pressure: not changing. Still at 180 over 90. Blood chemistries not changing but this is to be expected as the body needs to catch up with itself in regard to the rapid weight loss."

He didn't say anything, just backed up from her chair so they no longer touched. Morgan's insides chilled as she skipped a couple of file folders and went to the one marked a month later.

"Day 32. Weight dropping too quickly. Patient now at 300 lbs. Blood pressure spiking again at 198/100. Began administering beta-blockers again as a precaution. Glucose at 225 mg/dL, which is good to see. Cholesterol level still same at 300 mg/dL. Enzyme levels still elevated. CRP level very high at 47.5 mg/L, indicating inflammation within the body. Patient has begun to run a low grade fever and exhibits general malaise. Advised this might be a reaction to the extremely rapid weight loss."

Morgan's heart began to pound. Her stomach dropped to her knees. He hated her. He thought she was the murderer. So, she kept on reading. She kept on punishing herself.

"Day 50. Subject deteriorating rapidly even though all therapy halted fifteen days ago. Weight at 250 lbs. Skin folds becoming a problem because of bacterial infections. Blood pressure still spiking, even with beta-blockers. Blood chemistries normal. Cholesterol levels have remained high at 300 mg/dL despite the statin therapy. Liver enzymes have climbed to near critical levels. CRP levels extreme. Muscle and skeletal mass decreasing at an alarming rate. Debating hospitalization at this point. Patient exhibiting bodily stress akin to acute starvation. Patient on constant nutrient drip. Hypothesis: the more nutrients consumed, the more the body is burning. Considering halting all nutrients to see if metabolism slows down."

Morgan couldn't read anymore. She'd taken the same steps with Pinky and Louie. Once the metabolic rate reached a certain stage, it couldn't be turned off, even if the subject starved.

Morgan tried to swallow and found she couldn't. A hollow pit had formed inside, and she felt like she stepped outside her body.

"I'm sorry, Jack. I couldn't tell you. For your own safety." She closed the folder and sat staring at the computer screen for what seemed an eternity. "I've just made you an accessory after the fact. I didn't want to but you just wouldn't listen. Instead of listening to me and taking me to Atlanta, you brought me home. Back to Boston."

She tried to think. She tried to feel. Something. Anything. Warmth would be nice. But that might be too much to expect.

Funny how people tried to cope in times of stress. She seemed to enjoy out-of-body experiences. She wanted to throw herself into Jack's arms but found she couldn't move.

"Without my work, without my brains, this wouldn't have happened."

Jack didn't answer, he just stared at her, making her feel unclean. The complete horror of the moment hadn't even sunk in yet.

Morgan didn't move, she just kept staring into space, a space filled with facts and figures representing a young woman's death.

In a detached way, Morgan recognized that Jack coped by holding back on his emotions. But his refusal to answer was scaring her half to death.

Taking a deep breath, she looked him straight in the eyes and said, "You'd better take me to the police, Jack. I've got a lot of explaining to do."

"What?"

"We need to go to the police. Now!"

Galvanized into action, Jack gripped her upper arms and started shaking her, not hard but trying, she guessed, to get her to react.

She watched him take a deep breath and exhale slowly. The frown on his face deepened but he still didn't answer.

Cold seeped into her bones. "All my life, Jack. More days, nights, weekends than I care to count. Since I was a kid. Dreaming of the day when I'd find a cure for cancer or halt the effects of aging. Dreaming of the day I'd give mankind a gift. Because it burned inside of me. Because, I guess, I believed God wanted me to." She barked out a bitter laugh. "Now I've given them a nightmare."

He started shaking his head. “No, you didn’t. Please. Just look at me. Focus. You’re in shock.” When she tried to rise, he wouldn’t let her get up.

Morgan shuddered. She didn’t know how to explain. She swallowed, not trusting her stomach. “I think I’m going to throw up.”

“No, you’re not,” Jack told her, his voice stern. “You’re going to get a hold of yourself this instant.”

Morgan swallowed hard, realizing she’d never be warm again. “I checked the creation dates of each of the folders in the main menu. God, I should have seen it. I should have known. These were my experiments. This was my work. Two years’ worth of work. I knew everything that was going on. At least, I thought I did.”

He grimaced at her. “You are not a murderer, Morgan. Do you hear me?”

Morgan swallowed again as acid burned a hole where the emptiness was. Jack didn’t say anything else, he just waited for her to continue. She kept on talking. “Don’t you see, Jack? My work. I should have known. Should have paid attention. I should have seen a folder I never, ever, want to see again, the one with the data of a dying patient.”

“Someone used my process, *my* process,” she repeated. “On a woman. And she ended up just like Pinky and Louie.”

Morgan started laughing. There was a tinge of manic inside her. She had to be going crazy. Had to. Or else, in a moment, she’d wake up and find it was all a bad dream. She buried her face in her hands but she couldn’t bury the vision in her head. The picture of an emaciated body and the gaze of a frightened woman who wanted to be beautiful and ended up making a mistake that cost her, her life.

She imagined the joy the woman must have felt, shedding all those pounds so effortlessly. The return of physical energy with a renewed sense of hope that something was finally working, that she was able to lose weight. Then, the concern that the weight was coming off too quickly. Should it be happening so fast? This isn't right, is it? Then, not feeling so well. The constant craving for food even though she'd just eaten. Was this normal? Did the drug make you hungry too?

Then, the long silences and the unanswered questions. The not so cheerful smiles. The gaze that wouldn't quite meet hers. Until the day she found out the truth. That she was going to die of starvation even though she was consuming 10,000 calories a day intravenously. And that if the drip was turned off, she would still lose the weight. Less quickly, but the metabolic rate wouldn't stop, would never stop. Not until she was dead.

Morgan dropped her hands and wrapped her arms around her midriff, rocking back and forth. She still couldn't understand how everything could have gone so wrong.

Think! Focus!

Jack bent down and wrapped his arms around her. He rocked with her. "You're going to listen to me, now. Do you understand? Just listen. All right?"

Morgan nodded. She buried her head in his chest, knowing she had no right to let him make her feel so protected.

"Someone was stealing your data and your notes. We figured they were doing it from the get-go and they were."

Some of the ice inside her melted. Then, she shivered, her reasoning about thirty seconds behind her hearing. "We?"

He rose and urged her to stand with him. His arms wrapped around her, his warmth enveloping her, trying to expunge the chill in her heart. Then, as suddenly as his arms were there, they weren't any longer.

"Yes, we."

At first, Morgan didn't understand. All she knew was that a Siberian winter was warmer than the knot inside her belly.

"Wait a minute. I don't understand. We? Who's we?"

"Ian and I."

Morgan stared at him, still not comprehending. “You knew? You’ve known all along?”

He didn’t apologize, didn’t beg forgiveness, he simply answered. “Yes. Ian works for the FBI. I’m working undercover with him.”

Her arm arced before her mind registered the command. She landed one on his cheek, and his head snapped to the right, making the last time she’d done this pale in comparison. He didn’t even register the impact. He just swiveled his head back and stared.

“There’ve been more bodies than just this one,” he continued. “At first, the police didn’t connect them. Then, the ME’s started talking. No one could figure out what could cause such devastation. I mean, this kind of body mass and weight loss has only been seen once in all of our history—in the concentration camps during WWII. So they called in the FBI. The FBI started targeting all companies in the weight loss business. Ian saved my life during one of our tours of duty together. He called in a favor. Said the FBI needed my help. Told me about Sam.”

Morgan didn’t say anything. She couldn’t.

“With Sam in the security business, it was a perfect setup. I didn’t want to believe he was dirty but I had to find out for myself. I knew I was onto something when BioClin made their announcement to the banks. All of a sudden, Sam wanted me to find out everything about you. Then, he told me to go after you. When you skipped town, I was pretty certain you were involved. And when you asked, and I told you I didn’t want to know more, I wasn’t lying. I already knew.”

He took a deep breath and let the air out in a rush. “Then, you showed me your data.”

“And now?”

He didn’t answer. He didn’t have to. It was why he’d brought her back to Boston.

CHAPTER NINETEEN

"I'M SORRY KITTEN," HE SAID, MEANING EVERY WORD, knowing she had more than every right never to believe him again.

She shoved him. He faltered backward, then regained his balance. She shoved him again. This time, he didn't budge. And when she saw she couldn't move him, she started pummeling his chest. He didn't feel anything other than a well of remorse bubbling through his insides.

"When did you decide that?" she asked, raw agony making the question a knife that slid between his ribs.

Jack had no idea how to explain. He had no idea how to make her understand. "I already know you had nothing to do with any of this."

"Oh, really? How did you come up with that conclusion? Because I'm good in bed?"

"Our being together has absolutely nothing to do with trying to find out who murdered those people," he insisted, trying not to let the sneer in her tone add to the well. "Or finding out that my best friend was a criminal."

"Sue me," she fired back at him. "Because if you think I'm

going to feel sorry for you right about now, you know what will happen to hell."

He shivered, feeling about that cold inside. "Already there, kitten."

The look she gave him twisted the knife so he would feel her pain. "Why didn't you tell me? You had every opportunity since I showed you what happened to Pinkie and Louie."

"I couldn't."

She whirled away as if the sight of him sickened her. "God, what a fool you must think I am. You begged me to forgive you."

"Because I had to." He reached out to turn her around. She shrugged off his hand, daring him to touch her again. "Because I needed you to." Oh hell, none of that was coming out right. "Morgan, listen to me. There was nothing personal—" Uh-oh. Time to quit while he was behind.

"Nothing personal?" she nearly shouted. "So it was just slam, bam, thank you ma'am?"

"Absolutely not. One had nothing to do with the other," he insisted, lowering his voice in hopes that his calm might help deflect the oncoming explosion. "Do you really think we could have made love the way we did together if I thought you were a criminal?"

Rather than explode, her tone tightened, making him realize exactly how much he'd injured her. "Right now, I'd believe just about anything."

God, that hurt. And he deserved every mangled nerve. "Please try to understand," he begged.

"You asked me to trust you, you bastard!" Jack waited for another slap, waited for the punishment he rightly deserved. But instead, her shoulders hunched as if she wanted to crawl inside herself and never come out. "And you want me to understand why you betrayed me? Again?"

Each word kept on stabbing at his insides. "I couldn't let you know!" he exploded. "I was under orders!"

"And you always follow orders?"

He saluted. "Yes, ma'am, I do."

She stormed past him and Jack reached out to catch her just in time. "Look. I know how you feel."

"You do? Oh, I don't think you do. Because if you did—" She didn't finish. She couldn't. Her face turned a mottled red and then cleared as if she'd thought of something, something that might help him get her to listen.

"I don't care how you feel about me," he told her, his tone weary. "You can hate me into the next millennium, but you need to get something through your head right now. I wasn't supposed to tell you. I broke protocol. And now you're going to have to help me whether you want to or not. Because I need you to help me find out how involved Sam is. And I need your help in figuring out what's going on. We either have a really nasty sonofabitch out there or a serial killer. And he—or she—is going to kill again."

Her eyes widened as the truth of his words sank in. "All right. Let's cauterize the wound. You didn't trust me. I didn't trust you. That still doesn't absolve you."

Jack closed his eyes to the pain that caused. They were both beyond emotional overload.

"Once we catch the bastard, you'll never have to see or hear from me again," he promised.

Her soft laugh skittered across his psyche. "I don't have to do that now."

"True. You can leave. And I'll get into a heap of trouble with Ian. But don't forget who's going to be in even more trouble," he told her.

And then that laugh landed right in his guts. "Right now you're looking at accessory to murder, or if you're lucky, accessory after the fact. So, we can play this either way. Either you leave, or you help me. If you help me, it all goes away."

That got her attention. She looked up, catching her gaze. "Does that include you?"

He winced, a hurt sinking so deep inside him, he knew he'd never dig it out. "Including me."

She wrenched her gaze away, her tone giving away none of her feelings. "Deal. But if you come within ten feet of me, I swear to you, your fingers aren't the only part of your anatomy that will get cut off. Are we clear?"

He shuddered as a very vivid picture of her doing exactly that popped into his head. "Crystal."

JACK WANTED NOTHING MORE THAN TO LIE IN BED WITH her and listen to her breathe. He stared at the nondescript walls in the muted light, understanding the difference between light and shadow. He'd lived his life in shadow, never quite able to tell the truth about what he was and what he did. While Morgan, on the other hand, was all about the light, about saving lives, about making a better world.

You are so done, man.

How many times was too many to ask someone to forgive? If he was honest with himself, the answer was none. And yet, here he was, having not only gotten her to trust him twice, but then turning around and betraying her twice.

He didn't stand a snowball's chance in hell with getting her to forgive him again.

And yet, his gaze kept finding her. Instead of trying to sleep on a rather uncomfortable floor, he sat in an even more uncomfortable chair, watching her sleep.

Because he couldn't help himself.

And if he didn't start getting his head out of his ass, they would both be toast.

For the first time in his life, Jack wondered what heaven on earth might really mean. Because he couldn't be in a better place than he was in right now. Even though he was sitting in the middle of the worst cesspool he could have imagined.

Didn't matter. Because everything had changed. He didn't have to lie anymore. He could be a real human being for the first time since he'd met Morgan. The funny part was, Jack was falling, and he had no idea how to get up. Everything was so backward, so totally upside down, that he was scared of trusting his own judgment.

Thick sooty lashes framed her closed eyelids, resting on satiny cheeks. Her breathing told him she was asleep but not deeply, for every now and then she would shiver as if something haunted her in her dreams.

He couldn't even begin to imagine.

When a person works for most of their waking moments to save lives, it's hard to understand the harsh reality of death. She'd taken her brains and her heart and all the hours of working on projects to help, not harm, which made Morgan Mackenzie one of the good guys. And you know who just dragged her down below his level.

Way to go, Jack.

He had no trouble understanding the motivation surrounding their predicament. He'd seen enough of the uglier side of life to last a lifetime, and the reality was, he *wasn't* one of the good guys.

But he did believe in truth. And when someone screwed with him, they got Jack. And justice.

So what you just did to her was right? Didn't you do to her what Sam did to you?

Jack closed his eyes and tried hard to fire up his brain. Because beating himself up about it wasn't going to fix the situation. Finding a murderer would.

This whole mess hadn't been easy to figure out, especially while he tried to play both ends against the middle. On the one side, Jack was fairly certain that BioClin didn't know what was on Morgan's computer or her data stick. They wanted their property back so they could get their hands on their investment capital. The most logical way to do that was to hire a private investigator. After all, they figured the data stick was theirs to begin with.

What they didn't know about was the additional data in their computer. What they didn't know was that someone had taken a process that didn't work—yet, he said to himself with a small grin—and turned it into a murder weapon. Why?

Two possibilities. One, someone had decided to play Frankenstein and use human subjects to see if it worked. Or two, someone was a sick, psycho, serial killer.

Neither option made Jack feel warm and fuzzy inside.

So, he asked himself the next 'why.' Money. This someone had wanted to see if the process worked in order to sell it.

Who was this someone?

Every time he asked that question, he came up with one answer: someone at BioClin, someone within their organization.

More than one person? Possibly. Jack's guess was that the person who created the data and killed that poor woman Morgan described tonight, was trying to keep the truth from the company while pretending to act in the company's best interests.

So it was up to Jack, now, to protect Morgan and clear her name. Because she wasn't a geek, and he'd never met anyone smarter or braver or more beautiful.

She doesn't want you to save her.

Yeah, and at the moment it didn't really matter. He'd screwed up royally. Again. And he would never be able to make amends. But he could try.

Because he cared.

And though his first idea of getting things out in the open seemed like a really good idea at the time, this discovery changed everything. He hurt her—again. Not his very best move.

He'd also brought them right to the brink of disaster. Not his second very best move. So what he needed now was time—time to find out who was behind all of this and to try to make things right with her.

He listened to her turn over. Then, she tossed and turned over again. His stomach hollowed, and he wondered if it would stay that way forever.

"I thought you were asleep," he said as she leaned back against the headboard

"I can't. Too many nightmares. ."

He drew in a deep breath and let the air out slowly. "Can't say I blame you. I want you to know I'm not real fond of myself at the moment."

She didn't say anything for a long time. "How many more people are dead, Jack?" she asked, her voice flat and weary.

"Does it really matter at this point? All you're going to do is beat yourself up about it. You need to realize you're not responsible for someone else's actions."

She sighed. "You're right. Learning to live with what's happened is going to be tough. But not nearly as tough as keeping me away from whoever did this once we find him. Or her."

Jack laughed softly. He had personal experience with her ire. And fingerprints on his cheek to prove it. "I may just let you go on that one you."

She wiped at her face with her hands and Jack wondered if she was crying. He couldn't see in the semidarkness of the room, but his insides clenched at the thought. And that made him even more determined to make things right between them. The best that he could do now was what he did best: track a culprit down and turn them in. So, he cleared his throat and began talking out loud.

"Someone stole your data and copied your notebook to do what they did. Then, they hired Sam because Sam is very expensive but very secure. I'm also guessing that they assigned someone or asked for someone to handle the situation. I believe that person, or persons, we don't know which, is also the murderer. There are two big questions in all of this. The first is whether Sam knows what we know. For the sake of a friendship borne under fire, I'm going to bet he doesn't. That makes him stupid and greedy but not an accomplice to murder. The second is who else at BioClin knows what's going on. Because they're the people we're after."

"What about your friend? What about the FBI? Don't you need to contact him and let him sort this out?"

He shook his head, amazed that she still wanted to do the right thing despite the consequences. "No. The first person they're going to throw in jail is you. You wiped BioClin's files and ran. If that doesn't make you look guilty, I don't know what does."

Jack realized she'd already figured out her predicament. "Then take the data stick," she told him. "I offered it to you once before. Give the FBI the data stick and let them catch the killer."

Jack smiled to himself. He wished he had one ounce of Morgan's integrity. "I can't. I'd rather use it to prove your innocence once we catch the bastard who's done this."

"How kind of you."

Her words held no rancor, just weariness. He closed his eyes, wondering if they'd ever get beyond the past. "Hey, I certainly deserve everything you might decide to dish. But that's not going to solve any of our problems right now."

"*Our* problems? What do you mean?"

"That there are a few things you need to understand."

"Like what?"

At least she was listening. "There's a flaw inherent in your logic. I'm an accomplice now. I can't help find the truth if *I'm* in a jail cell."

"Makes sense."

Jack took a deep breath, letting the air out slowly. He hated listening to her monotone. However, it seemed like a step in the right direction. "Look, I can't trust Ian to help me sort this all out. He's a by-the-book kind of guy. He'll follow his book first and figure it all out later. So we've got to do this on our own for a while."

She didn't answer right away. Then she asked, "We, Jack? Our? Do you really mean that?"

"With all my heart."

"Seriously? I mean, all you'd have to do is tell your boss I seduced you, and that you couldn't help yourself."

Ouch! "That's true, I could. But I really am trying to help you."

"Why, Jack? Tell me. I need to know. I have to understand. Because yesterday you were willing to hand me over without batting an eyelash."

"Not true. Never true. I figured that out as I sat waiting for you to sneak out of the SeaScape."

"What?"

"Isn't it kind of obvious? Two words. I care." He didn't dare let hope grow but a tiny seed planted, and he couldn't stop it from taking root.

"Yeah, right."

"The word is called integrity. You've got a boatload of it. From trying to protect me by sneaking out of the SeaScape to trying to protect me in the parking lot in Delaware, to trying to protect me now by giving me the data stick."

"What do you mean?"

"That all you've ever tried to do is the right thing. No matter what you've faced. And all I know is that you're in the middle of a situation you didn't create."

"Yes, I did. This is all my fault."

"No, it isn't," he continued. "Right now, I can't even imagine how you feel. I know you never meant for your discovery to become a weapon of destruction. I also know you never meant for these last couple of days that were so right, so beautiful, to become so wrong. But they did. And that's my fault."

"Don't let my bad taint your memories," he begged. "That's all I ask. When all of this is done, hate me if you have to."

"I don't hate you."

She was saying that but did she really believe it? "Maybe. Just don't hate what we shared."

"Even though it was a lie?"

Damn, that hurt, but she had a point. "I guess that's what I'm trying to tell you. Out of this entire fiasco, this mess I've created, you were the one reality. What we shared was real, Morgan. And you know it. If you look deep inside yourself, you'll see."

She didn't reply. Because she was thinking? Because she was crying? All of the above? The silence nearly drove him mad.

He sighed, figuring he'd already lost the battle. "Right now I'm in the middle of Hotel California with no way out." She still didn't answer but there was a war to win here. And that meant pounding away at the beach until it was safe to land. "But there's a way to build a door if you're willing to work with me."

Would her fragile psyche allow it? He needed her cooperation. Maybe the forgiveness, at this point, was just a fairytale. Then again, maybe it wasn't.

"All right."

He let go of a breath he hadn't known he was holding. "Good. Then we need a game plan."

"Do you have one?"

"At the moment? No. My first priority was to figure out how to get some sleep. That meant trying to make you understand that I never meant to hurt you."

She laughed softly. "Jury's still out on that but I'm working on it."

"Morgan, I really do need to sleep. And I won't be able to do that unless you make one last promise."

"What's that?"

"Not to run. Because, that's your last option. And it would get me in a lot of trouble."

There was that wonderful non-answer again. Jack really was going to have to have a talk with the guy that said that silence was golden.

"As tempting as the thought is," she began, "I'm not stupid, and I'm not crazy. So, as much as I would like to watch you squirm, I have no intention of going to jail for something I didn't do. Besides, I rather like the idea that you work for me now."

Jack didn't dare groan at the relish in her tone. "You didn't promise," he reminded her.

She huffed out an indignant breath. "I didn't do a lot of things I should have. Like walk away from you in Cape May."

"I'm glad you didn't."

She didn't answer and Jack figured he'd have to live with that. For now.

CHAPTER TWENTY

SAM ORMOND SAT AT HIS DESK, DRUMMING HIS FINGERS ON the polished wood, waiting for the phone to ring. He didn't consider himself a man to be trifled with, yet he was caught in a situation spiraling downhill at an alarming rate. What he was about to do came very close to the hairy edge of his personal limits, and he wasn't happy about that at all.

The phone chimed and Sam jumped in surprise. His heartbeat soared through his chest and he took a deep, calming breath before answering.

"Ormond."

"To what do I owe this...displeasure this late in the evening, Mr. Ormond?"

Snide little creep.

Sam wondered if there were enough zeros in the world for this kind of abuse. "I think Jack Kent and your precious Dr. Mackenzie are headed for the Boston area. If they're not here already."

"Think, Mr. Ormond? Do you even know?"

Sam inhaled sharply. "Look. Jack is one of the best tracers in the business. He's going to go after BioClin."

A long silence told Sam what his "employer" thought about that statement. "That would not be wise."

Sam clenched his jaw, feeling the muscle in his cheek twitch. What he wouldn't give for five minutes in a sparring ring with this A-hole. "I think he's in Boston and he's getting ready to go to the police."

"There goes that word again, Mr. Ormond."

"Yeah, well, Jack is ex-Ranger. You don't want to be messing with him."

"Or you?"

Sam ignored the obvious answer. "You can take what I say, or you can leave it. At this point I really don't care. I just thought you should know."

A snort came through the phone and Sam read it for what it was, all shades of displeasure mingled with a hint of disbelief.

"Some of us take the time to plan, Mr. Ormond. We *think*. You do understand that word, don't you? It's the word that's going to keep you out of jail."

With his insides turning to shards of ice, Sam blanched. He snapped his chair upright and tightened his fist around his telephone receiver. "Jail? I'm not going to jail. Not for you, or for anything, you got that?"

The laughter in response to his words sent those icicles deep into the pit of his stomach. He nearly doubled over in pain. "So sorry to disappoint you, Sam. You see, you really are involved."

"Oh, yeah?" All right, his client was a fruitcake. The sooner he cut his losses, the better.

"Take a look inside your upper right-hand drawer."

Sam frowned and threw the drawer opened with shaking fingers. His Glock was gone. "You should know better than to leave your things lying around, Sam."

A cold wash of dread seeped into his bones. "What are you talking about?"

"Your gun, Sam. Your revolver."

"What about my gun?" he asked, not really wanting to know.

"It really is a shame." The sigh that accompanied the words bore not one hint of remorse. "It seems to have discharged itself."

"What? Where?" he bit out, not wanting to know.

"You have to understand. The end result was a merciful act. Believe me."

Oh God, someone's been murdered with my gun.

"Now, I want you to listen and listen very carefully," his client said. "This item will remain lost forever if you decide to continue our relationship. After all, business is business. Otherwise, I'm sorry to say, it will manage to find its way to the police."

Sam listened to the pointed laughter coming through the phone, knowing that if he ever got his hands on this crazy person —or people—someone was going to have pull him off.

"How do you know I'm not recording this entire conversation?"

"Because your recording device was removed from your phone when your gun was removed from your drawer."

Sam's insides hit the floor. He was tempted to look but realized that the person he was dealing with wasn't bluffing. Or stupid. Maybe insane but not stupid. "I'm listening."

"Good. Now, for every action, there is an equal reaction. The young woman in question will make her way into the hands of the authorities, one way or another. But without said weapon, the police will simply have another unsolved crime on their hands. Do you understand?"

"Yes," he growled.

"Excellent. If you had *thought* about the facts for a moment, you would have realized that Dr. Mackenzie came back here to find something, something she wanted very much."

"Her Gucci bag," Sam muttered.

"Tsk-tsk, Mr. Ormond. However, I suppose I deserved that from your point of view. But I must warn you, don't do that again. My patience is wearing very thin."

Sam bit back another smart reply. "And your point is?"

"She came back here because she knows there's more to this story, Mr. Ormond. A very damaging file is probably in her computer. And by now, I'm sure she knows what has happened. Unfortunate for her. Unfortunate for your partner, Mr. Kent."

"Hey, I don't do murder."

A chill racked his spine as he listened to the voice on the other end of the line laugh. He never wanted to hear laughter that cold ever again.

"Yes you do, Mr. Ormond. Yes, you do."

AT A RATHER INDECENT HOUR IN THE MORNING, IAN'S personal cell phone went off. He'd been dreaming of his most recent lady and found he'd been smiling.

"Ian? It's Jack Kent."

At this hour of the morning? "What's wrong?"

The smile on Ian's face faded slowly and his brows began to draw together when his friend didn't answer right away. And, from the sigh, Ian knew something was wrong. His fist tightened around his cell.

"I'm in trouble."

Uh-oh. "What kind of trouble?"

"The kind you can't know about. But I think there's something else you're going to want to know about."

Jack double-speak. Before my morning coffee. Just what I need. "Ah, crap, Jack. Did you break protocol?"

He could just picture Jack and his grimace. He swung his legs over the edge of his bed and ran a tired hand through his hair. And when Jack didn't respond, Ian had his answer.

"Why?"

"She's innocent, Ian. I know you probably don't believe that, but I do. And as much as I don't like them, there's a gray area this time."

Jack didn't believe in gray. He was a black and white kind of guy. "You're kidding, right? You almost got me killed because you don't believe in gray areas, remember?"

He could imagine Jack wincing even as he listened to him bark out a laugh. "Yeah, I remember."

Ian rubbed his eyes and looked at his alarm clock. "Jesus, you know how to wake a guy up," he groused. "How far are you in this?"

"Up to my eyeballs."

There could only be one reason why Jack would go out on a limb like this. "Oh hell, Jack. Don't tell me you fell for her."

"No." It was said way too fast and too emphatically.

"And now you don't want to bring her in?"

"Well, yeah, until you decide to consider me an accessory after the fact."

Ian shook his head. Wow, talk about turnarounds. The Jack he knew would've arrested first and asked questions later. "Then, just talking to you puts me in jeopardy, you know that?"

"Of course. But I also need to find out how bad Sam's involved."

"He's already in this up to *his* eyeballs. You won't be able to protect him much longer."

"I know. But it's Sam, Ian. I just can't believe..."

"You think I do?" Ian cried. A piercing pain started right between his eyeballs. He tried to rub his forehead with his fingers.

"I won't leave him stranded.

Ian wouldn't either.

"She wants to help," Jack added.

It figured. People would say anything to get out of jail.

"Wait a minute," Ian replied, his thoughts coming together slowly. Jack believed her. Jack didn't trust anyone. So, this wasn't just a hollow promise. "How?"

"If I tell you, you may cross a line you don't want to cross."

Ian frowned and shook his head. "I think you'd better tell me."

"Morgan Mackenzie created the process that's killing these people. There's no doubt about it."

"Then you need to bring her in. Now."

"You didn't let me finish," Jack cried. "You need to listen. She stole all her data and the information on the process *so no one would get hurt.* Someone at BioClin was copying her work."

That was plausible. "I see."

"Now, either this someone wants to try selling the formula Morgan created on the black market or we have a really sick psycho on our hands."

Hmm. Jack's logic makes sense. That's not good.

"Tell her to come in. We'll talk it over," Ian decided.

"That would make finding the bastard who did this very happy," Jack answered, cutting him off. "It would stop you from searching for him. Or her."

"I see." Jack had another really good point.

"As far as I'm concerned, she's done nothing wrong. She's caught in a mess she can't get out of."

"All right, Jack. I can check with my sources and Interpol to see if anyone's heard about a possible formula sale. But you don't have much time. Right now, my superiors still think you're playing the game to find out if she's more than just a suspect. If you don't come in soon, I'll have to go by the book."

"She didn't do anything wrong," Jack insisted. "Give me some time, and I'll prove it to you."

Ian sighed. Sometimes Jack could be as stubborn as a mule. "So, what do you want to do?"

"First, I want immunity. Immunity in writing. Not just a promise but in fact. In return, Dr. Mackenzie's agreed to become the bait."

"I don't know, Jack."

"In my opinion, she's a hero."

"That's an opinion of one."

"Ian, I don't think you're listening well this morning." Jack's voice had dropped and Ian knew that tone all too well. "I'm not going to dick around with this. Immunity. Got that? And not just a promise. In return, she's agreed to become the bait. She wants to nail whoever's doing this to the wall."

Ian hated to ask but had no choice. "Think she's using you?"

Jack bit out a bitter laugh. "Other way around, compadre. I was using her to get at the truth."

"You were supposed to."

"Yeah, I know."

Ian thought about their conversation for a moment. "You wouldn't be thinking of going out there and playing vigilante, would you? Because that would make me very unhappy."

"Tough."

His boss. Uh-oh. "Mike won't like it, either, Jack. That would make *him* very unhappy."

"And your point is?

"This isn't the Army anymore. You can't just go out and do whatever the hell you please. Mike's not going to agree to put a civilian in the line of fire unless she's under our protection. And you *know* he doesn't want you rolling around playing Wyatt Earp."

Jack snorted and Ian knew exactly what his friend thought of his warning. "Tell him she'll be under *my* protection and I'm better than Wyatt Earp ever was."

Ian sighed. Ian knew how good Jack was. He'd have been an excellent field agent if his heart hadn't been broken by the Army. No, that wasn't right. By circumstance and decisions that were made beyond his control.

"He's not going to understand."

"Then make him understand!"

Double crap. There was only one reason he could think of that Jack would put his life on the line for this woman.

"Jesus," he muttered as horror filled him. "Don't tell me. You're not just falling for her, you're in love with her?"

Dead silence greeted him. Then, Jack answered, "My life. My business."

Oh, this was not good. "Bad move, Jack. You won't be able to stay objective."

"That's my problem, not yours. You just get Mike's okay and let me worry about the rest. Until then, consider me hostile. I'll call you in twenty-four."

Ian sighed. "I'll see what I can do."

"Do better, Ian. Otherwise, I'll play this my way. And if I do, people are going to end up hurt. Even dead. I don't want that and neither do you."

Despite their friendship, Ian felt a tiny shiver run down his back. He wouldn't want to be on the receiving end of Jack's ire, and he knew Jack meant business.

"All right, Jack. We play this your way for now. Twenty-four."

He didn't hear Jack's sigh of relief as much as he felt it. "Thanks, old buddy."

"You're welcome. Just remember, it's her life too."

CHAPTER TWENTY-ONE

MORGAN'S HEART HURT. MORE THAN HURT. HER WHOLE body had emptied, leaving a gaping hole inside. She looked up from her computer screen, dragging her brain with her.

Jack opened the door of the hotel room. "Hey."

Oh, wonderful. A peace offering. At five forty five in the morning. Then, she spied the bag and smelled the coffee. One point for him.

"What are you doing up?" he asked.

She watched his gaze flip over to the clock as he handed her the bag. Then, he moved away and sat down at the table. His distance made her sad.

"Couldn't sleep," she answered.

"Neither could I."

For different reasons. "I don't want to think anymore, Jack," she confessed.

He played with his coffee cup before catching her gaze. "I know. But running away from a problem isn't going to solve it. The truth will still be waiting for you."

"Truth? You lied to me. So many times I've lost count."

His lips quirked, and she read the self-loathing in them.

"True. Is it going to change anything?"

He had a point. "No."

"Listen, I don't want what's going on inside of you right now to fester."

"And how do you know what's inside of me?"

"Because betrayal comes in all forms. But this isn't about me and what I've done or about you and what you've done."

"How can you say that?"

"What I did to you was unforgivable. You won't ever be able to forgive me. You feel what you did to that woman was unforgivable. So you need to accept both and move on."

Could she? Did she want to? God, she was tired of fighting with herself. "Someone used my discovery to kill another human being. Are you telling me I shouldn't be angry about that?"

"Of course not. But I want you to think this through for a moment. What I am telling you is that you had no more control over someone stealing your work and using it than I had over being forced to keep my silence."

Morgan didn't answer. She couldn't. Guilt soured the coffee sitting in her stomach.

"You're not going to believe me right now but there's only one way for me to explain."

"Do your worst," she challenged.

"The caveman who picked up a dinosaur bone didn't automatically think to himself, hey, this would be a great thing to bop old Bruno over the head with. He said to himself, hey, this is going to help me put dinner on the table. It wasn't his fault that Bruno didn't like Charlie and that Bruno figured out if he could bop dinner over the head, he could bop Charlie too."

A cartoon picture of cavemen running around with dinosaur bones started rolling around in Morgan's head and she started to laugh. Then, she started crying. Jack had managed to put things in Jack-like perspective once again.

He half lifted out of his chair to go to her and then thought better of it before sitting down. But she recognized his dilemma by the way he tried very hard not to crush his fist around his coffee cup.

"I know," she replied, finally getting herself under control. "And without those bones we'd have probably become extinct. I just don't understand why there always has to be a catch, a caveat to life."

"I don't know, Morgan."

At least he'd taken her at her word and not used kitten.

He shrugged again, his fingers twirling his coffee cup in place. "So, what are you doing up so early?"

Morgan didn't answer right away. She had no idea how to feel anymore, what to do, or where to begin. She wanted them, she and Jack, back the way they'd been, and that could never be. "Trying very hard not to remember yesterday. Can't you go away again for a while?" she asked.

"No."

Near defeat, she queried, "Anyone ever tell you that you're beyond a royal pain?"

"Yes." He laughed gently. "My mother."

"Egads! You have a mother? Poor woman."

His face registered surprise as he answered, "I'll have you know my mother loves me."

"She has no choice."

Glad for the chance to zing him, Morgan sat back in her chair and caught his gaze. He tipped his head in acknowledgement.

"When you started talking about how bad this mess really was," she began, half speaking out loud, "And I was able to see past the horror, I started thinking. You said the FBI was targeting other companies that were performing research on the same type of process."

"I did."

"I mean, I'm supposed to keep up with that kind of stuff but worrying about the competition wasn't high on my priority list. I was spending fifteen hour days in the lab. So, I went downstairs for a while. I've been checking the internet."

"The internet? Why not ask me? I would've gotten you a list of possible suspects from Ian."

"The reason is that I wasn't looking for the obvious. I was looking for a piece that I might be able to fit into the puzzle. A scientific piece. A paper or an abstract that might connect to my work."

"Any luck?"

"No. It's been rather slow going. Part of the problem is that I don't have access to every database on the net, and most of the databases want you to sign up for their services before they'll let you upload a file. So far, I'm coming up with a major dead end."

"At least you tried."

At least they were speaking with each other and it didn't feel like razors were slicing her insides.

"If we could just find out who was in the market for something like this."

"I've already asked Ian to check."

Stunned, she didn't know what to say. She'd forgotten it wasn't just the two of them against the world anymore. There were more players and a whole lot more at stake than she could have imagined.

"I thought you didn't want him to know about me just yet."

"I figured we needed the help so I called in on my friendship. He gave me twenty-four."

"I see," she said. "Do you think whoever used this woman as a guinea pig has already sold the 'formula'?"

He pursed his lips in thought. "No. Not yet. Why are you asking?"

Morgan hesitated, hating that she did. It was hard to deal with someone when every time she said something, a niggle of doubt crept into her brain. But that was what lack of trust caused.

"I was cutting through several departments one day. In a hurry as usual. I overheard one end of a telephone conversation that may be important. I mean, I just realized it might be important."

"Do you know who was talking?" Jack asked. She could hear the interest in his voice and the tight control on his emotions that made his response sound urgent.

"No. There were too many instruments running. It was too loud and I was too far away to tell."

"What makes you think it's relevant?"

"Because, at first, I thought it was someone, you know, having an affair. The voice sounded...the conversation was....."

"Intimate?" he pressed.

"Pornographic."

"All right," he replied, his tone thoughtful. "What else?"

"Then, I figured whoever it was, despite the tone of the conversation, was possibly talking to someone else about one of our distributors in Europe. The end of the conversation was distinctly about Gateway. Maybe this person was looking for a market."

"Possibly. But I still don't think whoever it is has found one yet."

"Why?"

"Because Sam hasn't gotten all his zeros. He's still looking for us. So, it stands to reason, his client doesn't have his or her zeros either."

Morgan nodded. "That makes sense."

"It does, but I'm still not sure that we're not dealing with a serial killer. We can't rule out that possibility yet."

Morgan shuddered. "I know."

She took a deep breath and let the air out in a soft rush. Despite hating him for betraying her, Morgan's desire to make things right let her confess, "I need to do something, Jack. I need to fix this."

"I understand, Morgan. And I promise you, we'll make this right."

She watched Jack close his eyes and realized she wasn't his only problem. "What about your buddy, Sam? He might end up going to jail."

She watched Jack frown and open his eyes. He snared her gaze with his, as open and honest a gaze as she'd ever recognized. "He's responsible for his actions. He's created his own problems, and he's going to have to get himself out of them."

Morgan nodded, trying hard to believe that she had his loyalty. "Was this all about money, Jack?" BioClin. His buddy, Sam. Her voice broke as she repeated, "Was it really all for the money?"

He winced at the pain in her voice. "I don't know." He took a deep breath. "But I swear to you, as God is my witness, knowing you don't believe a word I'm going to say, I'm gonna find this bastard. Or bastards. They're going to get Jack. And they're going to get justice."

A DIM LIGHT CAST EERIE SHADOWS ALONG THE WALL, glancing off a bank of stainless-steel doors and gleaming countertops. Rows of cabinets lined the opposite wall filled with beakers and test tubes waiting to be used. Evenly spaced work areas, now silent before the day began, waited patiently to start their work again.

Only the sound of a man's heavy breathing broke the silence.

Anton Dvorak sat straight in the vinyl cushioned lab chair, his hands tied behind his back. He shivered with pleasure as a long red fingernail parted the folds of his once perfectly pressed dress shirt. His tie held his hands, just tight enough so he couldn't break the bond, just loose enough to allow blood to flow. He'd learned the hard way not to fight. The knot tightened if he struggled.

She'd left him squirming in his chair for hours when he protested.

That insidious finger drew lazy swirls over his abdomen. *Go lower. Go lower.*

He dared not even whisper his plea for fear of her reprisal, not the least of which would be an abrupt end to his night of pleasure.

Her finger traveled aimlessly, and Anton sucked in his stomach, holding his breath, hoping her finger would slip. Just one touch, one graze of skin on skin. He released the air slowly, knowing she would never make that kind of mistake.

A hint of perfume danced through the air. His nostrils widened to catch every delectable morsel of the scent. The finger of both pleasure and pain dipped just below his waist, reminding him of the prize.

But, oh God, the torture.

His cock strained for contact, swollen until he was certain it would break. She'd opened his shirt and pants and allowed him to be free, yet there was no freedom in the room—only submission and the insanity of reward.

Anton swallowed hard as she blew a soft breath over his straining flesh. She strutted her body in front of him, dressed in red lace, her breasts pushed up until they overflowed their confines, her dark thatch shiny and wet from his oral ministrations.

"That was good, Anton. Very good. You have a talented tongue. But not good enough. And you know if you don't please me, I won't please you."

Words tumbled to the tip of that talented tongue. Words like one touch, one suck, one millisecond in that warm wonderful haven of femininity. His lips parted, his chest heaved. He stared at her crotch, as if by thought alone, he could bring the prize to him.

She laughed.

Merciful heavens, she laughed. Today was going to be a good day. Today, she wouldn't watch him shame himself with that derisive smile on her face. He hated that smile.

Oh, the joy. Today, she was going to let him in.

His cock jumped in answer, and she crooned to the organ. Her palm cupped his balls and he shuddered. He didn't dare come now. He bit the inside of his cheek, welcoming the pain. He couldn't come now. She'd deny him for days if he did.

He reined in his mind, concentrating on chemical equations, performing routine calculations in his head. She rolled them in her fingers.

Ah, God. She was doing it on purpose. There was that grin again.

"Bitch."

She laughed. "You cannot come until I come at least two more times. Do you understand?"

He nodded. It was a test of wills. A battle of the sexes.

She straddled him. She rubbed her hot, wet core all over his erection. Without giving him a chance to protest, a chance to breathe, she lifted up and thrust herself all the way down on his cock. She started riding him like a horse, up and down, each movement sheer torture, incredible delight. But he didn't dare come. Not yet. Not until she did. Two more times. Then, she would give him the reward he so richly deserved.

But in every battle, there were ebbs and flows. It was his turn to make her sweat. Literally and figuratively.

"Sam Ormond has a partner. A guy named Jack Kent. He's with Mackenzie. I'm positive they know what happened."

His lover didn't even break stride, just kept pumping up and down with her mouth parted and her lips glistening in the dim light. A tiny thrill of fear helped take the edge off his lust, and Anton was able to keep his composure as she played with her nub and then orgasmed all over his thighs.

She lifted one leg and climbed off him, her face still an unsatisfied mask of desire. Not for him. He'd understood that long ago. For sex. And more sex. And more sex. She pushed her mound over his face, nearly smothering him in an attempt to quench the unquenchable. He stuck his tongue out and lapped at her core. She ground her thighs against his face, begging and pleading until she came one more time.

Thank God, he thought. He'd withstood her demands. Again.

"That's your problem, Anton. Not mine."

He frowned. "But you told me we wanted to find a buyer." Fear and concern caused him to shrink. "You told me we would make a fortune and no one would know."

She laughed. He watched her stick her finger deep inside her core and pull it out. She waved it under his nose. His erection grew to full length once more.

"No one will know I had anything to do with it, Anton. Your word against mine. Your notations, your experiments."

"And if I told you I taped our conversations?"

She laughed even harder. "I'd know you were lying. You know why?"

The next thing he knew, she had his balls in her hand. Her fingers tightened slowly. At first, the pain made him even more engorged. Then, the pain reached deep into his belly.

"I'm sorry!" he yelled. "I'm sorry," he cried, real tears filling his eyes and falling down his cheeks. The pain. Oh God, shooting through his brain.

Just when he thought he was going to pass out, she let go. And she swallowed his cock whole. She brought him back to full strength in seconds, then slid her steaming, wet heat over him.

He watched her throw back her head and open her long slender neck to his gaze. Such a pretty neck. White and smooth and flawless. Such a shame to mar such lovely skin. She lifted up and down on top of him and he lifted his hips to match her movements. She tweaked his nipple with her thumb and forefinger, and intense pleasure shot through his groin. With one part of his brain, Anton acknowledged that he was about to come.

With the other, he realized he was going to regret losing her. And as he reached the peak of sensation, as his mind reached parity with his body, one thought pounded along with the pounding of their bodies.

He had the formula. He had what remained from their experiments. And he was going to enjoy watching her die.

CHAPTER TWENTY-TWO

"TOUCH ANOTHER ONE OF MY FRIES, AND I'LL BE FORCED to remove your fingers from your hand."

Taken aback, Morgan had to look at Jack twice before she saw that little grin of his. She yanked her fingers back and stared at them to make sure they were all there. "I'll remember that."

He sat back in the booth of the restaurant, seemingly at ease with himself. She frowned, wondering how he could look so unaffected. As if telling her to get over it already would wipe the slate clean.

Jack waved his hand for their waiter and asked for a check. Then, he finished the last of his French fries. By himself.

Morgan threw herself back into her seat and started fidgeting. "I don't want to go back to the hotel. I'm tired of being cooped up."

She watched him cock his head. "So am I."

"Since the only way I want to communicate with you right now is about finding a murderer, let's try to be productive, shall we?"

He smiled. "I'm not sure how much we can do until I contact Ian again. Why don't you try to relax?"

"I can't. I need to find out who's behind all of this so I can put an end to it once and for all."

He sighed. "I always thought scientists were patient people. One step at a time? That sort of thing?"

"We are. I mean, I am. Normally. Well, I try to be."

"Ahh. So it's the lack of control that's bugging you."

"Yes. No." Morgan snared his gaze with hers. "I think you know exactly what I'm feeling right now."

He nodded, his face turning grim for a moment. Then, he brightened. "I have an idea. How about we free-mind for a few minutes?"

"What's free-mind?"

"It's like playing with a gigantic white board. Anything you think of, we write down. And somewhere along the way, we get dots we can connect." He cocked his head at her. "I'm kind of surprised you haven't heard of this before. I'd have thought in your line of business, it would be a first step."

She shook her head. "I'm so linear you can use me as a level."

He smiled, and she realized how much she'd missed his smile. "I'll remember that."

"So, what do you want me to do?"

"Let your mind go."

Morgan knew that would be nearly impossible. "I can't, Jack. Every time I do, I feel responsible for an innocent woman's death. I get angry and I can't think anymore. I want justice. For her. For all of them."

"And absolution for yourself?"

"Yes! No!" She grabbed her head with her hands and then covered her face with them so he wouldn't have to look at her. "Oh God, Jack. It's tearing me up inside."

He reached out across the table and gently pried them loose. His touch felt so good, so right. "I know, Morgan."

She could feel his reluctance as he let go. "I keep thinking I missed something. Something simple. Something really stupid. Something that's going to make me hate myself more than I do already. Just help me find the bastard or bastards who did this so I can try to sleep at night," she begged.

He sat back and pulled a hotel pad and pen out of his jacket pocket. He gave her a couple of sheets of paper and she pulled another pen out of her pocketbook.

"All right. Let's start at the beginning," he began. "Before you began to think there was a problem, you must have had contact with upper management."

She threw him a look. "Of course. I even gave two board room presentations."

That piqued his interest. "Who was there?"

"The COO, the CFO, the VPs of Marketing, Regulatory, R & D, two senior members of my staff to explain some of our findings, and the heads of the other departments."

She watched him frown. "The heads of other departments? Why were they there?"

"Courtesy, mostly. But you also have to understand the implications of my work for the company. This was bigger than Lipitor and Viagra put together. So, at the time, I also thought they were invited to ask questions. Of course, you throw enough PhDs into the mix, you get back alphabet soup."

She watched him grin at her quip. No, she decided. She missed the grin more. "Point taken."

"Okay," he continued. "So, you gave your presentations. Everyone went gaga over your findings and then they leaked the information and all started painting dollar signs on their office doors. Is that about the size of it?"

She nodded. "Yeah, that's about right."

He kept thinking out loud. "Good. Now, some time had to pass, right?"

Morgan tried to think back. "About three months or so."

"And then you found out the process didn't work."

"Yes."

"So, you cried foul and they didn't like that?"

"Very much so."

"All right. Then the first important question is...who notified you they were taking the project away?" he continued.

"My direct boss, Dr. Ralph Bernecky, the VP of R & D."

"When?"

"A few days after my last project meeting."

"What was the reason he gave you for taking the project away?"

Morgan lifted a brow that asked if this was the third degree, but he just rolled his eyes. "He said it was too big for one person and one team to handle." She sighed, trying hard not to remember how much that had hurt. "Reading between the lines, he was telling me I failed so they were going to find someone else to handle things."

"Did he know about Pinky and Louie?"

"Of course. He was one of the first people to know."

"What happened then?"

"I begged Ralph to let me continue. To let me sort out what went wrong."

"What was his answer?"

"That two heads and two teams were better than one."

"Did you believe that?"

"Not a chance."

He raised a brow at the force of her answer but kept on going. "And that's when he told you this other guy...what was his name?"

Her stomach knotted with bitterness. "Anton. Anton Dvorak."

"That Anton was getting the project?"

"Yes. Ralph tried to tell me it was only temporary, but I knew. I'd gone from hero to goat in less than a week. They were going to find someone else who could fix the problem. By any means necessary. That was when I went ballistic. I already knew they were going to go after the bankers. Now they were just being stupid and someone was going to get hurt."

"What did you do next?"

"After realizing the Arctic was warmer than my office? I

backpedaled. I apologized. Profusely. So I could keep the project. But it didn't seem to matter. I took that to mean that they wanted me out of the way so they could make the data work any way they could. That the bankers were more important at that point than reality."

"Probably were. What happened after that?"

"I overheard a conversation, in the ladies' room of all places, that my days at BioClin were already numbered. That was when I realized doing the right thing meant nothing to these people." Morgan sighed. "Ralph fought for me to a certain extent, I suppose, but not really."

Morgan remembered the disbelief, the shock, picking up the broken glass from the beaker she'd thrown in the sink. "Helluva lesson to learn. Lose your temper and end up killing someone."

"Un-unh, kitten. No pity party allowed. Keep thinking. You're on a roll. Keep going."

"At that point, I knew something was wrong. Kind of like driving along on the freeway and then missing your exit. Suddenly, you wake up and everything is off kilter, out of focus. Someone had been stealing my notes from my notebook. Then, I got pulled off the project and was going to be fired. As if each piece was being engineered or choreographed."

She watched Jack nod. "They were."

"Yeah, well, they underestimated their opponent. I knew I didn't want anyone else working on the project but me. So I took my personal computer with me to work the next day, not my work computer, by carrying it in my work computer case so no one would know. Then, I downloaded all the files from the server and took my personal computer home with me. The next day I called in sick. I spent the day copying every file onto the memory stick and deleting them from both computers. When I returned to work with my regular work computer, they confiscated it. I left the office before they found out I'd deleted the files, and never went back."

"Wait a minute. Didn't you also tell me you deleted all the files from the server?"

She smiled. "I'm not that good. I had help."

He raised a brow, seeming to wonder if she was going to elaborate. *Not yet.*

"Very well, we'll get to that later. Right now, I think we need to talk to Ralph," he decided.

Morgan smiled. A real smile. One from the heart. "You know something? I do too. How many minutes do you have left on your phone?"

"Enough."

"Good. I'm going to call him and have him meet us. And I know just the place."

He turned serious. "Somewhere very public, okay?"

Morgan shook her head and threw him a look. "Of course."

O'DONNELL'S WAS EXACTLY WHAT ITS NAME IMPLIED, A small Irish pub. If they hadn't already had lunch, Morgan would've insisted they eat again. The shepherd's pie was to die for. And she knew Ralph would feel comfortable meeting here.

Portly, balding, Ralph didn't fit the physical profile of a highly respected PhD. He looked more like a kid's little league coach. And he was one, for his son. But the man knew his science and he managed to orchestrate multiple projects by multiple project teams at one time. Which could be called art rather than science.

As Ralph sat down, he hesitated and shook his head at her. "Jesus, Morgan. You look...different. I almost didn't recognize you."

Morgan watched Ralph's gaze flip to Jack. "Jack, this was my boss, but since I left the company before I was ever officially fired, I have no idea how to introduce him. Dr. Ralph Bernecky. Ralph, this is Jack Kent."

"Pleased to meet ya," Ralph replied, shaking hands with Jack.

"Likewise."

"Thanks for coming, Ralph," Morgan said.

He grimaced back at her. "Puts me in a bad position, ya know. But I had to come. You need to make peace with the company. If you give me the files and walk away, I can help. I'm sure I can get the company to let bygones be bygones. They won't press charges."

Relief washed through her as Morgan realized Ralph had no idea what was going on with the rest of it. Ralph was working from the point of view that she'd committed industrial espionage, nothing else. Yet she couldn't help feeling sad. She'd hoped for a little more loyalty. But hell, she didn't have two kids, two car payments, and a mortgage. Just integrity, which meant more to her than all the mortgages in the world put together.

"That's not why I called you, Ralph."

Confusion creased his forehead at the flat tone in her voice. "I don't understand. You mean you're not turning yourself in?"

Morgan flicked her gaze to Jack. His features appeared neutral but she could tell he was judging and processing Ralph's every word, his every expression.

"Let's just say there's a little more to the story. So no, not yet. The reason I called you was to ask you some questions."

"Questions?" her ex-boss asked, his tone guarded and his gaze not quite meeting hers. "What kind of questions?"

Ralph's mistrust hurt big time. Obviously, he'd known some of what was going to happen. "Oh, like when you knew they were going to take the project away from me."

"I didn't until right before I told you."

Morgan felt Jack stiffen. She watched him lean forward against the table and stare at Ralph for several long seconds. She wasn't sure how he knew Ralph was lying, but he did. "The lady asked you a fair question, Ralph. I suggest you answer her honestly. I'm not in the mood to dick around with anyone from BioClin right now."

Ralph's gaze shot to hers. "He knows? How much? Do you know what kind of trouble you're both in?"

"More than you'll ever know, Ralph," Morgan replied, her tone sad.

But Ralph wasn't listening to her. He was staring at Jack. "Just who the hell are you, anyway? Are you a cop?"

Jack simply smiled. "Something like that."

Ralph didn't look at either of them. He stared at the table and started shredding a cocktail napkin. His fingers shook ever so slightly. "Can I have a beer?"

Jack stopped their waitress and ordered one. Once it arrived, Ralph swallowed a healthy draught. "I didn't do anything wrong."

Except for sticking a knife in my back, Morgan thought bitterly. "You sold me out."

"Sort of."

At least he had the decency to look her straight in the eyes when he said it. "What do you mean, sort of?" she asked, dread growing in the pit of her stomach.

"It was all internal politics. You should have paid attention. But you didn't want to know about that kind of stuff. You just wanted to be left alone to do your job. In a way, I admired you for that. But in another, you were incredibly naïve if you thought you were going to be able to get away with that kind of behavior."

"Dog eat dog," Jack muttered, his tone none too happy about her treatment.

"I tried to warn you, Morgan. But you wouldn't listen. The moment you walked out of that project meeting, you killed the goose. They were already counting the money, don't ya see? They were already trying to figure out who they could hire with the biggest name that would garner the most prestige. They were looking at this as the biggest breakthrough since Viagra. And then you went and blew it all to hell and back again."

"Tell me about it," she answered bitterly. "I need to know more, Ralph. Did they say anything else to you?"

Ralph frowned back at her, not quite understanding the question. "You mean, about your test mice? About the process?"

"Yeah, that teensy-weensy little problem that was going to end all those lovely dollars for BioClin. Did they tell you anything more?"

"More? I'm not sure I follow."

Jack laid a gentle hand on her arm before she could explode. When she looked up, he gave a slight shake of his head. It was obvious he didn't know the process had been used elsewhere.

All right. There were other questions she could ask. "Did anyone ever talk to you about Gateway in Europe?"

Ralph looked a bit astonished. "Regarding this project? Of course not."

So that meant Ralph truly had no idea of anything else going on. Funny, though, how this piece of his innocence didn't make her feel much better. Maybe asking the one question that was burning a hole deep in the pit of her belly would.

"How much did they pay you, Ralph? To keep quiet? To keep their plans alive?" she asked, learning from Jack. Her tone betrayed little of the turmoil that raged inside her.

"They didn't. I—"

"How much?" Jack asked again, cutting him off.

"It was a bonus."

Morgan was certain she was going to be sick. The one person she'd thought she could trust. "How much?" Morgan cried, slamming her palms on the table.

"Enough to put one of my kids through college. Private college."

"Bastard," she hissed. Then, she felt Jack's hand tighten on her arm. She didn't want to make a spectacle. "You're the one who sold me out."

Ralph looked up, and she could see the misery warring with remorse in his gaze. She almost felt sorry for him. "No I didn't! Honest!"

"Do you really expect me to believe that?"

He shook his head. "You don't understand, Morgan. You're smart. You get it. You have the ability to think outside the box. I don't. I just barely got my doctorate. I'm a people person. I can manage things but I'm not good in the lab. You are. So I rode your coattails. And when the fountain stopped flowing, I took the money. I'm sorry."

Morgan swallowed, not trusting herself to answer. She let Jack do that for her instead. "How sorry, Ralph?"

"Sorry enough to know that I don't want Morgan going to jail on my account."

"Good." Jack gave her arm a light, reassuring squeeze. "Then you can help Morgan stay out of jail by telling us if anyone else in that meeting who knew the process didn't work came to you after the meeting."

"Yes."

Morgan whipped her gaze up to stare at Ralph. Ralph dropped his gaze. And then Morgan realized. "You don't work for BioClin anymore, do you? You took the bonus check and you ran."

"I got an offer I couldn't refuse."

Jack caught her gaze with his and she realized there was a 'we' in Ralph's prior statement. The person who gave him the offer. "Who, Ralph?"

Ralph didn't answer; he just kept staring at the table, making more and more shreds of his napkin. Morgan didn't know whether to laugh or cry. Was integrity truly dead? Was it really dog eat dog out there?

Morgan shivered, turning cold inside. Someone she knew, someone she'd worked side by side with for two years screwed her over. But that didn't matter. That same someone had used the process to kill.

A part of her didn't want to ask the question. Because that would mean she would have to know the answer. The other part of her knew she'd never sleep until she did.

"Who gave you the job, Ralph?"

He didn't answer. "Who gave you the job, Ralph?" she asked again, her tone tight and brittle with anger. "I'm not going to ask again."

Ralph lifted his anguished gaze from the table and said, "Anton Dvorak."

CHAPTER TWENTY-THREE

MORGAN WAS CERTAIN SHE'D NEVER BE WHOLE AGAIN. AS soon as they reached their hotel room, Jack wrapped his arms around her and refused to let go. She fought him. She fought herself. A huge emptiness gaped before her. He didn't say anything. He simply let go, made her lie down on the bed, and tucked her in under the covers.

"Make the pain go away, Jack."

"I'd like to, darlin.' But I'm on the wrong side of everything right now."

Honesty. When she'd least expected it.

Integrity. When she'd least expected it.

Morgan slid onto her side, and scooted over so Jack could lie down and wrap his arms around her. His chest labored with furious abandon against her back. "Why, Jack? Why?"

There were two parts to that question. The first was obvious. Why did Ralph hurt her, but most importantly, why had Jack?

"Because people feel they have to do what they have to do to survive. There's no justification to it, just fact I guess."

"But it hurts so badly."

"I know. I thought what I was doing was for my country. There was honor and pride in that. I was willing to lay down my life, no questions asked. But when I balked, when I questioned what happened, they told me to forget about it."

He chuckled, the sound as bitter as she felt. "Forget?" he continued. "Forget that I killed innocent people? That mistakes were made in war? The truth was they wanted the target dead. And they didn't care if his kids got killed with him. End of story."

"I faced a choice," he added. "Same as you're facing right now. Live through it or don't."

That wasn't exactly what she wanted to hear.

"Morgan, listen to me. I hurt you the first time because I thought you were a criminal and it didn't matter if I hurt you or not. Jack and justice. That's me."

He sighed, the breath cleansing for both of them. "But it's funny how life turns around on a person. I found out you're as far from a criminal as a person can get. But by the time I did, you'd already played right into the web I was weaving. You ended up trusting me. How in God's name was I going to tell you I was following orders? So, I hurt you a second time. And you know what the irony of all this is? I thought I was in complete control and ended up with no control at all. Things just happen, Morgan."

"No joke."

"People will tell you to get on with your life, just like I've been telling you, but you'll never really believe it until you can tell it to yourself in the mirror."

"I can't. Not yet."

Was he smiling? She thought so. She could feel his cheek move against her hair.

"Listen, this isn't about me anymore. It's about you. Or maybe I just need to go get Bruno so he can bop you over the head a couple of times.

Her shoulders shook slightly. Maybe there was hope after all.

HE'D GOTTEN HER TO LAUGH. JACK COULDN'T BELIEVE IT. He twisted his body slightly so they faced each other. Jack looked down at her. They were about to kiss. His insides were firing on all eights, yet his thoughts couldn't go beyond the warmth radiating from her eyes.

He melted.

He should have been gone by now, should have run in the opposite direction, put the moment into Jack-like perspective. But he couldn't. Because hooks like hers didn't simply come out, they ripped out. And while Jack wasn't afraid of the pain or the scars that would follow, he was terrified of *her* consequences and the hurt he would inflict on *her*.

For the first time in his life, Jack put another person ahead of himself. And he liked it that way.

"Morgan, I want to make love to you in the very worst way. But I'll get up out of this bed right now if you say no."

"Why would you do that?"

"Because I don't want to hurt you again. Because I don't deserve a third chance. Because you're beautiful and strong, you're honest and honorable—things I've dragged through my muck for way too long now."

"Why, Jack? Why did you hurt me?"

"Because I wasn't thinking about you, I was thinking about me. It's that simple."

"Nothing's that simple."

He chuckled. "I know. I also know you won't forgive me anytime soon. But I can't stand to see you like this. I want to make it better."

"You can't."

"We both know I can. But if that's going to end up hurting you even more, I'll get up and walk away. Now. Before we both regret it."

Jack held his breath. The ball was in her court, the decision was hers. *Do I stay, or do I go?*

She shook her head, lifting up and covering his mouth with hers. Molten fire spread through his veins. He was certain he was going to die right then and there.

Tearing his mouth away, he gasped, "Are you sure? I don't want to...once I—"

She nodded with an abashed grin. "I'm sure."

He rolled them both over and bent his head down to kiss her again. She knew. There was only one way to heal the ugliness. With all the feeling that was in his heart, Jack covered her mouth with his. He licked her lips, his tongue rimming the outside and then he slipped it inside. They didn't fence, they danced to the glory that was theirs and theirs alone. Just as they had on the terrace of the hotel in Cape May.

In the eyes of the world, what they were doing might be wrong. But Jack only knew right. Just as he knew someday that Morgan would realize she was a hero and not a villain in all this.

"Morgan, I—"

Jack stopped. She wasn't ready for that confession yet. She had a mountain of emotions to climb over first. But she was ready for some healing. The Jack kind. So, he lifted her up to a semi-sitting position and removed her sweatshirt with a single pull. She rolled away and off the bed and shucked her jeans in ten seconds. Then, she gave him a sly and shy look and unsnapped her bra.

Jack decided he could get very used to this.

She started to climb back onto the bed when he gave a go ahead signal. She hooked her fingers in the waistband and slid her panties down her thighs one inch at a time. Jack's heart double tripped and slipped from his throat to his knees as he watched. He wasn't sure he'd make it if she didn't climb back on the bed that instant.

He urged her to slide back into his arms but she shook her head. Instead, she flipped her leg over his body to straddle his chest. Hot honey from her core warmed his skin.

"You're awfully ready for me, kitten."

She laughed. "True. But I want to go slow. As if this is the first time."

He didn't know how to answer. Was she really giving him another chance?

She cocked her head at him, her hips rubbing her core against his chest in an unconscious rhythm. "That doesn't mean you can't enjoy the fruits of my labors for a little."

"That's an offer I can't refuse," he answered with a smile that came from the heart.

She grinned down at him. "All right. The first rule is, you can't move."

"I can't?"

She shook her head. "Second rule. I run the show."

He grinned. He'd taken control away from her, not given her a choice because of the circumstances of their predicament. But here, where they were most vulnerable, he could give it back to her.

"No argument."

"Third rule. There are no rules. I'm running the show."

With that declaration, she started sucking on his fingers. *Oh no, she isn't. Is she?* Right into her hot, greedy, little mouth. No one had ever done that to him before.

Ah hell, now he was in trouble. Real trouble. He wasn't allowed to move. And if she didn't start paying attention to his lower half, he was going to end up shaming himself all over her.

Now that would be a waste.

Jack wrapped his arms around her and pulled her down for a sinfully deep kiss. Sometimes a man's gotta do what a man's gotta do.

"Hey, I thought I was running this show," she complained as she lifted back to look at him.

"You are," he agreed. "It's just that, well, I—"

Jack had never really let go of himself. He'd let people in, but only so far. Even when he thought he cared, he was cautious. He calculated and weighed options, made sure that his heart was always protected.

His gaze told her everything. Being together wasn't about the sex, it was about being together. Morgan was more important to him than the sex and always would be.

She bit her lip in uncertainty. Her gaze swirled with heat and softness, but deep inside, also a touch of fear. He knew that fear well. He'd just figured out how to tame it.

"I know, kitten," he whispered. "No pressure."

Tears welled in her eyes. He didn't want her crying again, so he blurted, "Except… I mean…well, you know, I really need some relief."

She choked out a laugh and answered with a roll of her hips. "Which one would you like first? Right or left?"

He answered with a huge smile. "Doesn't matter. Just bring 'em on, baby."

She did, allowing him to feast on one and then the other. Of course that just put more of a hurting on his already enormous erection.

"Greedy, aren't you?" she asked after they shared another mind-blowing kiss.

"Yeah," he answered, flexing his hips, which were begging for attention.

She slid back, and for one hopeful moment, Jack thought she might change her mind and let him in. When she didn't, he knew she was hurting and that she needed more persuasion. Then, all sane thought ceased. She cradled him in her hands and went down on him like he was her favorite candy.

Done. Gone. Sweet heaven, there ought to be a law about something that feels this good. Of course, that also meant he had zero willpower and her suggestion of complex chemical equations wasn't helping one bit.

Jack wanted the sensation to last forever. The tight pulls and the warm swirls. God, she had a talented tongue. But sometimes a man had to do what a man had to do.

He let go and with a mighty roar, came from the tips of his toes to the top of his head and back down again. He came and came and came. And she just kept drawing him in.

Sweet heaven on earth. It didn't get any better than this.

MORGAN SAT BACK ON HER HEELS WITH A SATISFIED SMILE. "I am so not done with you yet," he choked out in between huge gulps of air.

"Just a diversion."

"You call that a simple diversion?" he asked, his tone incredulous. He pulled her down to lay across his body.

He didn't speak at first. Just held her tight. And each time she moved, his arms would band around her even tighter.

"We put the cart way before the horse, you know," he told her.

"I kind of like it that way," she confessed.

"Someday, we'll have to go out on a real date. Where I pick you up, bring you flowers, and take you to a really quiet, really expensive restaurant. And hope and pray I'll get lucky."

"You've already gotten lucky," she replied with a soft laugh.

Morgan made sure he understood the double entendre. And when he answered, she'd never seen nor heard him so serious. "I know."

"All you know about me is the 'dark' side, Morgan. Someday, I hope you'll give me a chance so you can see the other side."

"I'm trying, Jack. I really am."

He bent his head and kissed the top of hers. "Now it's my turn."

He flipped her over onto her back. Then, he scooted down to the bottom of the bed. The next thing Morgan knew, he was doing to her toes what she'd done to his fingers. And being terribly ticklish, the feeling was insane, running all the way up and down her spine as she got hotter and hotter.

Brutal man that he was, he left no toe untouched.

Then, his tongue swirled up each one of her calves as he rested her legs, one on each shoulder. He pulled her down on the bed as he inched his way closer to the prize, rising to his knees to get a better angle.

That wasn't the only thing rising.

Morgan watched him grow, her body heating with desire. She tried to bury the pain of his betrayal and found she couldn't. So she pushed it to one side and compartmentalized. Eventually, she would have to make a decision about how she would deal with that, but right now, he owed her. Big time. And if she wanted to take that out in trade, that was her choice.

Because this time, she did have a choice.

So, she caught his gaze. He gave her a slight nod and a very naughty grin as he bent down to continue working his way to her core.

At first, he simply breathed. That was all. A light breath, a lick here and there. She was so ready for him that she knew she would explode the moment he touched her.

He did too.

So, he avoided her nub and licked his way around her core, his tongue dancing everywhere but the one place she wanted.

Did he want her to beg?

No, the times for one-upmanship were over. They'd seen each other naked, truly naked, soul-bearing naked. Neither one of them was beautiful. But together they created a masterpiece of art.

He flicked at her nub and she jumped, all sane thought centering at her core. She squirmed and moaned, trying to get him to give her release, but he didn't give into her. And then, she realized why. He wanted her to not just explode, he wanted her to have the most mind blowing orgasm of her life.

"Oh, God, Jack."

As if that was the switch, he covered her core with his mouth and started sucking and flicking her nub. The pressure built inside her until she thought she was going to die. Then, her body hitched and she screamed, coming from the very depths of her being. Her core convulsed and he let go of her legs, sliding into her body in one long thrust.

At first, Morgan thought she needed to stop. But this had happened before. He'd built her up to such a frenzy that one orgasm wasn't going to be enough.

He lifted up onto his elbows, pulling out as far as he could and thrusting hard into her body. Each time, he made sure to rub his cock against her nub. In and out. He kept thrusting as the sweat of their bodies mingled.

He swallowed hard, and she watched his face grow tighter and tighter as he held back and waited for her. He was trying to tell her without words that he was willing to do whatever it took to make things right between them.

Morgan's body answered for her. She climbed with him. He opened his eyes to look straight down into hers.

"Fly with me, kitten," he begged. "Fly with me."

She did. She reached the precipice and spread her arms wide, diving off the cliff into space. She soared, screaming her joy at the top of her lungs, his voice joining hers in a song they'd never forget. She felt his warm wet fluid shoot into her body and drank greedily.

And when he collapsed on top of her, when their bodies heaved with lungs filled with air, when her core pulsed with the aftershock of an earthquake she knew she'd never duplicate, Morgan realized he was telling the truth.

Jack was Jack. She was going to have to take him or leave him exactly as he was. Simple as that.

CHAPTER TWENTY-FOUR

IT'S FUNNY HOW IT DIDN'T MATTER WHERE JACK WAS AS long as he was with her. Morgan was sitting on the couch the next morning, with her bare feet curled underneath her and her arms crossed over her chest. She didn't look happy but all he could think of was how he'd sucked and nibbled on her toes last night. And the response that he had elicited.

Not her ire at his decision to meet Ian alone.

He watched her rise in one fluid motion, her gaze stormy and her anger growing. "I thought you said we were both going to the meeting."

"I changed my mind."

She thrust her hands deep in her pockets as if to keep them from hurting him. *Fat chance.* "I thought you trusted Ian."

"I do. But Ian's the type of guy to put his ducks in a row first and sort things out from there. Worst case, one of us needs to stay free and mobile to continue searching out who's behind all this."

"Tag, I'm it?"

He nodded, trying hard not to smile. "Can I trust you to stay out of trouble while I'm gone?"

"Sure," she replied, her tone sarcastic. "I'll just stay here, go downstairs, and play solitaire and surf the web."

"Morgan—"

She thrust out her chin with a look that asked, *What did you expect?* Pillsbury dough-girl his woman wasn't. "All right. I'll behave."

He snorted, as much as for what she said as she didn't say. Then, it hit him. *His* woman. He liked the sound of that very much.

If she would have him.

"I wish I could go home and grab some clothes."

"Not your best idea, although I like you better without them," he quipped to hide the horror of his next thought. "You wouldn't be thinking of going there, would you?"

"No, of course not," she exclaimed.

"I mean it, kitten." A knot began to form in his gut. "I want you to stay out of trouble and off everyone's radar, you hear me?"

"I *get* the message."

Boy, this learning how to trust thing was hard. For both of them. "Do you?"

"Sheesh," she groused. He watched her pick up a pack of half-eaten Oreos they'd gotten from the hotel vending machine. "I feel like one of these damned cookies. I've got BioClin on one side and the FBI on the other."

Fighting hard not to laugh, Jack answered, "Yeah. But think of it this way. You're the cream and I get to lick you all I want."

"God, you are so one-track," she cried, throwing the cookies back on the table.

"Morgan." She refused to look at him. "Morgan, listen to me."

You've got to give a little. Take a little.

With his heart pounding high in his chest, Jack waited for her to turn. When she did, he snared her gaze with his. "Come here."

She shook her head. *And let your poor heart break a little.* "Please."

Reluctantly, she stepped toward him. "What?"

He reached out and drew her close. He wrapped his arms around her and leaned back so he could stare deep into her eyes. "I've never said this to anyone before."

At first, he thought she would try to bolt. Instead, she tore her gaze from his and let her eyes shutter. All right, so she wasn't ready to reciprocate. That was okay with him. For now, all she had to do was listen.

"I know my own heart, kitten."

That's the story of....

"Don't Jack. I'm not—"

He smiled down at her, giving her all the love that was in his heart. "If anything happened to you, I think I'd put a gun to my head."

Horror rose in her face, followed by anger. "That's not funny. Be serious."

"I am."

Her gaze came back to his and she read the truth of his words. "Jack, I—"

That's the glory of...

"I love you, Dr. Morgan Mackenzie."

He let go of her with one arm and placed a gentle finger against her lips. "I don't expect an answer. Hell, I don't expect you to even talk to me once this is over. But that won't change how I feel. Or that I've never said this to another woman."

He watched tears fill her eyes. "Except your mother."

He laughed softly. "Yeah, except my mother."

He swallowed hard and bent his head. He gave her all the love in his heart and tried to make sure she knew it in his kiss. When he broke away, they were both breathing hard.

Jack didn't want to let go, he never wanted to let go, but he had no choice. His arms dropped to his sides. Without her touch, it felt like a piece of him was missing.

"If I'm not back by five o'clock, check out of the hotel. Take a taxi into Boston and a train, bus, whatever, to Cape May. Take the ferry and get my car. And while you're at it, pray the damned thing hasn't been towed." He handed her the keys. Her fist closed over them so tight, her knuckles showed white. "You'll find cash, credit cards, and another prepaid cell in the trunk. Don't keep the car too long. Ian'll be following you. When you ditch the car, find a limo to take you a few hundred miles. I don't want to know the direction. Just stay away from your original plan to get to Dr. Lee for now. Get lost. As lost as you can. Make Ian work for the right to use you. I'll try to convince him to stop looking for you and look for the real culprit instead."

She didn't say anything, and that scared him. He didn't want her to close herself off to him, but she was already putting on her armor, protecting herself in case things went south. "You hear?"

She nodded. "I hear."

He let go of the breath he didn't know he was holding. "Tell Ian," she continued, a Jack-like grin growing on her face. "That he'll have to deal with me if he starts messing with you."

"I will," he choked out, reaching for the door handle.

Suddenly, he turned and hauled her up against him. "We'll get through this together, kitten. I promise. And when we do, we'll do things normal people do. We'll go dancing. We'll go shopping." He gave her one of his own grins back. "I'll pay you back for that suit I owe you, as long as you promise we can make a stop at Victoria's Secret."

She opened her mouth to laugh, and he accepted the invitation. Their tongues mated in a familiar dance. Jack loved everything about Morgan, but this moment most of all—the moment her body melted into his as they kissed.

A kiss isn't always a kiss.

He let go and yanked the door open, not trusting himself to say another word. The door clicked shut behind him with a finality that rang through his body and ended in his soul. But he couldn't stop smiling. Because that truly was the story of and the glory of...

Love.

MORGAN STARTED OUT BY TRYING TO WEAR A HOLE IN THE carpet of the hotel room. Events were spinning out of control at an alarming rate and she had to do something. But what?

You promised.

She rubbed her face with her hands and let them fall.

She acknowledged how funny it was. She did her best thinking while her hands were busy. So, Morgan went into the bathroom and reapplied the makeup she'd just wiped away.

She was just reapplying her lipstick when it hit her. She picked up the cell phone Jack had left her with shaking hands. "Dewy? It's Dr. Mackenzie."

"Mac attacks. How the heck are you? Long time, no talk. Where've you been?"

Morgan smiled. That was why Dewy was such a treasure. He truly lived in a cocoon, his own world, a world of technology and science. He had an incredibly brilliant mind but people scared the hell out of him. "I needed a change of scenery."

Dewy didn't answer. But that was Dewy. "How's everyone at work?" she asked, trying to keep things as normal as possible. "How's Rebecca doing with her diet?"

Dead silence. Morgan frowned. "Dewy?"

"Rebecca's not here."

Did she get fired too? Morgan's heart sank at the thought. And even more anger churned in her guts.

"Is she all right?"

"I don't know. I guess so. She hasn't been here for a while. I'm sorry, Mac. You know I don't pay attention."

"Yeah, Dewy, I know."

"You remember I told you about Dr. Lee, right?"

He paused. "Oh yeah, I remember."

"And you remember when I asked you to help me wipe the files from my project off the server? Because the process didn't work, and I didn't want anyone to get hurt?"

"Sure, Mac. I remember. We're not gonna get into any trouble are we?"

He must have heard the concern in her tone. "I promised you, you wouldn't get into any trouble. And I meant it."

She listened to him sigh with relief. "So, what's up?"

"I found a file folder that I didn't create. But my copy doesn't have any signature on it. I just need to know if you remember a name attached to it."

"What date was it created?"

She told him the date. Then she told him where she'd found it.

"Give me a sec."

Morgan waited patiently, listening to the silence as Dewy processed. She'd always wondered if he had a photographic memory. Or close to it. Her hand hurt from gripping the cell too tightly as he went through his memory banks.

"Umm. No name that I remember. Just letters. Yeah. Letters. A, D, E, T. I remember it because of the last two. E. T. Kinda fit, ya know?"

No joke. She wrote the letters down on a pad and asked, "That's all you can remember?"

"Sorry, Mac."

She nodded. Not much to go on but something. "Hey listen, you've been a big help. Thanks."

"No problem. You're my fave, doc." He paused and asked, "So, when you coming back to work?"

He missed her. Her heart swelled. "As soon as I can, Dewy. As soon as I can. Take care of yourself, okay?"

"Will do. Later."

Morgan sat down. Her stomach clenched. She tried not to think that Rebecca had been fired because of her actions but she expected no less from BioClin. And that made her angry. More innocent people paying for her mistakes.

Morgan wrote the letters down and tried to create words from them, anything that would help her figure out who created the file folder. Even though everything pointed to Anton, she had no real proof. This was her problem and her mess.

When she couldn't get the word sets to make sense, Morgan left the room and walked down the hallway to the vending machines for a soft drink. She put her money into the slot and waited for the machine to read her dollar. Research was more failure than success, so she took a deep breath and told herself to go back and try again. As she did, she read the service label on the vending machine. It read 'I.T.A Service.' And then it hit her.

Initials.

The signature line on the file folder was made up of initials.

She ran back down the hallway and had to put in her key three times to open the door because her hands were shaking so badly. Throwing open the portal, she looked at the letters again. A. D. Anton Dvorak. Of course. But what about the other one?

She paced, looking at the initials every few moments and then down at the floor. One set of the initials belong to Anton, one set of the initials had to belong to someone else who was in the meeting. Her mind clicked again. That other set of initials had to belong to the other person of the telephone conversation she'd heard. The person who'd already killed an innocent woman. Morgan shuddered.

Think, deduct, reason!

And then it hit her. *E. T.*

With horror filling her belly, Morgan realized that when this whole thing blew up, and it would, BioClin was going to go down the tubes for something its board probably didn't even know about. They were being snowed, lied to, by two of their top managers, the heads of two of their best departments.

And now she knew exactly who they were.

CHAPTER TWENTY-FIVE

THE DIN OF THE DINER GRATED ON JACK'S NERVES. HE'D arrived early and waited for the last booth against the wall, not feeling comfortable until his back was against the vinyl of the seat. With a full view of the diner, he waited for Ian to arrive. There was always the possibility that Ian wouldn't believe him.

But there was something else that might just swing the scale in his favor...they'd eaten sand together...saved each other's lives more than once.

He couldn't help smiling as he watched Ian approach. For a moment, Jack thought he caught a worried look in Ian's gaze. Then, he dismissed it and rose from his seat to greet his friend.

"Good to see you, bro," he said, giving Ian a bear hug and a couple of back slaps.

"Wish I could say the same," Ian threw back at him as he sat down.

He watched Ian look over his shoulder at the rest of the diner, and then back at him, as if to say he got the message and wasn't happy about having his back exposed. Jack grinned.

Ian signaled for their waitress and asked for a refill on Jack's coffee, another cup, and a couple of danishes. Once she was gone he said, "You sure do know how to cause trouble."

"Always have, always will," Jack replied with an unrepentant grin.

Ian sighed. "Mike is flipping out."

"He's not the only one. I need the immunity, Ian."

"I only have so much pull, Jack. He's not going to make any kind of deal unless he knows everything that's going on."

"This isn't about me, Ian. It's about her. I need the immunity."

"And I can't give it to you until we know what you know."

The waitress returned with their order, and Jack played with his coffee as he tried to decide what to do. Morgan meant more than the world to him now.

"Listen, I'm not here because I want to screw you," Ian continued.

Jack sighed. "I know, man. I know."

"And as my boss, if Mike had wanted to, he'd have made me walk in here with handcuffs, not a hello."

Jack took a sip of his coffee and then put the cup down. It all came down to trust, he realized. He had to trust the sand and himself.

Jack sighed. "You arrest me, she runs. You got that?"

Ian nodded. "Loud and clear."

Jack relaxed. But only slightly. "All right. Here it is..."

Jack explained why he believed Morgan was innocent, how much he thought Sam was involved, and what they'd discovered from Ralph Bernecky. God knew it sounded more like the plot of a suspense novel than reality, but he knew Ian would be true to his word. Ian would never forget the picture of that emaciated woman.

"I want to catch the sonofabitch who's done this," Jack told Ian, struggling to tamp down his anger. "Bad."

"Trust me, I do too."

He watched Ian's features tighten, and knew his friend was struggling as well. "When all of this began, and I asked you to trace

Dr. Mackenzie, I also started a quiet investigation of domestic and international drug channels," Ian continued.

Jack closed his eyes, willing himself to focus on Morgan, knowing it was up to him to keep her safe. "So far, we haven't come up with much, so don't get your hopes up."

"It's still worth a shot," Jack said. He shifted in his chair, needing a three hour workout in a gym to get rid of his angst. "This whole thing is a mess. Bernecky doesn't even work for BioClin anymore. Said he got a 'bonus,' then split to work for another company. He got paid off to keep his mouth shut."

Wow, that came out bitter, even to his own ears.

"Can't charge him for being a prick, you know," Ian asked. Then, he must've realized who he was talking to.

Jack gave him a pointed stare. "Thanks."

Ian shut his mouth, figuring he'd better not answer.

Jack pulled a piece of paper out of his pocket. "She's made a list of anyone she could think of who might have been privy to any information, starting with her immediate supervisor and the guy they gave the project to."

Jack watched Ian take the paper and then put it in his pocket. "Second," Jack continued, "she keeps mentioning a company in Europe called Gateway. A distributor that BioClin worked with. You might want to do some digging on them."

"Thanks, I will."

Jack frowned. "You know, I have a feeling if you dig into this company Bernecky is working for, that might lead you to the guy Morgan believes killed that poor woman. And maybe the others."

"Who's that?"

"Used to be her direct competitor within the company, she said. Anton Dvorak."

"Do you think she's right?" Ian asked him.

Jack nodded. "Someone inside that company's been orchestrating things. I'm sure of it. Now, that person might tie into the other deaths, and then again, he might not. I don't have any way to tell yet."

"Guess we'd better keep digging then."

Ian hesitated and Jack wondered why. "Ian, listen. You know I'm right. She's a hero, not a murderer," he continued. "She was trying to do the right thing and keep everyone safe."

She was a hero. Except for that small glitch called the law, of course. Which might get them both thrown in jail if Ian couldn't work some magic.

"All right, here's the deal," Ian finally said, nodding in agreement. "You hand over all the evidence. I'll 'persuade' BioClin not to press charges. When they find out what's been going on, I believe they'll be more than happy to cooperate."

Jack took a deep breath and let the air out slowly. A huge weight lifted from his shoulders. "What if they're all dirty?" he wondered out loud.

"You let me worry about that."

"Not good enough. She's really upset that someone used her process to kill. She wants to help set up the murderer. Become the bait."

Ian frowned. "You want me to set up a meeting and hand her over to the lions in the lion's den?"

"Yup."

"Why?"

"Because of the people who've died. Because whoever is doing this is crazy. I don't care if these murders occurred in the name of greed or science, there's no doubt a crazy is on the loose."

Now it was Ian's turn to decide what to do. He hesitated again, making Jack wonder. "That might be out of the question now."

"What do you mean?" Jack stared at him, confusion and hurt racing through his guts.

"There've been...developments."

Jack's insides clenched as the temperature in the diner dropped. "Developments?"

"Yeah. While she's been running you on a wild-goose chase, another murder has been committed. This time, very close to home."

"What? Who? How? Where?"

Ian didn't seem sure of which question to answer first. "It seems someone has been able to speed up the process. A young woman who worked for BioClin, Rebecca Daniels, disappeared right after Morgan Mackenzie."

"Oh my God, her admin!" Jack exclaimed.

"Interesting that Dr. Mackenzie would have told you about the young woman, don't you think?"

Jack didn't answer. He couldn't. Ian had things backward.

"She's dead, Jack," Ian told him.

His stomach soured. "The same as the others?"

Ian didn't reply. He didn't need to. He simply nodded. "And you think Morgan killed her."

Ian didn't reply again. Was Ian testing him? None of this made any sense.

"Motive and opportunity, Ian. Killing her own admin would put her right in the spotlight. Why take that chance?" He swallowed hard. "She told me one of her reasons for working on this drug was to help people like Rebecca Daniels. Why tell me about her? It brings attention right where she wouldn't want it."

"Because the perp we're dealing with is sick."

Despite the cold dread filling his gut, Jack clung to the mantra that a person was innocent until proven guilty, not the other way around.

"She didn't do it, Ian. She's a hero. She stole the data so no one would use it."

"Someone did."

"She's innocent, Ian," Jack insisted. "And I'm going to prove it to you."

"How?" his friend asked with a worried frown.

"By any means necessary."

JACK DROVE BACK TO THE HOTEL IN A QUANDARY. HOW WAS he ever going to tell Morgan that Rebecca was dead? He wanted to play it straight with Ian, but there was no way Morgan was getting arrested for murder. And Ian had made it clear he was going to do what he had to. His priority was the FBI. Besides, his buddy had a habit of following the rules.

The same way Jack had a way of bending them.

He sighed. He didn't want to go it alone. There were simply too many things that had occurred that could be misconstrued into a mountain of circumstantial evidence. How could they prove that Morgan didn't steal those files to cover herself? The dates of the files were during her tenure at the company.

No, they needed proof. And there was only one way to get proof. Somehow, someway, Morgan had to become the bait. Not only that, he was going to have to convince her to trust Ian when he wasn't so sure that was a good idea.

You're going soft, man.

Yeah, well, he'd never been in love before. So, all of this was uncharted territory. And that made him very uncomfortable.

Jack pulled into a convenience store. He wasn't hungry, but Morgan might be. He figured he'd pick her up a sandwich. Stepping up to the counter, he spied a basket of fresh flowers. His hand reached out and plucked a bunch from the rest.

You're going soft, man.

He drove back to the hotel with a slight smile on his lips. His heart sped up as he put his key into the hotel room door. He wasn't exactly sure what he was going to say. But there was one thing he was certain of—he loved her—and he'd give up his life to protect her.

Maybe that was a good place to start.

The moment he walked in the room, Jack knew she was gone. Adrenaline spiked his blood stream and caused his fingers to tremble. He put the bag from the store down on the table along with the flowers. Then, he searched the room for a note, anything that would tell him where or why she'd gone.

Damn her. She was so dead when he caught up with her.

If you catch up to her.

Jack called himself every name in the book. But he was a tracker. The best of the best. And she was now one sorry-assed, oh-what-he-was-going-to-do-to-her-ass-when-he-found-her target again.

Her pocketbook was gone and so was the small stash of money he'd left her. But she'd left the cell phone on the table. *That's odd.*

He went into the memory to dialed numbers and saw a number he didn't recognize. Before he could form his next thought, his thumb was hitting Send.

"Hey, Mac attacks. What's up? Did you remember something else you wanted to ask me?"

Jack drew in a deep breath. Morgan's life depended upon his ability to convince whoever was on the other end of the line that she was in danger.

"This isn't Dr. Mackenzie. But please, don't hang up. I need your help."

Desperation bled through his voice and he hoped it would convince the man on the other end of the line to talk to him.

"Who is this?"

"My name is Jack Kent. I work for the FBI."

"FBI? For real? Oh wow. I mean, oh no. Is Mac in trouble?"

Jack knew he had to play along. "Yes, sir, she is."

"Man, she didn't have to lie to me."

Lie to him? "Exactly what did she tell you—uh, I don't know your name, sir?"

"Oh. Mac calls me Dewy. My name is Bartholomew Douson."

Jack wanted to scream in frustration. "I need to know what she told you, Mr. Douson."

"Dr. Douson."

In a minute, he was going to rip his hair out. "It's all right, Dr. Douson. Dr. Mackenzie is working with the FBI on a sting operation. We already know about the file. But—" Jack hesitated. Did he tell the guy the truth? "Dr. Mackenzie is missing. I'm very worried that she might have tried to go out and put an end to the operation by herself."

A soft chuckle reached him through the phone. "That would be Mac. She's not very patient."

"Tell me about it," Jack exhaled slowly.

A short silence ensued. "She wanted to know if there was a signature on the file before it was deleted from the server."

And Dr. Douson would know this how? Jack thought hard about his answer for a moment and then breathed, "You were the one who deleted it for her."

Dead silence. "Am I gonna get into trouble?"

"No, of course not. I give you my word."

"I told her the signature line consisted of letters. Yes, sir. And I've been thinking about them ever since Mac's called me."

Jack took a giant leap of faith and said, "You know what they stand for, don't you?"

"I think so. I think they're initials. A. D. is probably Dr. Dvorak. But we have several people that work here with the initials E. T."

"Thank you, Dr. Douson. Thank you very, very much."

"No problem man. And if you're a friend of Mac, you can call me Dewy."

"I owe you one, Dewy. Seriously owe you one."

"No, you don't. Mac is my friend. Just take care of her for me, okay?"

Jack grinned. Oh, he had something in mind for "Mac" once he found her, something very painful, something that would teach her to trust him once and for all.

"Will do."

Jack hung up and dialed Ian to explain that there was a monkey wrench in his plans and that he was going to have to improvise. But that was what he was good at. Finding people and improvising.

The funny part was, he already knew where she was going. The problem was trying to get to the truth before someone else got hurt.

His gaze narrowed. Someone was going to hurt all right. Especially when he got his hands on her.

IAN SMILED AS HE DROVE BACK TO WORK. HIS MIND flashed vignettes of the past as he thought of them. The three amigos. Raw recruits with special talents, talents they'd put to use for their country.

One for all and all for one. He could no more turn his back on Jack or Sam than he could his wife—if he had one. They were joined in a way few people are.

Army strong. And then some.

Ian walked into the office and headed straight for his boss's office. He knocked on the door and opened it. "Got a minute, sir?"

Mike Grady was a good man, dedicated to upholding the law. Would he understand there were times when loyalty went beyond the law?

"Sit."

Ian cleared his throat once he did. "I've got a problem."

His boss grunted. "Didn't think you'd knocked on my door to play tiddledywinks, Spencer. Personal problem or work related?"

"Both," he replied with a sardonic smile.

A long silence followed a glare from beneath a deep brow. "Don't have all day, Spencer. Spill or leave."

Ian nodded, taking a deep breath. "I served with two Rangers in the Army, sir. Jack Kent, you know about. The other is Sam Ormond. Seems they're both caught up in a bad situation."

As unflappable as always, Ian thought as he watched his boss. "How bad?"

Ian shifted in his chair, trying to look comfortable but knowing he wasn't convincing anyone, least of all the man across the desk. "Not sure yet. It's complicated."

His boss simply stared at him. "It's about the murders, sir. Jack's trying to protect Dr. Morgan McKenzie," he began. "Says she stole the data on the formula from her company that's been killing everyone because she knew it didn't work and she was afraid they'd try to make it work anyway."

"You mean, they weren't above cheating."

"Yes, sir. Exactly."

"Go on."

"As you know, Jack Kent is one of the best tracers in the business. So, I called in a favor and asked Sam and Jack to find her and bring her and the formula back to us."

"And this involves your friends...how?"

"Dr. McKenzie found out about the 'additional testing' on human subjects. And when Jack caught up to her, he realized she'd run to keep the formula from killing anyone else. Even so, Jack was willing to stay with her and see what else she knew, see if she could help lead him to the real culprit. But Sam decided to try to bring her in on his own."

"That's kidnapping on your friend Sam and aiding and abetting on your friend Jack."

Ian grimaced. "I know."

"And hell, she stole company property," his boss continued, clearly unhappy. "That's theft."

"Believe me, I know."

His boss sighed and leaned forward to brace his arms on his desk. Then, he smiled. "All right, this is complicated. What do you want to do?"

"Jack says Morgan's willing to become the bait and set up the real murderer. But she—they—want immunity."

"And your friend, Sam? You looking for immunity for him too?"

Ian smiled. "Oh no, sir. With your permission, I have an idea you might be interested in."

"Go ahead."

Ian started to relax. It was going to be all right. Maybe not perfect. But all right.

"Well, sir, this is what I'd like to do..."

CHAPTER TWENTY-SIX

MORGAN KNEW THERE WAS ONLY ONE WAY TO END THIS fiasco—confront Anton Dvorak—and make sure the E. T. she was thinking of was the right person. To do that, she needed to do some digging, and maybe even a one on one with the suspected E.T. And the only way to accomplish it all was to wait until the people at BioClin had gone home.

Her advantage was that she'd worked at BioClin for two years. She knew the place and the habits of the people who worked there. Most of the staff left by six. The guys finished shipping packages around seven, and her staff usually left by then as well. So, the best time to sneak into the building was right before everyone left.

Funny enough, Morgan had no idea how to kill time. Minutes dragged into hours as she wandered through the strip of stores she used to frequent. One was a department store that tempted her to purchase new clothes. She settled on a couple of necessities instead.

She spent the rest of the afternoon in a mega bookstore, trying to read a bestseller, and sipping free refills of coffee. It didn't take long before Morgan realized her life, at the moment, was much more bizarre than any novel on the bookshelves.

And no matter how hard she tried not to let them, her thoughts always drifted back to Jack.

Morgan put her book down for a moment and stared out at the scene that unfolded through the huge picture window in the front of the bookstore. People were hurrying home to their families before darkness fell, running last minute errands before dinner, and doing things normal people do.

PhD geek-scientists aren't normal.

Why not?

Morgan thought about her parents, really thought. This was something she hadn't done for a very long time, and she admitted to herself that she was still angry with them for leaving her alone. Their deaths had forced her to live her life for her work instead of herself so she wouldn't have to go near the gaping emptiness they had left behind.

She shook her head and picked up the book, trying to read again. But the pain wouldn't go away. Then, she realized why.

Jack.

Being "in sex" with him was perfect. It was safe. She didn't have to worry about opening the box that held her emotions. And just like Pandora, she knew how dangerous lifting the lid would be.

Did she dare? Morgan took a sip of coffee, letting her fingertip trace the outline of the cap. She watched a tree sway in the wind. She observed a mother lifting a baby higher on her hip, opening her car door, and putting the baby in a car seat. And that was when it hit her. She knew she wanted it all. She wanted what her parents had, that thing that made her so jealous inside. She wanted that look two people shared that she could never understand until now.

Until Jack.

He loved her. God, it was so insane. The man who could have any woman he wanted, wanted her.

Why?

Morgan shrugged. The scientist in her wanted to examine every nuance, string together logical motivations, and come up with an indisputable answer. Then, she realized it really didn't matter anymore. He did.

Fait accompli.

What are you going to do, Morgan? Stay a geek for the rest of your life, or go after the captain of the football team? Go for the gusto, or crawl back into your safe little hidey-hole?

Morgan smiled. Tears filled her eyes. Jack's grin filled her vision.

She lifted the lid.

SAM SAT AT THE BAR, NURSING A BEER. THE DOOR OPENED, and he didn't have to look over to know who'd walked in. He simply signaled the bartender to pour another draft.

"Hey, bro."

Sam rose and clapped Ian on the back. "Hey."

Sam sat back down and watched Ian pull a long draught from his frosty mug before he asked, "What's going on?"

Ian smiled and watched his friend sit on the bar stool next to him. "That should be my line," Ian replied.

Sam frowned. "Why?"

"Jack came to me for help."

Sam's stomach pulled a high dive right into the sewer. He stared at the foam in his mug, watching it disappear, wishing he could be as lucky. "I should've known you weren't calling to go find some women and bump uglies."

"Not this time, Sam."

Uh-oh. First-name basis. I'm in real trouble now. He took a long pull on his beer. "I'm an ass."

"Yeah," his buddy agreed. "With really long ears."

Sam watched a line of condensation roll down his mug, figuring he was the one who should be running. But there was one thing Sam Ormond wasn't. And that was a coward. "Guess I'll have to turn myself in."

He watched Ian give him a funny look. "I'm not here to arrest you."

Surprise stopped his brain cold. Long minutes passed before he exclaimed, "You're not?"

"Nope. I'm here to play Let's Make a Deal. You game?"

Adrenaline spiked through his bloodstream and he gripped his mug to keep his hands from trembling. "You kidding?"

"Not the kind of joke I'd play with you, amigo."

"Then, hell yeah. I'm interested."

He caught Ian's gaze and they stared at each other for a long time. "What do you know about this guy Dvorak?"

Sam wanted to spew. "Egomaniac with a bad superiority complex."

"Hmm. When I asked you to get involved, we already knew that people were dying. I don't normally handle cases like this, but this was different. Maybe you'd better look at these a moment."

Ian threw a manila folder onto the bar. Sam opened the envelope with cold dread filling his belly. By the third photo, he wanted to heave. Instead, he jacked his spine back into place and met Ian's stare.

"What I didn't tell you was something Jack found out. He said this Dvorak was looking to sell the formula, probably overseas. We're already looking into the distributor over there that Jack mentioned."

Did he tell Ian the whole truth now or wait to see what his friend offered? Sam hated holding anything back, especially since Ian was willing to cut him a break. "I see."

"Well, here's the deal," Ian continued. "I'm going to need someone to do some research. My boss wants to go after Dvorak. Especially if he's got overseas connections."

"He struck me as a pompous ass, but not that bright." Sam

sighed and gave Ian a small dose of the truth. "And I can't make this any clearer. I'm sooo sorry I ever hooked up with BioClin."

"You should be."

There was more, but Sam wasn't sure if he could tell Ian everything yet. He didn't want to blow this chance. "Tell me about it." Sam frowned. "Dvorak's a weasel. All glory and no guts. Underneath, he's a coward. Push comes to shove, he'll run."

"That's what we're hoping for. We want him to run to his buyer, if he has one."

"I get the gist of this, but not my part," Sam continued, wanting just a little more information before he threw in the prize. "How do I come into this?"

He listened to Ian explain. The more he listened, the more he liked the idea.

"All right," he bit out, very unhappy with himself. "I like what I'm hearing. But you're not going to like what else is going on."

He watched Ian frown. "Spill."

"As usual, I thought with my dick."

Ian smiled. "That's nothing new."

"Yeah, well, I just put two and two together and you're not going to like how things add up."

He watched Ian frown. "You withhold information now and the deal goes out the window," his friend threatened.

"I figured as much," Sam answered. "Dvorak has a partner. And she's sick enough to do what you just showed me."

"She?" Ian frowned, his face filling with distaste. "Ahh, you really are a dickhead."

"Very funny," Sam bit out, really hating himself. "She's a bitch. But a smart one. Stole my gun and threatened to pin a murder on me if I said anything."

"Wonderful," Ian groused. "Just fucking wonderful. How the hell am I supposed to get you out of that one?"

"I don't know. But you're going to have to. It's part of the deal."

He watched Ian nod. "I'll see what I can do. But you're going to owe me big-time."

Sam nodded. He understood more than Ian would ever know. "I made a mistake and I'll do my time for it. But BioClin—hell, everyone—gets theirs, right, compadre?"

"My pleasure. Just make sure you don't get nailed in the process. I wouldn't want to have to explain that one to Jack."

MORGAN'S GAZE SLIPPED TO THE CLOCK ON THE WALL across the room. The bookstore was changing shifts. It was time to leave.

She rose, stared at her half-empty cup of coffee, and threw out what was left as she walked out of the store. A block away, she waited at the bus stop and then caught the six-fifteen to Framingham. She stared out the window of the bus and tucked Jack deep into her psyche. Now was not the time to think about love. Now was the time to remember she had a job to do. Now was the time to remember that innocent woman and acknowledge she'd died for greed and no other reason.

Anger churned in Morgan's stomach, making the amount of coffee she'd consumed roll like a sick drunk in a bad storm. *No mercy.* She would get no quarter from her motion sickness. She would give no quarter to the bastards who used her work to kill another human being. End of discussion.

The bus let her off about half a mile from BioClin. Hunching her shoulders against the cold and the wind, Morgan walked off the sickness in her belly and pushed her anger deep inside. She needed to keep her wits about her. She didn't need her emotions clouding her judgment. She'd save that for after she got Anton to confess. Maybe she could even get him to implicate his partner in this terrible crime.

A small smile grew on her face. She'd make Jack proud of her.

As she approached the building, Morgan hid her face with her hood, and walked across BioClin's back parking lot. She slipped behind one of the huge green dumpsters by the shipping dock and checked her watch. Seven on the dot. Not bad. Not bad at all. She wouldn't have to wait too long.

Morgan huddled against the dumpster, using it to shield herself from the wind. She started shivering and knew no matter how short the wait, it would feel a whole lot longer. She kept checking her watch, and about fifteen minutes later, she saw Paul, the shipping manager, walk to his car, get in, and leave. She waited another five very long minutes before she walked up the shipping dock steps.

Peeking into the warehouse through an open bay door, Morgan didn't see a soul. That's because she knew the shipping guys took an extra break as soon as Paul left. Always. Nights and weekends. It didn't matter.

Inside the shipping area, sitting several pallets back in a deserted corner of the warehouse, sat boxes of deionized water. The boxes were stacked almost five feet high. But there was enough room between the wall and the pallet to hide until the shipping guys finished, had their packages picked up, and left the building for the day.

At least waiting inside would be warmer than outside. But it still meant she had to cool her heels and kill time, even though she itched to dig around and find any incriminating evidence she could, then ram it down Anton's throat.

Looking at her watch, she saw it was nearly eight o'clock. Damn, damn, damn. Of all nights, they had to work later than normal tonight. She kept on peeking around the boxes, then slipping back unnoticed. She listened to their banter, wanting to scream at them to hurry up and just go home already. She wanted to prove Anton was behind this. She wanted to confront Anton, push his buttons, and get him to talk and incriminate himself. She wanted to get him to incriminate his partner, right onto the little hand held voice recorder sitting in her pocket—one of the necessities she'd purchased at the store.

What Morgan got was way more than she bargained for.

The lights finally went out, startling her. She listened to the shipping guys lock up the outer doors, tell each other good night, and leave. As she listened to the door slam, Morgan breathed a sigh of relief. But she stayed hidden. Just in case. Patience was a learned virtue that was rewarded in the long run. And she wasn't about to screw things up now.

Her watch didn't have a lighted dial so she had no idea how long she had waited. She finally scrambled out of her hiding place, straining to see in the darkness, and skirted her way around larger objects, heading toward the offices and labs. There were two entrances to the main part of the building, one by the warehouse conference room and one leading to the labs.

As she entered the hallway leading to her office, ex-office she reminded herself, Morgan thought she heard voices. Her heart rose in her throat. Trembling, she wondered who the hell would be working this late?

You would.

During off-hours, most of the building wasn't lit up to save on electricity. But today, there were lights coming from the chemistry lab. Morgan skirted by the door with care, so as not to make noise, and headed to the front of the building where the offices were.

She passed by a bank of cubicles, where most of the technologists and scientists working for BioClin had their desks, and headed for her office. She wasn't surprised to find it practically empty. Her personal items had been thrown in a box on top of the desk. But she went through her drawers anyway, just to see if they'd left anything behind. They hadn't.

Turning quickly, she continued down to Anton's office. The door was closed. She reached out to turn the doorknob when she heard voices coming toward her. Damn.

Morgan had no choice but to get the hell out of there. She

continued to the front of the building and tiptoed across the marble entrance and into another bank of offices. She hurried down a hallway past a set of cubicles and turned into the molecular biology lab. Maybe she'd get lucky and find something Anton left behind.

She combed through stacks of papers in the corner of the lab, but they were all package inserts and control inserts for the equipment they were using. Then, she went into the prep room. She found a notebook and scanned its pages quickly. No help there.

By ducking through the refrigeration area, where huge stand-up refrigerators and minus seventy degree Celsius freezers lined the walls, Morgan would come out on the other side of the building. It was a shortcut to her lab she had often used.

At first, she thought she was losing her mind because the floor should have been empty. It wasn't. There was a man's dress tie in the middle of it.

That's odd.

Without thinking, she picked up the tie and put it in her pocket. It smelled of dry-cleaning fluid and something else. Something familiar. Something on the edge of her mind, but she couldn't quite place it.

Morgan shook her head. She couldn't waste time worrying about it now. She needed to find evidence. Hard evidence. Anything that would link the notations in that file to Anton Dvorak—and his partner.

A mixture of hurt, regret, and anger ripped through her as she stepped into her lab. It was funny she'd thought she could walk right back into her cocoon again. Her hand skimmed a countertop as she remembered the hours spent here, the lonely hours and the empty hours. Jack had changed all that. She didn't need her cocoon anymore.

In her line of business, to prove that something works the way it's supposed to, a scientist needs to ask why at least five times. As she searched through her lab for clues of any kind, Morgan started asking those questions. Why would Anton want the project? To have something he coveted from the get-go. Why? Because he wasn't smart enough to get it on his own.

Okay, so he got what he wanted and then found it didn't work. Why take the risk of endangering someone's life? Money. But somehow that didn't quite ring true. Anton was the type of person to put his efforts into corporate politics, not actual work, and then take the credit for the accomplishments of others. Prestige?

Perhaps. But that would only be part of it. Anton was an egomaniac. He had to be the best. One-upmanship. He was trying to prove he was better than everyone else. Prove it to whom?

E. T.…Elaine Tanner.

He killed a woman because he was competing with Elaine? Possibly. But there was more. He killed that woman because he was competing with—*her*, with Dr. Morgan Mackenzie. Now that made a whole lot more sense.

What else made sense was that, because Anton wasn't the sharpest tool in the shed, he'd stolen her notes and experimented on that poor woman because he wanted to prove he was smarter and a better scientist than all of them—especially Morgan Mackenzie.

Morgan's fists tightened. Anton Dvorak was going to burn for this. She was going to see to it personally.

CHAPTER TWENTY-SEVEN

MORGAN LEFT HER LAB, ANGER AND BETRAYAL SIMMERING just beneath the surface of her skin. She desperately wanted to find something, anything that would slip the noose around Anton's neck.

But all she had was the tie in her pocket.

Frustrated beyond belief, Morgan was about to slam the door when sanity returned. Along with voices. She didn't dare get caught. Not now. Not until she could prove what was going on.

Morgan's heart sped up as she slipped into the hallway that led back to the warehouse. She'd come full circle, made an entire circuit of the building and come up empty. Except for the tie. And as disappointing as that might be, it was time to leave.

As she walked closer to the warehouse doorway, Morgan realized the sounds were getting louder. She stopped near the warehouse conference room door. It wasn't quite closed and what she was listening to sounded like—what the hell? Damned if it didn't sound like a porn movie.

Now that was just ducky. Here she was, in the middle of putting her life on the line, only to stumble onto an interoffice tryst. She shook her head. Could things get any worse?

Probably. She could get caught. Better to get the hell out of there while she could.

Her focus returned, and she shook her head. She approached the room with caution and realized the door was partially open. Morgan didn't consider herself a prude by any means, but this was way too kinky, even for her. She paused, needing to make a decision. Slip past the open door and pray she wasn't noticed or turn around and go back through the building, facing the risk of getting caught by someone else?

At that moment, one of the participants in the porn movie decided to get vocal. Really vocal. Morgan stood stock still. Her blood ran cold. She knew that voice. And, suddenly, she knew why Anton had done what he'd done. But the other participant?

Cats had nine lives. Morgan hoped she had more than one.

She stood tall, flipped on the tape recorder in her pocket, and pushed the door all the way open. The other participant wore very distinctive cologne, the same cologne she'd smelled on the tie.

"Well, well, what have we here?" she asked, anger and betrayal simmering inside her gut. "I believe this belongs to you, Doctor," she added, holding out the tie for him to retrieve.

The scene that greeted her reeked. Dr. Huan Chuan Lee and Elaine Tanner. Intimately embraced.

He jumped and twisted his head around, crying out in disbelief as she walked into the room. Morgan tried not to think as her heart shattered in a thousand pieces. What greater betrayal could there be than a surrogate father fraternizing with the woman who'd used her process to kill? A ball of ice formed in her belly.

She closed her eyes, unable to believe what refused to leave her sight. When she opened them again, it was to find the one person in the entire world she'd least expected to find in this position, disengaged and zipped up, thank goodness. He had turned away to put himself together before turning back around. When he did, his gaze refused to meet hers.

"Why, Huan? For the love of God, why?"

He didn't answer. He turned away as if the sight of her reminded him of what he'd done.

However, Elaine Tanner didn't seem fazed at all. She gave Morgan a knowing smile before turning her attention to Morgan's mentor.

"You didn't finish, Lee. Come back here right this instant!" Elaine commanded her lover. When he didn't, she screamed at him again to continue making love to her. Morgan swallowed hard to keep from getting sick.

"No." His face grew red and his gaze never left the floor. "I can't."

"Of course you can," Elaine scoffed. "It's more fun when someone watches," Elaine added, looking straight at her, giving her that smile again.

In shock, Morgan didn't know what to say. Or do. But Elaine was a different story. She had this glazed look on her face. She sat on the conference table where they'd been going at it, her blouse still half-open and her skirt barely pushed down to cover herself. Morgan looked away before her stomach contents reached the point of no return.

"Huan, listen to me," she told the man she'd looked at like a father. "There's no mistake that can't be rectified. Remember that."

"Mistake?" Elaine cried. "Why would you think this is a mistake?"

"You might not care about anyone," Morgan answered. "But Huan—" He stared at her a moment, a guilty flush rising up his neck, before looking away again.

"Really, Morgan," Elaine retorted. "You're so plebian."

Plebian? "You won't get away with it, either of you. Murder is murder." Morgan threatened. "And you definitely won't be able to explain if anything happens to me."

This time, neither of them answered.

Morgan stared at Elaine, her gaze accusing Elaine not just of murder but torture as well. Unfazed, Elaine simply crossed her legs in what was supposed to be a sexy pose. Morgan thought she would really hurl. She had to swallow several times not to.

"Oh, this is going to be so delicious. Darling," she continued, turning to Dr. Lee. "I have an even better idea now. You're going to do her right in front of me. Then, you're going to do me."

Horror filled Morgan's soul at the reality of the truth she'd stumbled upon. But a part of her still couldn't believe it. "You arrogant, stupid fool. Did you really think I came here without any backup? The FBI knows all about what's going on. You murdered poor, defenseless women and then you tried to pin it on me."

She caught her mentor's gaze this time and watched him go pale. "I didn't kill anyone, Morgan." His gaze flipped from her to Elaine and back again until the reality of his situation finally sunk in. "Tell her, Elaine. You have to make it clear. I didn't kill anyone."

Elaine licked her lips, a glazed look entering her gaze at the thought of murder. "Oh, Lee, where are your balls? You truly are spineless. And believe me, when it comes to lovers, I've had much better."

A terribly hurt look stole over her mentor's face along with disbelief. As if he couldn't believe Elaine would say such a thing. "Elaine, please. You can't mean that."

Elaine merely laughed. "Be a good boy. Do what I tell you to and shut up."

Huan stiffened. It was one thing to be humiliated in private. And for pleasure. It was another to be humiliated in public.

"No."

Taken aback, Elaine's gaze narrowed. "What? What did you say?"

"I said no."

She let her legs part for his view alone. Morgan watched him stare at what was being offered for a long time before turning her face away from the scene in disgust. How could he not know what a bitch this woman was?

"Oh God, you're both sick." She shook her head, bile filling her mouth, and swallowed heavily before continuing. "In a way, I almost understand Elaine. She's always been off center. But you?" she asked Dr. Lee. "How could you? All your principles. All your values, your integrity."

Her friend and mentor raised his head and met her gaze for the first time since she'd entered the room. Several moments later, his shoulders slumped and his gaze turned sad. "Look at me, Morgan. Really. Look at me."

"I can't. At the moment, you disgust me."

His eyes closed in pain but when he opened them, only resignation remained. "You wouldn't understand."

"Try me."

Elaine laughed, the sound brash and harsh, grating on the ears. She jumped off the conference table and sauntered over to him, trailing a finger across his crotch and outlining his semi-erection. "Men are men, Morgan. They all think with this. And only this."

Morgan had to turn away as the man she knew and respected crumbled before her very eyes and became a psycho's lap dog.

"I can't believe that. You have one of the most outstanding minds I've ever encountered, Huan."

"Mind? You cannot see a mind, Morgan."

"I don't understand."

"I am not very beautiful, am I Morgan?" he asked her, his tone beyond bitter. "On the outside?"

"So what?" she cried. "It's what's inside that counts." He raised a sardonic brow in answer. "You have a wonderful family, a respected career, and the ability to save the world, not destroy it."

He shook his head, the truth of his words swirling in the misery of his features. "I have an arranged marriage and an icicle for a wife." He paused, his gaze resentful. "I have a career where I reached the top of my profession at the age of twenty-eight. Do you know what happens when you reach the top?" She didn't answer. "There's only one place to go. And that is down."

"Don't expect me to feel sorry for you."

"I'm not."

Morgan snorted, beyond angry. What a waste. She stared at him, condemning him with her gaze. "Why couldn't you have waited? You knew I was working with test mice. Poor innocent women that you don't know..."

He blanched and had the grace not to even try to meet her gaze. And that's when it hit her.

There was someone else. Another victim. Someone that made him unable to meet her gaze.

"You've killed someone else? Another nameless victim?"

CHAPTER TWENTY-EIGHT

SHE LOOKED OVER TO SEE AN EXPRESSION OF DESPERATION and delight steal across Elaine's face. "Sorry to disappoint you, Morgan. You see, you did know her. She worked for me. And you."

"Rebecca," Morgan whispered, dread filling her soul. "Oh, God, no, I beg of you. Tell me I'm wrong. Please," she begged.

"You use the word so well. Well, Rebecca begged me," Elaine blurted in a rush. "She knew what we were working on. She wanted so badly to lose weight. She'd been obese all her life. I was just giving her what she wanted."

Tears filled Morgan's eyes. Pain ripped at her insides as she thought of that sweet, tenderhearted young woman whose only mistake in life was to trust.

What little respect remained for her mentor died as had her friend. "You'll both burn in hell for this."

She watched Elaine shrug and begin to button her blouse. Then, she walked over to where her suit jacket and pocketbook sat on a counter. Elaine made sure to catch and hold her gaze. A cold, calculating look entered her eyes. "I'm sorry to disappoint you all, but I have no such plans. No more fun and games."

"I don't think so," Huan told Elaine. "Enough is enough."

"What? After all this time you're finally growing a spine?" Elaine shot back at him.

Morgan stared at her, not quite understanding. But obviously Dr. Lee did. A frown creased his forehead. "You were always such a fool, darling," Elaine began, as she rummaged around in her bag. "So oblivious. But I tolerated you because it's so hard to find true submissives."

She turned and stared straight at Morgan. "You thought I was screwing Anton, didn't you?"

Morgan nodded. "Well I was," Elaine answered. "But he was starting to get tired of our little games."

A horrible thought came to her. "You murdered him too?"

Elaine smiled. "Now that's where he surprised me. He split before I could. So, he's next on the list."

She watched Elaine shrug into her suit jacket and then turn to Dr. Lee. "Get on your hands and knees, Lee."

"I think not, Elaine."

Surprise crossed her face. "Get on your hands and knees, Lee. Now!"

Morgan watched them stare, each one fighting for the upper hand. "I'm not going to jail, and I will not crawl," Huan stated. "Not now. Not ever."

To her surprise, Elaine merely waved her hand in dismissal. "You were such a wonderful wuss, darling. You still want me, though, don't you? You see, I'm never wrong about that. Come here and tell me you don't want what I can give you."

He barked out a shaky laugh and caught her gaze. He seemed bewildered, as if the day had turned surreal. Morgan had to warn him it was worse than that.

"Don't give in to her, Huan. If you do, she'll kill you. Don't think she won't. She's crazy."

He blanched as reality reached him. "No you won't. Come on,

Elaine," he cajoled, trying to buy time. "Let's get out of here, and I'll take care of that insatiable appetite of yours."

Elaine smiled at him and Morgan felt a chill run up her spine. "I'm sorry, darling. I really would love to, you know. But you've become a liability now. So, it's time to clean up the loose ends and get out while there's still time to leave."

Huan tilted his head as if he didn't quite believe what he was hearing. Elaine turned and pulled a gun out of her pocketbook. She caressed the muzzle, lust flaring in her gaze, and then she shook her head.

"Do you know whose gun this is, Morgan?" Morgan shook her head and watched as Elaine pulled on a pair of rubber gloves. "Do you know Sam Ormond?"

Morgan nodded in shock as Elaine pulled on a pair of latex gloves and wiped her fingerprints off the gun. Her gaze flicked to Huan who simply stood there, frozen, unable to believe this betrayal.

"You know, screwing Sam wasn't that much fun," Elaine continued. "Really. He was boringly straight. But I had no trouble stealing the key to his office one night. This is his gun."

Morgan's throat locked up. She tried to swallow as disbelief hollowed her belly and the barrel pointed straight at her. "Put it down, Elaine. Now. You don't want to hurt anyone," she cried, having no idea how to deal with insanity.

"She's right, Elaine," Huan exclaimed, his tone terrified. "You really don't want to kill anyone."

For a moment, her mentor seemed not to be able to accept the reality of the situation. Then, a stern frown creased his forehead. He swallowed hard, and his shoulders locked. "Elaine," he repeated. "You need to put the gun down. Now. Before someone else gets hurt."

Elaine looked up and a light of genuine regret flashed across her features as she whirled to Dr. Lee. "Sorry, Huan. It was fun while it lasted, but now the fun's over."

Morgan tamped down on her horror as she realized she had no idea which way the woman would turn. Heads toward her, tails toward Dr. Lee. “Elaine,” she cried, trying to take the woman’s attention away from her mentor. As she did, she realized she had to figure out how to stop Elaine and not get killed in the process.

Suddenly, the woman drew in a deep breath and pointed the gun, not at her, but at him.

“No, don’t!” she cried as Elaine very calmly shot Huan once, right in the chest. He crumbled to his knees and fell to the floor. Morgan wanted to scream and keep on screaming, but no sound would come out. She ran to Huan and slipped to his side. He stared up at her in shock. Falling to her knees, she watched his gaze grow sad.

“Huan. Oh, Huan,” she said, her tone laced with pain, tears filling her eyes, as she cradled his head in her lap.

He looked up at her, begging forgiveness. “Please.”

“Of course, Huan. You know that.” Tears dripped down her cheeks. “No one should die because of a mistake.”

Morgan watched the life drain out of his gaze and then lifted her own to Elaine. “You bitch!”

Elaine stared at her as if the whole situation had become boring, as if she were above reality, as if nothing could touch her—that the mundane couldn’t hurt her. She gestured toward Morgan with deceptive nonchalance.

“I’m an expert at everything I do, including marksmanship. So, be warned, your death will be harder to explain, but I’ll explain it.”

Morgan stared down at the trail of blood flowing out of her friend, knowing there was no way to save him. Her soul cried out in agony at the waste and then ice filled her veins. There was no way this bitch was going to get away with murder. Too many people had died, people she knew, people she’d loved.

Morgan let go of Dr. Lee with reverence and closed his eyelids. When she lifted her gaze, she hid the anger roiling inside, and refused to acknowledge the tiny sliver of fear. Instead, she decided to press the woman's buttons, keep her talking, and find a way out of the mess she was in.

"You're not that good, Elaine. I know. I've seen your work."

Elaine tilted her head as if considering her words. "You think so? Did it occur to you that this is very easily explained?"

She frowned. "How?"

"You never realized that, in order to be a great scientist, you also need to be a student of human nature. What are the most common, most visceral emotions that rack the human psyche?"

"I don't know. You tell me."

She inclined her head as a teacher would with a beginning student. "Greed and jealousy, my dear. In this case, both work just fine."

Greed and jealousy? "How the hell are you going to work those angles?"

Elaine's brow furrowed in thought. Then, she grinned. "We were having an affair."

Ewww.

"You're gay and I'm bi," Elaine told her, licking her lips as if the thought were delectable. "I broke it off to be with Huan. You found out and came searching for me. You found us together and you shot him in a jealous rage."

Morgan snorted in disbelief. "No one is going to believe that."

"Yes, they will. They'll believe it because you were also jealous that BioClin gave the project to Anton instead of you. And you found out I was screwing him too. Double motive."

Morgan couldn't fathom how Elaine could justify murder so blithely. While she struggled with that, Elaine paused, a slow smile growing on her face. "Yes. Yes. This will work out so well. You decided to kill two birds with one stone, no pun intended. You removed your rival, and you hurt me the only way you could."

Really? She smirked at Elaine, certain the woman was totally out of her mind. "You're a fool, Elaine. That might have worked except for this other company you started."

She watched Elaine's eyes widen in confusion. "Company? What company?"

"You know. The one that gave Ralph Bernecky a job."

Morgan watched the woman's face fall like a balloon with a slow leak. "First off, I didn't give Ralph Bernecky a job. I wouldn't. He's a fat little pig without an ounce of brains."

After his treatment of her, Morgan was inclined to agree.

"Second, I have no idea what you're talking about."

Elaine doesn't know? What the hell? Confused, Morgan realized she needed to keep Elaine talking. "Maybe Anton did. And I'm going to bet he made sure you weren't going to be a part of it. I'm going to bet that he was going to keep on trying to create a legitimate drug. It's possible he even arranged that this company would be a subsidiary of BioClin. Unbeknownst to them, of course."

Elaine frowned and shook her head. "Impossible. I would have known."

Now that's a woman talking from a secure position. Which made her wonder. "I don't know, Elaine," she taunted. "I think you might have to ask Anton that question before you decide to kill him, don't you?"

"No. I know everything that goes on in BioClin. There isn't an executive I haven't slept with. They all tell me what I need to know. Or their wives find out little tidbits of information."

Morgan laughed. "How would you know they weren't lying to you? Just to get you off their backs?"

Elaine smirked at her. "Domination, my dear. Domination. Fear works wonders."

With a sinking heart, she had to admit Elaine had a point.

"Now, as much as I would like to hang around and chat, I have a plane to catch. And a little worm to find. But before I do, I have one more experiment to perform."

"Over my dead body," Morgan cried.

Morgan charged Elaine at full speed, pushing her with all her might. Once the woman was off balance, Morgan planted her feet to stop her momentum and turned to get the hell out of the room. She was just about out of the doorway when pain exploded in her skull.

"That can be arranged, my dear," she heard as the world went black.

CHAPTER TWENTY-NINE

MORGAN CAME AWAKE BY DEGREES. SHE MOVED HER HEAD, and pain shot through her neck, making her want to sink back down into the darkness. But something kept niggling at her, warning her, forcing her to open her eyes. She fought the warning for a few moments and then focused on the pain. When she'd willed it into a manageable ball and tucked it down deep inside, she opened her eyes.

She was in a laboratory. Her laboratory. In BioClin. Cabinets lined the walls, filled with shadows and shapes that were beakers and graduated cylinders.

She tried to move and found herself tied to a lab chair. The chair was on wheels, and she tried pushing on her feet to get it to roll, but she only moved a couple of inches in either direction.

When she started struggling, Morgan bit her lip to keep from crying out. Pain scorched through her right shoulder. She had a feeling someone hadn't been too kind about how she'd been transported here.

Fear raced through her heart and closed her throat. She gasped, fighting for breath.

Think. Deduct. Reason.

Easier said than done, she acknowledged with a wry smile. Especially when her heart hurt almost as badly as her shoulder. Dr. Lee. Her mentor. A father figure for more years than she cared to count. She remembered family meals when Liu would insist she eat with them, knowing Morgan hadn't had a decent meal in months because she was working so hard.

A sad truth hit her like a ton of bricks. You never really know a person. And that made her think of Jack. Dr. Lee, a person she'd thought was good inside, honorable, and true, had turned out to be an imposter. The imposter, Jack, had turned out to be good inside, honorable and true.

By now, she prayed, Jack had to be on her trail. He'd told her he was the best of the best.

She willed her heartbeat to slow, and took several deep breaths to help the pounding in her head recede. What she wouldn't have given for a couple of aspirin and a glass of water.

Carefully, so as not to aggravate her shoulder, Morgan twisted her wrists and tested her bond with her fingers. Damn. Plastic strapping material that felt like a large tie-wrap. She looked down at her legs. They were tied together with the same type of tie-wrap.

All right, getting out of these bonds wasn't going to be easy.

But that's where she had a feeling her adversary had underestimated Morgan Mackenzie. Elaine thought of her as devoid of all common sense and deductive reasoning unless she was working in a lab. Well, hell, she was in a lab, wasn't she?

And she was surrounded by glass. A piece of broken glass would cut a plastic tie-wrap.

Morgan wiggled her arms and ignored the pain. Her hands had been bound underneath the back cushion of the chair. So all she had to do was wiggle her arms around the back cushion and she'd be free to get up.

All?

Her brain screamed with pain as she tried to separate her elbows enough to go around the edges of the cushion. Sweat beaded her brow, and she bit her lip to keep from crying out. Damn bitch had probably dislocated her shoulder.

Breathe!

Morgan sat back and waited for the pain to subside. There was no way to know how badly her shoulder had popped, but she did know one thing—she could make this work to her advantage. If she could dislocate it completely, she could get it around the back of the chair.

Taking a deep breath, Morgan put her right arm behind the cushion and pulled. A loud pop reverberated through her ears as pain roared through her. She closed her eyes and pictured Jack lying on a hotel bed, concentrating on that picture so she wouldn't pass out.

Once she was able to function again, Morgan leaned back and to her right as her arm, now hanging limply, slipped around the back of the chair. Then, she leaned to her left to unwrap her other arm and she was free.

The chair had been secured to a pole that carried water to an emergency shower. Every lab had one, which meant she was also by a sink. The easiest place to find glassware would be inside the sink. Anton wasn't the type to do his own dishes.

She planted her feet and lifted up to stand. When she looked inside, she found a 100mL beaker filled with water.

Now all she had to do was figure out how to break the beaker without making a ton of noise, grab a piece of the glass without cutting herself, and figure out how to start sawing at the plastic without bleeding to death.

Then, she bent over and looked at a dark shape next to the sink. *Eureka!* A boxcutter.

Morgan felt tears well in her eyes. She blinked them away, sent up a silent thank you, turned, and lifted up on her toes to grab the boxcutter with her good hand.

Oh, crap!

Footsteps. Someone was coming.

Morgan had only one choice now, and that was to act as if she hadn't broken free. At least she had something she could use as a weapon if she had to. She certainly wasn't going down without a fight.

A bank of bright lights came on, and she blinked several times to get her eyes to adjust. Elaine strode into the room in a lab coat, wearing a rather self-satisfied grin.

"Ah, Morgan. You're awake. How wonderful. And how lovely to see you again."

The comment had been made as if they were merely professional acquaintances greeting each other after a long absence, taking Morgan's breath away. Indeed, after experiencing true psychosis firsthand, she wondered if she would ever trust anyone or anything ever again.

Apparently unaffected by anything that had happened, Elaine walked over to the lab counter and began inspecting the items on it. Elaine wasn't playing with a full deck, making Morgan realize rather starkly, she'd better be careful.

Morgan bit down on the first comment that sprang to her mind, and with a snort, she replied, "The pleasure isn't mine."

"Too bad. Too bad. You see, I thought you might want to discuss your findings."

Is she serious? She wants to discuss experiments now?

Yes. And that meant her earlier appraisal was right on target. Elaine was seriously disturbed. Better to play along, at this point, than to antagonize. Her fingers tightened on the boxcutter and reassurance flooded her being. "What findings?"

"I've been able to speed up the process, you know. Rebecca took only two weeks to die."

She watched Elaine shrug without a touch of remorse.

*She was a human being! With hopes and dreams and...*Morgan choked back her anger. "Why Rebecca? You knew the girl. Hell, she was just as much your admin as mine. Why didn't you tell Rebecca no? She was no threat to you or anyone else."

"I told you," Elaine said, her tone exasperated. "She begged me to help her. In addition, I got an offer I couldn't refuse."

An offer? Morgan's stomach hollowed as she tried to figure out what that meant. "You were having an affair with Rebecca?"

"She was so lonely, poor dear. She confessed it all to me, one evening at dinner. Just poured her heart out. So lonely. So desperate for companionship. She hardly had any friends. Male or female."

"She was a sweet young woman who had a medical condition," Morgan cried.

Elaine's gaze narrowed. Then, she shrugged. "She gave great head."

God that hurt. Morgan wondered if there would ever be an end to this woman's madness.

"You know," Morgan continued. "If you'd waited, upper management at BioClin would have come to you. You know they would. They would've ditched Anton," she added, trying to keep Elaine talking. The more she stalled, the more chance she had to survive.

"Yes. Well. Timing is everything in life, my dear. You, of all people, should know that."

"I do—and a beautiful young woman is dead."

Her gaze narrowed. "That was my point."

Morgan drew in a deep but silent breath and let the air out slowly. Not only was Elaine's deck short on fifty-two at the moment, it was looking like she was totally psychotic with just enough smarts to be beyond scary.

"Why, Elaine? Was it all just about the money? Was it about power? Was it about security? Tell me."

"You poor fool. It's always been about the game. You never knew how to play. You were too honest, too righteous. They'd already decided to bring Huan in to finish the project months ago.

When I copied your work and sent it to him, he became as excited as a teenager."

"It was good for you too, wasn't it, darling?" she crooned to the dead body.

Ewww.

A strange look of pleasure and pain stole over Elaine's face, making Morgan realize she'd never understand how sick the woman truly was.

"What are you going to do?" she asked.

Elaine's face lit up like a kid watching fireworks on the Fourth of July. "You."

Is she serious?

Morgan snorted in disbelief, even as she shivered in disgust. "You're a sex addict, Elaine, and not the least bit discriminatory."

She didn't answer. Her gaze simply narrowed, telling Morgan to shut up and not ruin her fun.

Knowing this wasn't the best course of action but unable to help herself, Morgan goaded, "You're going to love prison, Elaine. Because there's right and there's wrong. Better yet, there's payback. Too bad I won't be able to watch as you get yours from the other prisoners."

She still didn't answer.

"You know I'm right. I can see it in your eyes." Morgan paused, not sure if telling an insane person the truth was such a good idea. She found out the hard way how bad the idea was when Elaine rushed over to her and backhanded her across the cheek.

Pain shot through her brain, and she swore her lip split as she tasted blood. But Morgan would be damned if she'd let Elaine see how hurt she was. Then, Elaine swiped a finger over her lip and sucked off the blood that welled.

Despite the cold dread filling her belly, Morgan kept on goading. "You're sick, you know. Really sick. So, you'd better quit while you're ahead. Don't compound the mistake. You're in this bad enough as it is."

"Another won't make a difference," Elaine sneered. "But not until I have my fun. Right, darling?"

Morgan shivered again as she talked to Huan's dead body.

Excitement filled Elaine's eyes and Morgan shivered despite herself. The woman walked back toward the gurney. But before she did, she went and picked up the gun. She hopped onto the end of the gurney and started to finger the barrel, sliding it up and down over the meta of the barrel. Her gaze filled with sexual expectation, and Morgan could only imagine what she had in mind.

"You see, my dear Morgan," she began. "I've been looking for a way to test a theory of mine."

"Oh, really?" Sickness invaded Morgan's stomach, but she dared not let her see.

She watched Elaine continue to stroke the barrel, the woman's face filling with need. Morgan shut her eyes. She couldn't watch anymore.

"Open your eyes!" Elaine commanded.

Morgan did, but made sure there was no way to miss the disgust in her gaze. "You're sick, Elaine. You need help."

"Don't be jealous, darling."

"Jealous?" she scoffed. "You don't have the brains to improve upon my work," Morgan continued to goad. Her only chance at survival was to get Elaine to make a mistake.

"So, you say, my dear. So, you say." At least Elaine had finally put the gun away. But that didn't mean there wasn't something even more devious following. "I'll always be smarter than you."

"Smarter? How could you possibly think you can explain all these murders?"

Elaine merely smiled. Obviously, she felt she wouldn't have to.

She walked over to a coat rack and pulled down a lab coat, slipping her arms into the sleeves. Morgan's heartbeat tripled as she pulled a syringe out of one of the pockets. She willed herself not to move as Elaine approached.

"We've always been professional competitors. What would you say if I decided to test my findings? Think of it as you against me. Let's see who's right and who's wrong."

Morgan was certain she didn't want to. *Damn it, Jack. Where the hell are you?*

CHAPTER THIRTY

JACK STARED AT THE PREPAID CELL PHONE IN DISBELIEF AS it began to ring. His heart started to pound. Could it be Morgan? Could she have come to her senses and not tried to play detective?

Then, he read the incoming phone number. "Sam?"

"Listen, Jack. You'd better get over here right away."

"What? Over where? How did you get this number?"

"No time to explain. The Mackenzie woman. She's in big trouble."

Jack's heartbeat sped from zero to sixty in the space of a second. "What are you talking about?"

"My men have been canvassing every hotel in the area. They found your rental, but I told them not to pick you up just yet. Look, this is a waste of time. I'm at BioClin. I followed Dr. Mackenzie here. She slipped inside. I started getting concerned when she didn't come out. I've been waiting to call you, but now I'm just plain worried. It's been over an hour."

"Give me the address. We're on our way."

"We?"

"Ian's got my back."

Jack listened to Sam sigh. "Six Mountainside Ave. Framingham."

"I don't know how this is going to go down for you, bro."

"Don't worry about me. Worry about the lady," Sam urged. "Move your ass, Jack. If you're not here in twenty, I'm going in on my own."

"I'm on my way. And bro?"

"Yeah, I know. No worries."

"I'll do whatever I can for you," he told Sam, his tone sincere.

"Appreciate it. Now move!"

Jack dialed Ian as he raced out of the hotel and into the parking lot. "It's Jack."

"What's—"

He didn't let Ian get in another word. "Sam just called me. Morgan's in trouble. If that bastard Dvorak lays one finger on her head, I'm gonna—"

"No, you're not," Ian interrupted. "You're going to let me take care of it. My next call is to Mike to round up our team. Where?"

"Six Mountainside Ave, Framingham. Sam says it's an industrial park. She's at BioClin."

"I'm on my way. And Jack?"

Jack didn't answer. He'd already opened the door to the car, jumped in, turned off the phone, and thrown it on the seat next to him. Besides, he knew what Ian was going to say. Ian was going to tell him to wait until he got there.

No fucking way!

While his heartbeat was fast enough to give him a stroke, Jack's mind stilled to startling clarity. Every movement seemed to be in slow motion. He acknowledged the sound of tires scorching the tarmac as he hit the gas pedal with his foot. His eyes registered the speedometer needle moving past sixty on the ramp to the highway, and his fists tightened around the steering wheel in frustration as he realized the car wouldn't go past one hundred. Oh, and there was that little voice in his head whispering that getting himself killed at this point wasn't going to help the situation.

And yet, none of that stopped him. Because all he could see was her face: her gaze full of the devil and smiling from ear to ear when they'd gone and crashed that party in Cape May. That was the moment he'd fallen totally head over heels in love with her—the moment he'd denied and kept on denying until she'd wormed her way so deeply into his heart, he knew he'd never let go.

Then, he remembered his answer to her. That he'd put a gun to his head if anything happened to her. Fear seared his soul. And he stepped down harder on the gas, begging the engine to go faster.

C'mon. C'mon.

At the last moment, sanity intervened. Peeling rubber into the warehouse parking lot was a sure way to alert everyone under the sun that the cavalry had arrived. Jack braked hard, swung the car into the parking lot, and scanned the area for Sam.

Sam leaped out of his car and ran through the parking lot. Jack jumped out and they met by a set of bushes bordering the building.

"You armed?" Sam asked.

Jack shook his head. "I've been traveling light, remember?"

"I'm figuring you know who's in there already. But there's something you don't know. It isn't Dvorak who's behind all this."

Surprise scorched through his brain. "What?"

"You know how my dick always gets me in trouble? This one's a doozy."

Scared of every second they wasted, Jack bit out, "Cut to the chase, Sam."

"It's Elaine Tanner. She's the VP of—"

"I know who she is." Wow. He'd never have guessed.

"Doesn't change anything, does it?" Sam asked. Jack shook his head. "All right," Sam continued. "I have my Glock 17. But I don't have any backup. Damned bitch stole my .22."

Jack threw his buddy a horrified look. "Why?"

"She planned on pinning at least one murder on me if I went to the police."

"Shit. When this is over—"

"Later," Sam told him. "We need to get Dr. Mackenzie out of there alive first. I'm not gonna have another murder on my conscience."

"Another murder?" Jack cried, the cold outside reaching deep inside. "You mean, there's more?"

Sam sighed. "'Fraid so. I think someone's dead. I heard a gun go off. Unless it's the other way around. I would've gone in without backup but..."

Jack's face must have said it all because Sam's mouth dropped open. "Oh crap. You're in love with Mackenzie?"

Jack nodded and swallowed hard. He didn't have time to worry, didn't dare let emotions get in the way of what he had to do now. "Listen. We do this quietly. R and S first."

Sam nodded, his gaze telling Jack he understood. "Just like old times, buddy."

Jack didn't smile. "Yeah, just like old times."

MORGAN SENT UP A SILENT PRAYER, BUT HER GAZE NEVER wavered from Elaine's face. She watched the woman uncap the syringe, a maniacal look growing in her eyes. Morgan dismissed the craziness and focused on the syringe.

Keep her talking. Stall.

As she did, Morgan inched the blade of the boxcutter out. There wasn't time to cut her bonds now, but she had to do something to distract Elaine and get her to drop that damned syringe.

"You really need help, Elaine."

The woman in question smiled, lifting her head. She smiled with what Morgan thought was supposed to be a rather benevolent look on her face. Instead, it reminded Morgan of the movie Psycho, the one with the shower stall and knife scene. "You know, before I finish this, I am a bit curious. How did you figure out that I was involved?" Elaine asked.

"The initials on the signature of the file. Dewey helped me."

"Dewey?"

"Bartholomew Douson. The young man you loved to ignore."

Morgan watched her draw herself up with pride. "Child prodigy," Elaine answered, her voice dripping disdain. "Needed a good ass-wipe."

Arrogant sonofabitch, wasn't she? Despite everything, it was still all about Elaine Tanner. "Whose idea was it, Elaine? To sell the process? Yours or Anton's?"

Keep her talking. Keep stalling.

"That doesn't make any difference now, does it?" she answered. "I've been working on the problem. Now all I have to do is test my theory."

Elaine continued to advance until she was almost in front of Morgan. Morgan knew she didn't have too many options, and just as she was about to move, Elaine turned. Elaine pulled out the syringe and began to caress the barrel. "You have a choice now, my dear. Undress for me or die."

Horrified, Morgan didn't know what to do. She tensed, knowing she'd have one chance and one chance only to survive.

"Before I do, tell me why." Morgan threaded as much sincere curiosity into her voice as she could. "Help me understand. You weren't always like this."

She nodded, and a slightly pained look crept into her eyes. "No, Morgan, I wasn't."

Elaine inclined her head and let out a huge breath, deciding not to say more. "You're the one I'm going to regret. I always respected your intelligence."

She yanked off the cap of the syringe as she approached. As soon as she was within touching distance, Morgan slid off the chair and rolled her entire body into Elaine's knees. She caught the woman at just the right angle, and Elaine lost her balance. The syringe went flying as she stumbled backward, and Morgan rolled, slashing at her ankle. The cutter wouldn't do much damage, but at least it would hurt like hell.

What was going to happen after that was what scared Morgan. She wasn't sure what to do. And she knew that hurting Elaine was going to make her very, very angry.

Elaine screamed in agony as she clutched at her ankle. Morgan thrashed around and rolled, trying any way she could to cut her again. Her shoulder hit the floor, and she saw stars for a moment. Then she realized, she knew how to fix her arm.

Morgan flipped over as hard as she could on the back of her shoulder, forcing it into the floor with all her might. She saw more stars again and then the pain subsided to a dull roar. She flexed her fingers, able to move them again. But the movement cost her time.

Elaine lashed out with her good foot, kicking Morgan solidly in the ribs. Morgan grunted in pain. But she didn't let go of the cutter. For a slender, wiry woman, Elaine was strong. Morgan buckled under the force as Elaine kicked her again.

"Drop it." She bent down and saw the blood dripping from the cut on her ankle and kicked her a third time. "I said drop it."

"Never," she choked out.

Now that she had the use of her fingers again, Morgan tried to saw at the plastic holding her hands. The cutter was sharp enough to make a good slice, but the blade got caught in the plastic. She had to waste precious seconds trying to free it before she could begin sawing again.

The next thing she knew, she was being hauled up by her armpits and thrown into the chair. Then, Elaine locked her hands around Morgan's throat.

Morgan wanted to claw at the hands closing off her airway, but they were still tied behind her back. Black spots swam before her eyes. Her throat was on fire, and her lungs begged for air. But she kept on sawing.

Suddenly, the plastic gave way. She lifted her arms and swung them around, clawing at her throat, but Elaine wasn't about to let go. Then she remembered a safety class she'd attended and punched her thumbs right into the woman's eyes. Elaine howled in pain and grabbed at her eyes, letting go of Morgan. Morgan fell, gasping for breath. But that didn't stop her from searching for the cutter on the floor.

A shoe came into her line of vision, and she listened to her weapon skitter away on the tile. She rested her cheek on the cool floor before Elaine lifted her head by her hair and forced her to sit back down in the chair.

"You're going to pay for that."

She saw fury build in Elaine's eyes and shuddered, realizing that whatever sanity had shown was now gone. Morgan thought of Jack and the love they'd made and then glanced back at this caricature of a woman, realizing that power is in the grasp of the beholder only if one is willing to be a victim.

There was no way in hell she was going to be anybody's victim.

Jack's love had taught her that.

Her only regret was that she would never get a chance to tell him she loved him back. Or how much.

Morgan started laughing. "You are such a piss-poor attempt of a human, Elaine. Give me a break. Do you really expect me to feel sorry for you? You're even worse at being a scientist than Huan was."

Morgan continued with her original plan, knowing that every moment she stalled was another moment for Jack to find her.

"One shot isn't going to hurt me. It isn't going to make a body waste away into nothing. Even I know that. Science is logical. And you have to let the process build before it can cause that kind of damage. So, go ahead. Do your worst. I dare you."

Elaine gave her an evil smile. "Oh, Morgan, I intend to. But not before I have you begging for your life. And believe me, you'll be begging."

Morgan stared right back at Elaine and laughed harder. "You see, I also put some poison in the syringe."

Indeed, Morgan realized poison was a distinct possibility. Her head was still smarting, but her eyesight cleared a little. Just enough to see that Elaine had found the damned syringe while they were talking. And the woman was coming after her again.

Well, Morgan decided, she'd have to deal with that when the time came. But first she had another, more immediate problem. Pain burst inside her skull, the room started to swim, and her stomach lurched. Was she concussed? She couldn't think straight. She went limp, her eyesight fading. Perhaps she'd have to deal with it sooner than she thought, she decided, as she felt herself being lifted off the floor.

CHAPTER THIRTY-ONE

JACK CROUCHED BACK DOWN IN FRONT OF THE DOOR AND gave hand signals to Sam, who nodded. He listened to Morgan laugh and thanked God she was alive until his skin started crawling. If that damned bitch hurt her, if she laid one finger on Morgan's head, he was going to—

Jack opened his eyes to find Sam staring at him. He got the message. No emotions allowed. Not until they had her safe and sound.

He nodded and pulled down on the handle of the door slowly. Once the lock was open, he pulled back with even more care so the hinges wouldn't make a sound. He wedged his body against the door and let go of the handle. Twisting around, he watched Sam take the door in his hand to allow Jack to slip inside the room.

Someone's back was to the doorway. Morgan was sitting in a chair, her head lolling against the headrest. He could only see an outline from his angle, but he knew it was her. He had no idea who else was in the room, or if either Elaine or Anton were aiming a gun at Morgan. He didn't dare try to find out.

Jack bit the inside of his cheek to keep from making a sound. He moved silently across the floor. Three evenly spaced rows of drawers and workbenches filled the room. He hid behind the first row and looked back over his shoulder. Sam was following.

Jack sprinted to the second row. He still couldn't see well but he could hear. And what he heard made his blood run cold and his stomach burn with anger.

"I should kill you right now."

Jack watched Elaine Tanner smack Morgan hard against the cheek. Morgan's head snapped around, and she looked dazed. Jack sent up another silent thank you that she was alive. Then, he tamped down his feelings and waited until Sam was behind him. Once they were both in position, he motioned to Sam to go around to the other end of the counter for a two-pronged attack.

"I have to think about this for a moment, Morgan. When they do an autopsy on you, I can't leave any incriminating evidence behind."

Jack squeezed his fists so tight his knuckles hurt. He inched around the cabinets and watched the woman walk over to Morgan. She was tall, wiry, but well-muscled. Overpowering her might look easy at first but Jack didn't want to regret that decision later.

"You won't get away with it, Elaine," Morgan told the woman, her words spaced as if she were trying to focus.

Elaine Tanner laughed. "Oh, but I will, won't I, darling?" she crooned. And that was when Jack saw the body lying on the floor. Asian man. No. Impossible.

Elaine Tanner and Dr. Huan Chuan Lee? They were behind all this?

Jack was so surprised, he almost missed Sam's signal that he was ready to attack.

He waited a moment longer, watching as the woman lifted Morgan to her feet so she could look her in the eyes. Morgan tried to pull her head away. Elaine wouldn't let her go and wrenched onto her arm, making Morgan scream.

Jack knew for sure he was going to hurt this maniac something awful.

"You all think you're so smart," the woman bit out. "You think you know everything," she sneered.

Morgan didn't answer.

"What do you know? Where were you when my father sold me to one of his friends? And then another? And another?"

"I'm sorry for you, Elaine."

"Don't you dare pity me!" the woman cried. Then, she swallowed, reining in her emotions. "I fixed him, you know. You bet I did."

She sounded like she was talking to herself, and Jack realized how far gone the woman was.

"And all the others. Daddy never guessed who he was dealing with. Not until it was too late. I had the power. I held his life in my hands. Now I hold yours."

He watched her calm herself and listened as she continued in a lower tone of voice. "I have the power. I'm the one who decides. I hold your life in my hands."

Jack's blood ran cold. Not only was he dealing with a murderer, but he was also dealing with a raving lunatic. He looked back over his shoulder to see where Sam was. Sam was waiting, ready to follow.

"I don't think so," Jack cried, springing up from his hiding place.

The woman moved so fast even Jack was surprised. By the time he was halfway across the floor, there was a syringe pointing right at Morgan's neck. He skidded to a halt.

"Put your weapon down. Now!" Elaine cried.

Jack scanned the room and realized Sam hadn't followed. Damn, he owed the man if they ever got out of this. Elaine had no idea he'd brought back-up with him.

"Morgan? Are you hurt?"

"I'm...I'm all right Jack."

She was lying. White-hot anger seared his gut, but Jack had no choice. He bent down and lowered his weapon to the floor.

"Good. Now kick it to me. Gently."

Jack followed the commands, trying to calculate how far away he was and how far he could leap if needed. He edged closer.

Morgan's head lolled against her chest, and he called out, "Morgan. Are you all right? Talk to me, kitten."

He kept edging closer. Elaine Tanner kept edging backward. Stalemate.

"Let her go. You don't need to do this. Let her go, and I'll take her place," he promised.

"A brave sentiment," Elaine replied. "But unnecessary. Though you are an exceptionally fine piece of masculine material, at this juncture I only need one hostage. A woman of her size will be much easier to handle than a man of your stature."

"True. But I'll go with you willingly. She won't."

Elaine merely smiled. "Do you take me for a complete fool?"

"Don't do it, Jack," Morgan choked out. Her eyes opened and focused, and her gaze begged him not to do anything stupid.

Jack watched Elaine force Morgan to bend by pulling on her arm. Morgan groaned in pain, and Jack swore the bitch was going to pay for hurting his woman. She made Morgan pick up Jack's gun and hand it to her. Then, Elaine threw away the syringe.

Jack didn't know whether to laugh or to cry. The syringe was a maybe at best. He knew the damage the gun could do.

"Let her go, Dr. Tanner."

"Ah, so you figured out who I am. Well, no matter. You're both going to have to die now."

With that, the doctor pushed Morgan away and just as Jack leaped into the air to get her, Elaine Tanner fired two rounds. Jack hit the floor with a thud, fire filling his body as darkness filled his vision.

MORGAN WENT AFTER THE WOMAN WITH A MIGHTY ROAR. A red haze filled her vision. She grabbed Elaine's shoulder and spun her around, unable to describe how good it felt to watch the woman's nose shatter under her knuckles.

She reared back, ready to repeat the action, but Elaine parried her punch and spun away. The woman staggered into the counter that held the lab sink. She watched Elaine turn, reach into the sink, and then lift something out. The woman had a beaker in her hand.

"It's acid," she hissed through her broken nose. Blood dripped down, staining the pristine white of her lab coat. "Back off, or I throw it."

Morgan had no choice. She straightened and stepped back several paces. Elaine held the beaker in a shaking fist. Her eyes darted to the left and right, and then she started moving toward the door. A moment later, she fell flat on her face.

Sam had come up from behind and tripped the woman. The beaker went flying and crashed against the floor as Elaine tried to scramble to her feet and escape.

Morgan ran and launched herself onto Elaine's back. She tackled her to the floor, letting the woman take the brunt of the fall. Elaine grunted as the air whooshed out of her lungs. A moment later, Morgan was staring at the barrel of a gun and the sandy-haired man she'd seen at the ferry. He nodded and jerked his head in the direction of the sink. And Jack.

Sam.

Not knowing how to question why he was there, Morgan scrambled to her feet and raced to Jack. Jack was lying on the floor, blood all over, when the door flew open and a bunch of armed men flooded the warehouse.

"No one move! This is the FBI!"

"Over here," Morgan cried. "Oh, please. Help him. Please. He's been shot."

Fear sizzled down her spine. Jack looked so pale, so helpless.

She felt a hand on her shoulder. She looked up at Sam, a plea in her gaze that he would make it, that he would be all right.

"Jack. Jack," she whispered. A cold ball of misery welled inside her.

Sam's hand squeezed her shoulder gently. "You need to get out of the way, Morgan. You need to let the medics take care of him now."

She rose and hovered, her heart in her throat. *My fault. All my fault.*

"Will he be all right?"

Sam shrugged. He turned and pulled her away as they lifted Jack onto a gurney. A man with raven-black hair and ice-blue eyes walked over to them. He looked terribly angry.

"I thought I told you both to wait until I got here," he yelled at Sam.

"We didn't have a choice," Sam blasted back. "I heard one gunshot. I couldn't take the chance of another."

"Look where that got you both." He nodded at Sam and then gave her a piercing stare. "Go on. Take her to the hospital. I can handle it from here. The good doctor and I have some unfinished business to attend to."

"You won't get anything out of her," she heard Sam warn.

"We'll see, Sam. We'll see."

CHAPTER THIRTY-TWO

MORGAN SAT. SHE PACED. SHE SAT. SHE PACED. SHE reached for a cup of cold coffee, stared at the black liquid inside, and then put the cup down again. Then, she sat again. And every few seconds she'd reach out and slip her hand inside of his or trail a tender finger down his cheek.

No one knew for certain if he was going to make it or not. He'd taken one in the shoulder, one a bit closer to his heart. He'd made it through surgery. Now all they could do was wait.

His vitals are strong. His vitals are strong.

With that mantra carrying her through every moment, Morgan sat. She paced. Sam called again to see how he was doing. She had no other answer to give.

Sam brought her up to speed. They'd found Morgan's tape recorder back at BioClin, and Elaine Tanner was going to go on trial for murder. A lot of murders. Which was going to be a very small consolation if Jack didn't wake up soon.

With her stomach in knots and fighting every second of every moment not to break down, she tried to concentrate on what Sam was saying.

"Ian's taken over the investigation. I think the police were glad."

Ah, yes. The FBI agent.

"I really don't deserve anything from you, and I know I'll never make it up to Jack, but I want you to know I'm sorry. I made a mistake. A big one that nearly cost you your life—" He choked. "And I don't even know about Jack yet."

"You cost me everything."

"I know."

"I'm going to testify in return for a reduced sentence. Elaine Tanner won't get away with anything. She's probably going to try to plead insanity."

A picture of Elaine's face loomed. "She'll get away with it. She really is insane."

He sighed. "I want you to know they're giving me probation with no time served. But my business is gone."

Morgan wasn't sure how she felt about his announcement, but he did put himself in harm's way to save her. "Don't ask me to say anything until I know Jack is going to be all right."

"Fair enough. Keep me posted. I'd be by his bedside if I could."

"I know."

She hung up. Ian stopped by the hospital to find out how Jack was. He didn't say much, just bent down and whispered something in Jack's ear.

Morgan went through her routine and finally leaned down so her forehead rested against their clasped hands. She didn't know where to start but figured it wouldn't matter, so she did something very un-Morgan-like. The woman of science prayed.

The next thing she knew, no she could swear, was that someone was rubbing her head with their hand. She looked up to see Jack smile at her, with so much love pouring from his gaze she was certain she would drown.

His eyes fluttered closed, and Morgan had to swallow several times before the words came out in a hushed whisper. "Thank you, God."

She'd known Jack was a fighter, but for a few minutes there, she figured he could use some help.

He closed his eyes, and Morgan waited until he fell back asleep before leaving the room to call Sam. He told her he would tell Ian. Of course, it took another twenty-four hours before Jack started to come out of it. But once they moved him to a regular room, Morgan knew she could begin to relax a little.

She had fallen asleep when an inner sense woke her up. She rubbed her eyes and checked her watch. Three thirty in the morning. Then, she sat bolt upright. Jack was awake, giving her one of his patented grins.

"You're awake." All her fears and anxiety washed away with those two little words.

He licked his lips and then tried to speak. What came out was a harsh rasp. "Dr. Lee?"

"Dead."

His gaze told her how sorry he was for her about that betrayal.

"Elaine Tanner?"

"In custody."

He nodded. "I've been cleared of all charges," she told him. "Elaine refuses to say a word, but it was a smart move to buy that tape recorder. Ian says he has all the evidence he needs to charge Elaine with first-degree murder of Dr. Lee, and he's gathering more evidence with Sam's help for the others."

His head fell back, but he never took his gaze off her. "How do you feel?" she asked.

"Like crap."

Morgan couldn't help smiling. "That's good to hear."

"Easy—for you—to say."

"Yeah. I suppose so."

Morgan swallowed and turned serious. "You took a bullet for me. Two bullets. I can't believe you did that."

He simply smiled.

"I guess there are no words to thank you for that."

He swallowed, trying to speak. "Don't try to talk," she told him, smoothing back the hair on his forehead. "Just listen. Please."

He nodded. "All my life I've been the geek scientist. I'm not beautiful, I can't cook, and I was never like the other girls. I had brains and that was about it."

"More—than—beautiful."

She nodded, smiling through her tears. "Are you going to listen, or do I have to hurt you?"

He grinned and squeezed her hand. "When you stood there, leaning against that doorjamb, I was certain you were waiting for a five-foot-ten-inch model in stiletto heels with a size thirty-six D bust and a two-inch waist. And yet, something sparked inside. I have no idea why. I probably never will."

"Don't—question."

"You made me feel like a princess that night. Our one enchanted evening. And you stuck with me. You made me feel like a princess every night. Talk about being thrown."

"Betrayed—you."

"Yeah, you did. And I've held it against you long enough."

He smiled and sighed. "Good."

"But there's more, and you promised to let me finish," she continued, feeling lighter, more human, than she had in days.

He stared at her, hope filling his gaze. "I've never let go of myself. All this time, just like at the party we crashed. You wanted me to run with you. But I couldn't. I was afraid."

He sighed long and loud, and lifted her hand to his mouth. But his arm fell back to the bed heavily and she admonished, "Don't do that again, Jack. Not until you're stronger."

Her gaze caught his, and Morgan let all the love in her heart shine out for him. "I love you, Jack."

He didn't answer. She swallowed and tried to get the words out in as normal a voice as she could. "I said, I love you."

He squeezed her hand and rasped, "I know, kitten, I know."

She smiled and squeezed his hand back. "Forever."

He grinned. "You... sure? Long...time."

She nodded. "I'm sure."

Jack must have liked the sound of that. He fell asleep again, promising he was going to hold her to it.

JACK WAS CERTAIN HE WAS GOING TO PUT HIS FIST through a wall. As a matter of fact, he was downright positive. If Morgan didn't stop hovering around him, he was going to kill her. He'd been home for two weeks, and Morgan was acting totally nuts around him. Every time he moved, she jumped up to help him. Every time he ate, she'd watch him like a hawk. And then it dawned on him. She was terrified. And would be. Until a certain part of their relationship was in full swing again.

"That is it!" he cried one afternoon after lunch. "I've had enough."

"Enough of what?"

"Of you. Go away. Leave. Before I find my gun and use it on you and we're both invalids."

She simply stared at him. "What *is* your problem?"

"You."

"What're you talking about?"

"You cringe every time I get up. You hover around me constantly. What's up with that?"

She didn't answer.

"If you don't tell me, I'm going to go find my gun," he swore.

"You didn't see yourself after you got shot."

"So what? I'm fine now. Clean bill of health."

"Are you sure?" she asked.

"Of course, I'm sure."

"Positive?"

He wanted to scream. "You keep watching me eat as if you expect me to relapse. Or as if you expect me to leave. You need to get it through that thick head of yours. I'm not going anywhere. I love you."

"Oh."

"That's all you can say? Just oh? You've been driving me nuts since I got home from the hospital. Read my lips. I'm fine."

"You sure?"

He sighed. "Very sure."

"Really, really, really sure?"

Jack was just about to lose it when he found himself locked in her arms. He didn't get another word out because her tongue was mating with his. His engine started revving when she moaned. Now this was more like it.

"I love you, Andrew Jackson Kent," she told him, breaking their kiss.

His hips meshed with hers, swaying to the song of love. "I love you more, Dr. Morgan Elizabeth Mackenzie. I have a great idea."

She started laughing. Only this time, she didn't look at him as if he'd lost it. "The SeaScape. I'm game."

He grinned and then his mouth swooped down to cover hers again.

She broke away one last time. "No more guns, got that?" He nodded in agreement. "No more knives, either," he replied, struggling to keep a straight face.

She pouted and ran a lazy finger down his chest. "I like the way you use your knife."

Jack laughed. "Good, because—" And he proceeded to reach into his back pocket.

Thank you for reading! Did you enjoy? Please add your review because nothing helps an author more and encourages readers to take a chance on a book than a review.

Don't miss more from Linda J. Parisi with her paranormal series, BLOOD ROGUE, available now. Turn the page for a sneak peek!

Also be sure to sign up for the City Owl Press newsletter to receive notice of all book releases!

SNEAK PEEK OF BLOOD ROGUE

Every city has a pulse, a vibration, a sound. Take New York City, for instance. The city that never sleeps; it's unstoppable, frenetic, and definitely treble. Then there's the *new* New York. Hoboken, New Jersey, the land of thirty-something's tired of living four to a one-bedroom apartment, the city across the Hudson, anchored in the bedrock of the Palisades. Hoboken pounded out bass, slow, deep, rhythmic, and solid, like the beat of a human heart, the one organ a nine-hundred-year-old vampire would never take for granted.

Charles Tower, Chaz to those who knew him best, stood in *Beans*— his guilty pleasure. He stared at the rows of jars with black beans, brown beans, beige beans, appreciating that in his human life, coffee would have been as foreign to him as a heavy metal band. As a human born in the year 1094AD, he would always wonder what the brew tasted like. He hoped it would be as heavenly as the aroma permeating the store, sweet, earthy, and pungent. He inhaled deeply and exhaled slowly, feeling a little bit like an addict.

Yes, he knew all about that word, as well as need and cravings, the likes of which a human could never understand. There was the blood, and there could only ever be the blood, even when he tried to enjoy something as simple as a coffee shop.

What the hell is wrong with me?

Would there ever be a time when he could step up to a cash register and pay for a bag of Arabica that he'd give away, without thinking about the river of life? Maybe he'd be better off thinking of the rogues, the out of control vampires that he'd had to kill too often lately.

Frowning, he turned, left the store, and stepped out onto the sidewalk. Mayhem assailed with a cacophony of sound. The blare of a car horn, the rumble of a truck over uneven pavement, to the thoughts of the hundreds of people he didn't want to listen to. He tried to block out the sounds, to no avail. He stepped right into the path of three lovely women who parted like the Red Sea then came back together again as they passed. One, the blonde with the ponytail, looked back over her shoulder.

Chaz stilled. Her round face could've used more chin and less cheekbone. She had dark brows and even darker rimmed glasses. But, there was something about the beautiful eyes behind the lenses. Bright, the color of a midday sky, filled with energy and curiosity and such life. God, he could drown in that gaze, never surface, and remain happy forever.

Except for the blood.

She turned to her friends, and the moment died the way moments like this do, except he heard her say, "Oh my God. I just saw the most gorgeous guy."

"What?" asked the tallest of the three. "Stacy? Stacy Ann Morgan? The geek-cop? Noticing—oh-my-goodness—" She placed a hand against her chest. "—a man?" Her tone oozed attitude.

"Ease up, Kels."

Stacy. He liked that name. Curiosity piqued, and the irrational need to see those eyes again had Chaz wanting to hear more. He turned and followed them at a safe distance.

"No way. This is simply too delicious. Maybe Stace'll try and dissect him first. Wait. No. She'll run a two-week background check on him right down to his seventh cousin's middle name."

"Low blow, Kels," the woman on her right said. Her shoulders drooped a little, then her back straightened. "You do realize she carries a gun, don't you?"

"Ladies…stop! I'm right here you know."

Yes, indeed, he thought.

She walked with a long determined stride and had a trim, athletic body. She seemed to assess everyone and everything around her as she walked. Was that out of curiosity or protectiveness? By blocking out the myriad of voices around him, he also blocked out hers, so he'd have to find out.

"Of course you are," continued the one they called Kels. "But we know all about you quiet ones, don't we? You may act shy around the opposite sex, but still, waters run deep and all, right?"

They walked a few steps into *Adrian's.* Chaz continued down the block. Sometimes prudence really was better. But then he pivoted, turning back. This time, not for the blood but for the want of simple human contact. Stopping in front of the steps, he hesitated again. There would only be one winner tonight, the blood, and for a moment that made him sad. He shook that off and walked through the door. They were standing in front of the bar like they were waiting for a table to the restaurant.

He walked over and ordered a glass of Cabernet and leaned on the wood as he took a small sip. He watched Stacy's gaze soften as she leaned toward the sad woman.

"How are you holding up, Tori?"

A woman wearing expensive-smelling perfume approached him, and he tore his gaze away. Every pore on her face was filled with artifice, and he shook his head, making it clear he didn't want to be picked up. Her lips thinned at the rebuff, but she turned around and went back to her friends while he focused on the conversation he wanted to hear.

"They say time heals. Some days it's almost bearable. Some aren't."

He watched Stacy reach out and hug her friend, wishing he had someone that deeply invested in his well-being, someone close. Vampires were singular and very territorial. They had to be to survive.

While Stacy and the one she called Tori spoke together, the

woman they called Kels turned to stare at him. Her brow lifted, her hips shifted so that the line of her leg drew his gaze. He palmed his chest and mouthed, "Who, me?"

She nodded, offering a sly, knowing smile. He took his time pushing off the wood of the bar and sauntered up to her, already feeling her claws dig deep. She entwined her arm with his, but Chaz had no interest and extricated himself with deft precision. He ignored her pout and flashed them all a huge grin.

"Good evening, ladies. I know this is incredibly forward of me, but might I buy you all a round while you wait? Charles Tower at your service." He bowed, gracing them with the manners which had been proper in his time, and they hemmed and hawed, all except *her*. Stacy simply stared at him, assessing, head slightly cocked as she made her judgment. Funny, for the first time in just over a century, he didn't want to be found lacking.

You can service me anytime.

How...unexpected. He nearly grinned. Then he heard, *Where the hell did that come from?* He wanted to ask the same question. Too bad this night was about need and not pleasure.

Kels, the dark-haired one who was all talk licked her lips like he was some kind of treat. She turned him off, much too full of herself to be inviting. Tori, the sad one, frowned and eyed him up and down a couple of times, her gaze filled with mistrust. He let her see what she wanted to see, someone normal, someone human, and she nodded slightly. Then he claimed the prize, sinking into that incredible crystalline blue gaze once more, made even more delectable by the doubts she expressed.

"Sir? What can I get you?"

He started and looked up, indicating that the ladies each give their order to the bartender. "Put it on my tab."

Kels refused to give up, wedging her body into the tight space between the other women so that she separated him from her friends. Chaz steeled his features, daring her to touch him again. Her human instinct warned her, and she stepped back, allowing him to reach out and move Stacy away from getting stepped on. He trailed a light finger across Stacy's skin as he let go, pleased to see her skin bead from his touch.

"Do you come here often?" She winced, and he held up his hand, feeling a touch of dismay. "I know. Lousy pick-up line, right?"

He cocked his head, gave her a rueful lift of the corner of his mouth, and let the truth ring through his words. "But I've been so overwhelmed by your presence that I don't know what to say."

She didn't answer.

"Okay, that came out a bit too much, didn't it?"

She nodded, and he drowned in her killer blues, which was hard to do for one already dead. "Shall I rephrase?"

She stared, disbelief filling her gaze as she shouted her thoughts. *Make that more than once.*

Outwardly determined and in control, that was very evident. But inside? How fascinating. "Perhaps I should start over?"

She still didn't answer.

"You don't talk very much, do you?"

Her gaze flitted from her hands to his chest and then after a deep breath, made eye contact. But at that moment, her shoulders squared and she gazed at him openly.

Her cheeks bloomed pink. "I work in a lab." She half laughed. "The extent of my conversations run from who took an evidence bag to why the damned mass spec is down again."

She tightened her fingers around her glass and stared down at her drink again. *Is this really happening?*

Now he couldn't help himself as he grinned.

Look at the simple curl of his lip—the arch of his brow.

"Perhaps we could start with your name?"

Her heart sped up, and he could hear the rush of her blood in her veins. His mouth watered. Chaz swallowed, hating his reaction to her. She seemed nice, too nice to simply be used.

"Sorry." Again, twin spots of pink tinged her cheeks. "Stacy.

Stacy Morgan." *Nice going, dumb head. Probably thinks I'm sixteen now.*

Actually, Chaz found the combination of her boldness and insecurity intriguing and decided to reassure her.

"I'm a bit rusty in the world of social gatherings myself," he said.

She certainly made for an interesting combination. Supposedly she was some kind of scientist, her friends called her a cop, but she carried an innocence about her he hadn't encountered in a very long time.

The bright light in her gaze dimmed with uncertainty. Chaz might be considered more human than his fellow vampires, but make no mistake, this moment was all about the blood and only could be about the blood.

"Me too. Umm, let me introduce you. This is Kelly." Chaz wondered if his message had been clear enough. She shook his hand and let go quickly. "And this is Tori." Her sad friend was much more reserved and much less trusting.

"Ladies? A pleasure to meet you both." He inclined his head with a slight smile and leaned against the bar again. He picked up his glass, his gaze studying them over the rim. "This place is really busy tonight."

Kelly agreed. "More than usual."

Tori didn't answer.

He turned his attention back to Stacy. "I gather you're here to celebrate? Special occasion?"

"No," she answered. "We try to meet up when we can."

"Then I wouldn't be tearing you away from your friends if I asked."

Her nose scrunched up, making her glasses fall. She pushed them up with her finger. "Asked what?"

"Would you like to get out of here? Grab a bite?"

She gulped a deep draught of her drink then put her glass on the bar. He followed with his glass, still holding onto the bag of coffee. She seemed caught as she hesitated.

"Somewhere quieter? I can hardly hear myself think."

Her heart began to flutter. "I'd like that."

With a nod, the bartender came over, and he handed the young man a hundred-dollar bill. "For the tab and anything else they want."

"Ladies? Again, a pleasure to meet you. I've given the bartender enough to cover your drinks and perhaps more. Stacy's agreed to have dinner with me. So if you'll excuse us?"

Are you kidding me? For real? Kelly practically shouted.

Tori was much more skeptical and cautious. She threw Stacy a look. He couldn't help but hear her shout. *If I don't get a text from the restaurant, I'm calling the cavalry.*

She had good friends. "Stacy, you won't forget to send a text, will you? To let everyone know you're safe?"

"Of course," she answered, nodding, looking ready to roll her eyes, so Chaz led the way outside, blowing out a deep breath before he gave her a smile.

"Much quieter."

She didn't answer.

"You have some very good friends."

"Sometimes they forget I can take care of myself." A wisp of hair had loosened from her ponytail to frame her face. She blew it off her cheek with a sideways breath.

"I'm sure you can, but they also care about you."

"A little too much, but I guess I shouldn't complain. Certainly not to someone I've just met."

He dipped his head, lifted a brow, and smiled. "Let's make this a special occasion then. Our first meeting. The Chart House?"

She shifted her pocketbook strap on her shoulder, and some of the tension in her shoulders eased. "I've been there. That would be lovely."

He inclined his head but drew his brows together as if he had a problem. "I have a favor to ask. Would you mind driving? My car is in the garage of my building. We'd have to walk a ways to get it. Or Uber."

"Sure." She turned, and Chaz followed, admiring the view before falling into step next to her. That long stride of hers nearly matched his. "You had everyone going, you know."

"Excuse me?"

"My friends. They're not exactly subtle."

He lifted his eyebrows, hoping he appeared ignorant or innocent, but she didn't seem to buy it.

"Come on. You mean you didn't see the drool all over the floor? Kelly tried to chain you to her."

"That's why I stood next to you. I'm not interested in the obvious."

"Okay. So if I'm not obvious?" she asked, heading down another block. "What exactly am I?" She stopped next to a beat-up Jeep.

A word popped into his head, and he hated it immediately. "Intelligent. Strong. Beautiful."

She tipped her chin, head tilted, eyes widened, and huffed. "Really?"

"Really," he repeated. He climbed in the passenger side while she got in behind the steering wheel. As she put the key in the ignition, he covered her hand with his. Her gaze lifted, filled with confusion, anticipation, and a bit of curiosity. He leaned in and breathed in her scent, a heady mixture of expensive perfume and hormones. Her skin pebbled as he blew lightly on her cheek. Chaz heard the distinct rhythm of her heart as it hammered in her chest, which rose and fell with short rapid breaths.

His incisors grew, and he swiped a taste of her neck. Perfect.

She moaned as he bit down. *God, she tasted sweet.* Much more like dessert than a meal. He sucked and swallowed, sucked and swallowed, and her heart slowed, pounding in his ears to the same rhythm as the city.

Chaz.

He reared back away from her neck. Had he taken too much? Horror filled his gut. No, her flesh was still warm, pulse low and steady, eyes closed.

Thank God.

He leaned over again and bit down, but this time it was to give her the Lethe, the drug that would make her forget he ever existed. He admired her beauty one last time, then reached in her purse and found her driver's license, committing her address to memory. *Shouldn't have done that, Charles.* He climbed out of the car and placed the bag of coffee in the crook of her arm. She would wake up in about an hour or so and not remember a thing.

Damn. That sucked.

Chaz walked home deep in thought. He couldn't get Stacy out of his head. He replayed every moment they spent together, and then he remembered a small detail he must have disregarded. She was a scientist *and* a cop? What if she could help him understand what was happening to his people, why there were more rogues now than he'd seen in the last three hundred years? The idea tantalized. Then his stomach hollowed. He'd be putting her in grave danger. The Council would never allow a human to know about them.

But she was strong. A police officer. She'd be able to stand up to The Council.

And if they decided to end her life anyway?

Chaz shuddered. Then his cell phone buzzed. He stared at the number and smiled. "Pitch?"

"Charles Tower, as I live and breathe."

"You don't."

"Semantics."

"Captain Pritchard. To what do I owe this pleasure?"

"I'm at your place. Apparently, you're not."

Chaz smiled. "I will be in two or three minutes. It's been a long time. You slumming?"

"Uh, no." Pitch hesitated.

"What's going on?"

"When you get here, Chaz. When you get here."

Pitch wanted to talk in private? His stomach clenched. He walked as fast as he dared without attracting too much attention and made it home in two minutes.

With the sun having set, a chill breeze picked up, adding to his unease. A police siren sounded in the distance, reminding him of his duty to protect, making him wonder if there was another rogue they needed to put down. Pitch pushed off the wall and stepped out of the shadows when he arrived at his building. Black hair pulled into a knot at the nape of his neck, slight of build, but with a wiry strength and determination that just wouldn't quit, Pitch was the one vampire Chaz would always want guarding his back.

He clapped his friend on the shoulder, gave him a quick hug, and opened the door. "Smells like you just fed."

Her address was a burned tattoo inside his brain. "I did. Do you need to go out and come back?"

"Nah. If I leave, I'm not planning on coming back. You feel me, bro?"

Chaz winced. There was something out and out wrong about a Colonial Army Captain trying to mimic modern slang. He stepped into the elevator, and Pitch followed. Still curious and out of sorts from wishing he was with Stacy and not Pitch, he didn't say anything. He opened the door to his loft and walked up to a credenza, opened a drawer, and pulled out a key, which he threw to his friend. "In case you need a place to crash."

"Thanks."

Turning, he pinned his friend with a stern stare. "Okay. So what's going on?"

Pitch rubbed the back of his neck and started to pace. "You're gonna think I'm crazy, but I'm worried about Mick."

Chaz snorted then let out the laughter he tried to hold in.

"I know. I know," Pitch answered. "I'm crazy, right? But I'm really worried about him." Pitch stopped pacing, and his brows drew together and two creases furrowed his forehead. "I've been trying to get a hold of him for two weeks. He's not answering my calls or texts. So I went by his place. Doesn't look like he's been there in a while."

"He's been off the grid before."

"Yeah, but if I'm a real pain in the ass, he'll answer. Eventually. Not only have I tried him like three or four times a night, I even checked out his cottage up in Vermont. No sign of him."

A chill crept down Chaz's neck. He dismissed it immediately, as the idea of the three laws and that robot movie filled his head. Vampires had their three laws also.

Vampire rule number one stated a vampire may drink but were forbidden to drain a human to death. Rule two: humans must never know vampires exist, and every human must be given Lethe, so they never remember anything after a vampire has fed. Included in this rule was an edict that, unless a vampire was willing to put his life on the line to defend his actions, he dared not turn a human into a vampire. A long time ago, Chaz figured that was because there weren't that many humans walking the earth. Now he figured this was to continue to safeguard their anonymity.

The final rule, the most important, Chaz believed, was that a vampire should not drink from another vampire. *Ever.* Drinking from another vampire created a connection for as long as their eternity lasted. Before Pitch was born, Chaz and Mick had been forced to drink from each other to stay alive. Chaz would've known if Mick was in trouble.

A chill settled on the back of his neck anyway. "Mick is a big boy. He's been taking care of himself way longer than we've been around."

Pitch waved his hand, dismissing Chaz's explanation. "I know. But this...this feels different."

"What do you mean, different?"

"Well, for one," he paused, glancing at the bottles of wine in the rack. "You gonna offer me a drink?"

Chaz walked over to his bar and poured them both a small glass of wine. Pitch chugged his. That chill on his neck turned ice cold. "The last time I talked to Mick, he sounded, well, I know you're not going to believe it, but he sounded concerned. Anxious, even. And we both know that's just not Mick."

What? How was that possible? Why didn't he know? Oh shit. What the hell was going on? Chaz sipped on his wine to cover his angst. "Did he say why?"

Pitch stared down at his glass like he wanted ten more. Chaz knew what kind of pain that caused. "Got mad and told me to quit bugging him, that I'd know what was going on when I needed to."

Chaz nodded. "Well, that sounds like Mick, doesn't it?"

"Yeah. Except that was the last time I talked to him. Over two weeks ago."

When Chaz clapped his friend on the shoulder, Pitch looked up. His gaze was filled with worry. "Listen. You need to feed. I'll check around. Try and find him, although we both know if Mick doesn't want to be found…"

Pitch nodded.

"Let's touch base tomorrow night, okay?"

"Hey, look," Pitch said. "Maybe I'm just being paranoid. But he's like a father to me."

"To us all."

He walked Pitch to the front door and gave his friend a quick hug. "He's probably doing it on purpose 'cause you've been bugging him."

"God, I hope so." He punched Chaz in the shoulder and straightened as if the weight on his back lessened. "Thanks, man."

"And not a word to Ozzie or the others yet."

Pitch nodded. "No need worrying them."

"Agreed." Chaz smiled. "Next time, let's go hunting together. Like the old days."

"I'd like that."

"Good. I'm glad you stopped by." But as Chaz shut the door, he knew he was lying. Mick had sent him a file a couple of days ago that made no sense. Pictures of an abandoned estate up in New York. No message. Just the pictures.

What the hell are you doing, Mick? And why aren't you talking to me?

A few hours later, Chaz was still trying to figure out what was going on when his phone buzzed. He read the number, and relief flooded his veins. "What the hell, Mick? You've had Pitch going crazy. Even had me worried."

Silence. Then a voice whispered. "Help me."

Don't miss more from Linda J. Parisi with her paranormal series, BLOOD ROGUE, available now. And be sure to discover all her books at lindajparisi.com

There is the blood and can only ever be the blood. So, how will love survive in a world of pain?

Vampire Charles Tower never knew anything sweeter than the taste of Stacy Morgan's lips. He never imagined anything crueler than her being marked for death by the only father he's ever known.

Mikhail reared him. Taught him how to survive. Now he's gone rogue and it's up to Charles to put the man down. But can he convince himself, and Stacy, that love between them is impossible?

That's hard to do with a woman like her, especially when she offers herself up as bait.

Now they must fight against the centuries-old customs that bar them from being together and the rogue vampire who wants every last drop of Stacy's blood.

Blood Rogue is perfect for fans of forbidden love, dangerous vampires, and heart-pounding paranormal romance.

Please sign up for the City Owl Press newsletter for chances to win special subscriber-only contests and giveaways as well as receiving information on upcoming releases and special excerpts.

All reviews are **welcome** and **appreciated**. Please consider leaving one on your favorite social media and book buying sites.

Escape Your World. Get Lost in Ours! City Owl Press at www.cityowlpress.com.

ACKNOWLEDGMENTS

My family and friends for believing in me. Always.

Tina Moss and Yelena Casale of City Owl Press for going the distance with this book. And all the others.

The members of Liberty States Fiction Writers for their incredible support. Always.

And, Dr. Elizabeth Aiden and Dr. Murray Rosenthal for their guidance in researching metabolics and cellular kinetics.

Thank you all.

ABOUT THE AUTHOR

As a major in biochemistry with a minor in English literature, Linda J. Parisi has always tried to mesh her love of science with her love of the written word. A clinical research scientist by day and NJRW Golden Leaf winner, N.N. Light's Book Heaven 2021 Paranormal Romance Award winner, and the 2022 HOLT Medallion winner for Speculative Fiction by night, she creates unforgettable characters and puts them in untenable situations, much to their dismay. Choices always matter and love conquers all, so a happy-ever-after is a must. Linda is a member of the Board of Liberty States Fiction Writers. She has served on the boards of other writing organizations, and loves to teach the craft of writing at workshops and conferences. She lives in New Jersey with her husband John, son Chris, daughter-in-law Sara, and Audi and Archer, a pair of pooches who had her at *woof!*

lindajparisi.com

ABOUT THE PUBLISHER

City Owl Press is a cutting edge indie publishing company, bringing the world of romance and speculative fiction to discerning readers.

Escape Your World. Get Lost in Ours!

www.cityowlpress.com

facebook.com/CityOwlPress
x.com/cityowlpress
instagram.com/cityowlbooks
pinterest.com/cityowlpress
tiktok.com/@cityowlpress

www.ingramcontent.com/pod-product-compliance
Lightning Source LLC
LaVergne TN
LVHW091107080826
845145LV00008B/1835